Lady Emily's Matchmaking Mishap

Merry Spinsters, Charming Rogues

Sofi Laporte

http://www.sofilaporte.com

GPSR compliance:
Alice Lapuerta
c/o Block Services
Stuttgarter Str. 106
70736 Fellbach, Germany
sofi@sofilaporte.com

Editor: Rebecca Paulinyi
Cover Art: Victoria Cooper

Dear Forest Fay,

They say if you leave a wish in the hollow of the forest's oldest oak, the forest fay who lives there will grant it. Will you grant me one wish?

Yours, most humbly,

Little Wren

Yes.

Chapter One

SURELY, IT COULDN'T BE THAT DIFFICULT TO CATCH A duke.

Emily White's gaze locked on the gilded crest emblazoned on the carriage door as it swept into the courtyard of the inn with a flourish. The crest was unmistakable: a wolf, two crossed swords and a crown. Her breath hitched as she recognised the crest, and her steps faltered.

It might be difficult, yes—but not impossible. Although, Emily mused, some might argue that catching *this* particular duke might be impossible, indeed. A fool's errand, they would say; and perhaps not an endeavour worth pursuing in the first place, and certainly not worth contemplating.

Yes, it would be folly.

Most definitely so.

And yet...

Yet here she was, contemplating it all the same.

Emily's mind reeled with a whirlwind of possibilities and probabilities. Her fingers clenched around Cissy's woollen cloak, damp and muddy from their long journey, which she'd taken to the well across the courtyard to wash.

She might as well not have bothered. For as the Duke's carriage rolled past her, its wheels hit a puddle, sending a spray of mud over her. She froze, standing in the middle of the yard, as the steaming horses came to a halt just behind her.

Emily hissed, ostlers shouted and rushed past her to attend to the horses, the coachman bellowed orders, footmen leapt from the back of the carriage. The inn's courtyard, silent only moments before, burst into life as people ran from every corner to attend to the newest arrival. Even the innkeeper himself appeared, carrying a tray of steaming mugs of cider.

Muttering under her breath, Emily wiped the mud from her skirt and wished, not for the first time, that the owner of this coach would be cast into the deepest, most infernal pits of hell, whence he'd undoubtedly come.

Then the carriage door opened.

A pair of well-polished Hessian boots appeared, followed by elegant legs and a tailored coat that billowed back as the owner stepped down, pausing for a moment in front of the carriage to survey the inn through his quizzing glass. Then he stepped around the puddle— which was now half empty, as most of its contents adorned Emily's dress—and, without so much as a glance at her, strolled into the inn, where he promptly disappeared.

Emily's mouth dropped open.

So that was him.

Wolferton.

The Devil Duke.

His reputation had preceded him long before he'd even set foot here.

He didn't look as sinister as she'd imagined, Emily thought as she stared after him. Nor had she envisaged him to be the picture of fashion. His dark hair was elaborately swept back in an affected style known as à la Brutus, his cravat intricately tied, his shirt points so high and starched they almost poked him in the cheeks. A tulip, that was clear. A dandy and a nincompoop. Who could have known?

Emily snorted with disdain.

Shaking her head, she turned to see the coachman leap from his seat, skilfully dodging the puddle, and shouting instructions to the ostlers. He was a tall, burly fellow with broad shoulders, wearing a double-breasted greatcoat, leather breeches and a hat. His boots were muddy.

"I say, sir," Emily called out. "Are you blind?"

The man glanced over his shoulder.

"Did you not see me standing here?" Emily walked up to him, pointing at her mud-stained dress. "Not only did you almost run me over, you splashed me when you drove through that puddle."

The man towered over her. His gaze swept across her, down her figure, then back up to meet her eyes, which inexplicably made her blush.

He had unsettlingly piercing amber eyes, framed by dark lashes.

He raised an eyebrow.

She forced herself to hold his gaze.

"A miss like you has no business standing in the middle of the yard of a busy coaching inn woolgathering," he growled in a deep voice. "And if you do, expect to get splashed." He turned to leave as if the matter was settled.

"A 'miss' like me?" Emily gasped.

"Aren't you a miss? A missus then?" He gave her a second, more lingering appraisal. "But no. You look decidedly unmarried."

Emily stuttered, not because he was wrong, but because he'd hit the nail on the head. Was 'spinsterhood' written on her forehead for all to see? And even if it was, how dare he point it out so rudely?

He strode over to the innkeeper, took a mug of cider, downed it in one gulp, and returned the mug before turning towards the inn.

"Wait!"

Emily's mind whirled.

This was an opportunity if ever there was one.

He paused and turned. "What else do you need? Your coat to be brushed? Your shoes to be polished?"

Ignoring the sarcastic undertone in his voice, she sidled up to him as if they were best friends.

"That man—" She pointed her chin towards the door where the Duke had disappeared only moments earlier. "That nincomp—I mean, that gentleman who just went into the inn earlier, the one whose coach you are driving. He's the Duke of Wolferton, isn't he?"

The hand that reached out to open the door froze. "And if he is?"

She shrugged. "Nothing. Just curious, nothing more.

4

It's not every day you cross paths with a real duke and get splashed by a duke's carriage. An experience to tell my grandchildren about one day, God willing, if I ever have any." She looked up at him with wide eyes, placed a hand on his arm and lowered her voice confidentially. "They say he's very rich, isn't he?"

Something flashed in the man's eyes. Once more his penetrating gaze swept over her, taking in her travel-worn, mud-stained gingham dress and crushed bonnet. Then he lowered his face. "Very," he growled. "He has three thriving estates and twenty thousand pounds per annum. Not to mention a mansion in London and a castle in Scotland."

Emily pressed her lips into a thin line. She'd known, of course, but she'd needed confirmation. Who better to verify these facts than his servants?

Her grip on his arm tightened briefly as her mind raced.

"They also say," she continued, "that there is to be a grand country party at Ashbourne House."

His face remained blank. "Is there, indeed?"

Emily nodded. "They say it is unusual because His Grace never entertains. They say he likes to keep his own counsel. I wonder why he's holding it at Ashbourne House of all places, where he never resides... " She stopped, noticing his openly curious gaze.

"How extraordinarily well informed you are."

"Just kitchen gossip." Emily shrugged, as if her words had no meaning. "I hardly believe half of it. You wouldn't believe how much the maids chatter. And as a lady's maid myself, I can't help but overhear." She lowered her eyes to avoid his unsettling stare. "But one servant to another, tell me: is there any truth in it?"

He crossed his arms. "There may be. This kitchen gossip is most amusing. What else do they say, I wonder?"

"It is said that he is looking for a bride, which is the sole purpose of this country house party. Is it true?"

The corner of his mouth lifted. "Why? Are you thinking of throwing your hat into the ring?"

Emily smiled sweetly, unimpressed. "Silly." She slapped his arm playfully with her other hand. "Of course not. I am but a lowly servant. A duke and a lowly servant? That could never be. But my sist—that is, my lady, of course—should not miss this once-in-a-lifetime opportunity. I am enquiring on her behalf."

He stared at her, openly fascinated. "Your lady? Why?"

Emily put her hand to her heart and sighed dramatically. "Because she is so very beautiful. As beautiful as Aurora, the Roman Goddess of Dawn. In fact, more beautiful."

"Egad. Is she really?"

She nodded eagerly. "She would be a perfect choice. Lady Lydia has the looks and breeding of the perfect duchess. She is an earl's daughter, you know. Why, if she were to meet the Duke, it would save him the trouble of hosting an entire house party to begin with. It must be such a nuisance. He'd find his bride on the spot. Think of all the time and effort he'd save! Men cannot help but see her and fall in love immediately."

"How absolutely terrifyi—I mean, of course, what an incomparable she must be."

"She is indeed. She is well known in the ton." Emily waved her hand. "And generally very well liked. She is not only beautiful, but gently bred, with a kind disposition. Which brings me to my point." Because he was so very tall, she grabbed his arm as she rose on tiptoe to whisper in his ear, but even then she barely reached his neck. "Can you help us get an invitation to Ashbourne House? My lady would be so very grateful if you could."

He looked down at her with an unreadable expression on his face. "My dear. I am a mere coachman, not His Grace's personal secretary. And even if I were, I don't think I'd have that kind of influence on His Grace's guest list."

Emily sighed. "I was afraid of that. I thought, since you so ruthlessly ran me over with your horses and brutally splashed me with mud from head to toe, that you might go out of your way to help me in this minor matter... who knows, His Grace might be very grateful if you helped arrange the match of the century. In the end, you might even find yourself promoted to Head Groom or Master of Horse, or perhaps even Estate Steward?"

"Match of the century, eh?" He lifted an eyebrow.

"Indeed. Of course it's no use expecting a mere coachman to grasp the importance of the matter at hand." Emily sniffed.

"Alas. I'm afraid you're right. The fault is definitely mine. I seem to lack the ambition for the role of head groom." He looked pointedly down at her hand, which was still clutching his arm.

Flushing, she dropped his arm as if it were a burning log.

His lips twisted into a smile, and then, to her utter astonishment, he winked.

"What an insufferable boor of a man," Emily stammered, red as a beetroot, as she watched him swagger away.

He paused and turned once more. "But for what it's worth. I truly did not see you standing there, Miss... "

"Meggie Blythe is my name."

"Meggie Blythe. I shall instruct the maids to have your clothes cleaned at our expense. I do apologise."

The apology was so unexpected that it left Emily speechless.

"No need," she called after him, raising her voice. "I would rather die than have His Grace inconvenienced on my account." But he obviously chose not to hear her, for he continued to stride towards the inn.

She turned to the well, where she began scrubbing at the mud stains on her skirt and shawl, muttering under her breath. "Really, like master, like servant. Why am I surprised? High-handed, arrogant, insolent, chuckle-headed oaf." She scrubbed the cloth vigorously with each insult. "Insufferable lickspittle. Maddening lackwit. Preposterous beetlebrain."

Did she mean the Duke? The coachman? Both? She wasn't sure who she was referring to. An involuntary chuckle escaped her. There was no point in fuming. It wouldn't change anything about her situation.

It was unfortunate that the man she hated most in the world was so close and yet so unreachable. As she worked, her anger subsided, and she heaved a sigh. Then she began to hum to herself. Gradually her voice rose, sweet and clear, with the melody of a childhood folk song she often sang while doing her chores.

A shadow fell over her.

She looked up, shading her eyes with one wet hand, to see the coachman hovering over her, with an odd expression on his face.

"My goodness, you gave me a fright," she gasped, almost dropping the shawl into the dirty water. "Why are you standing there scowling at me as if I just cursed the King?"

"That song. What is it called?" His sharp amber eyes bored into hers.

Emily tilted her head, studying him. "Why? Do you collect folk songs in your spare time? Or is this part of a new hobby for His Grace's servants? Cataloguing peasant laundry melodies?"

A muscle twitched in his jaw, but he didn't smile. "Where did you learn it?"

She shrugged. "I don't know. My mother used to sing it. Why?" She wrung out the shawl and shook it out with a snap, splashing some water on him.

"Was she from around here?" he pressed, not taking his eyes off her face. "Are you from this area? Meggie Blythe, you said your name was?"

Emily shifted uncomfortably under his stare. "What if she was? What if I am? What's it to you? Why this interrogation? Would you like to know my age, weight and shoe size while you're at it?"

He said nothing for a moment, his expression unreadable. His gaze lingered on her for half a beat too long, and he opened and closed his mouth as if he wanted to say something but thought better of it. Then, without a word, he turned and walked away, his boots crunching on the gravel.

Emily stared after him with a frown. "Well, what an excessively strange man. Charming manners, too."

She shook her head and bent over her work once more, scrubbing the fabric with more vigour than was necessary.

Then it came to her—an idea, bold and reckless, but thrilling in its simplicity. She froze, her hands stilling in the cold water.

"This could be it," she whispered. A rush of excitement shot through her, banishing all thoughts of mud, songs and strange coachmen. "This might actually work."

Dear Forest Fay,

Oh! You can't imagine how startled I was to reach into the hole of the tree and to find your answer! You truly do exist! I always believed you did! How happy I am!

Here is my wish: I wish Mama to be alive again. I miss her so.

Most sincerely yours,
Little Wren

Little Wren,

I cannot summon back the dead, little one. If I could, I would have done so already and summoned back my own mother. I do know what it feels like to miss one's mother...

Sincerely yours,
Fenn, the Forest Fay

P.S. Wish for something else.

Chapter Two

"Cissy, I've got the solution to all our problems." Emily burst into their room, breathless, for she'd scrambled up the stairs in a very unladylike manner, two steps at a time.

Cissy was sitting in an armchair, her foot propped up on a cushion, looking up from her embroidery with mild interest. "Really? What has happened? And what on earth has happened to your dress? It's all wet—is that mud? And you're all red in the face and your hair is in disarray, worse than it usually is."

"Is it?" Emily glanced into the mirror hanging over the fireplace and grimaced as she saw her brown, wispy hair more out of its bun than in it. "No wonder he looked at me like I was Medusa. I look terrible!"

"Who do you mean, Emmy?"

"Him. The coachman. A most annoying, oafish person." Emily knelt beside Cissy and took her hands in hers. "I meant it when I said I had the solution to all our problems."

Unimpressed, Cissy picked up a pair of scissors and cut a thread in two. "I can't wait to hear what story you've concocted now."

"You won't believe who just arrived at this very inn." She gripped her sister's hands with excitement.

"The King of England?"

"Almost." She drew in a breath. "The devil himself."

Cissy paused, threading a new needle. "Who?" She looked at Emily with a slightly tilted head. Then her eyes widened. "Surely you don't mean, you can't mean... "

"Wolferton," they said in unison.

"The devil, indeed," whispered Cissy, pale. "He's here? Truly?"

"He arrived the moment I stepped out into the yard. This is courtesy of his coachman." Emily gestured at her mud-splattered dress and grimaced.

"I told you we shouldn't have come here. Nothing good will come of it," Cissy wailed.

"Hush. But think about it, it's perfect! You know what we overheard last night, in the taproom." The two ladies at the next table had not been at all discreet when they had discussed the exclusive house party to be held at Ashbourne House. "Wolferton has arrived in person. He is on his way to Ashbourne House, which, as you know, is only a few hours from here. His coachman confirmed it." Emily bit her lower lip for a moment as she recalled her interaction with the coachman. "Come to think of it, he didn't actually confirm that there was to be a country house party, but he didn't deny it either."

Cissy tugged the thimble from her finger. "The maids are talking about nothing else. He wants to settle down.

Could there be some truth in that? Could he really be looking for a wife?"

Emily nodded. "Imagine that: England's most sought-after bachelor finally puts himself on the marriage mart." She clasped her hands in mock reverence.

Cissy shuddered. "Apparently, he is ruthlessly pursued by every creature in London who wears a petticoat, so he mostly avoids social events. On the rare occasions when he does show his face, such as at Almack's, he causes quite a stir. The dances are disrupted as all the women flock to him. Or so the maids say. You know how unreliable all the on-dits can be." She wrinkled her nose. "Honestly, I don't understand it, Emmy. Who on earth would want to marry that hateful man?"

"I know exactly who'd want to marry him." Emily paused dramatically, then pointed a finger at her. She took a big breath before proclaiming, "You."

Cissy blinked back in incomprehension.

Emily stood in front of her with her hands on her hips. "I'm terribly sorry, Cissy, but you will have to marry him."

"Emily White!" Cissy threw down her embroidery. "This is not a joking matter."

"I'm not joking. I am deadly serious. If there is to be a party at Ashbourne House, with the sole purpose of Wolferton choosing a bride, you will, most definitely, be there."

"No, Emily. Never." Cissy shook her head.

"Yes, Cissy. Absolutely. You will be a smashing success. You will bowl him over and marry him." Emily paced the floor in front of her. "Think about it! It is the solution to all our problems."

"Marry the Devil Duke?" Cissy shrieked. "Are you out of your mind? He's awful!"

Emily dropped down beside her and grabbed her hands. "Yes, he is, you're right. He's awful, and terrible, and everything that's bad under the sun. Like, like—" She lifted a finger and crunched up her forehead in thought, searching for a simile. "Like a rotting carcass that stinks to high heaven." She pinched her nose for emphasis.

"Overflowing cesspits," Cissy added with a shudder. "That's worse."

"The slaughterhouse."

"The urine pots of the tanneries." Cissy choked.

"Rotting fish."

"Unwashed feet."

The girls looked at each other and burst out laughing.

"But you know what rather surprised me?" Emily said, still catching her breath. "When I saw him, my first impression was that he didn't look like rotten fish and unwashed feet, Cissy. On the contrary; he was young, and very well dressed, and as he walked past me he smelled of violets, blast the man. You know how much I like violets." Her nose wrinkled, as if it hurt her to admit that there was something admirable about the Duke. "He's an out-and-outer, looking more like a dandy than a devil. Not bad looking at all, if you ignore that silly hair-style of his." She gestured with her hand to her forehead, mimicking the Duke's hair with an exaggerated sweep of her hand. "There is nothing terrifying about him in the least."

Cissy's hand flew to her chest. "What are you saying, Emily? That you like him?"

Emily's eyes widened. "Like him? Good heavens, no! I mean, he's just a man. A corrupt man with too much money, power, and a title. A man who needs to be taught a lesson in humility. A man in search of a wife. You. You will be a duchess!"

"A duchess?" Cissy echoed weakly.

"Yes."

Cissy shook her head. "You know I don't care about any of this. Least of all a title." She stuck out her lower lip stubbornly.

"But we both care about Meadowview Cottage." Emily resumed pacing. "And about finally returning home."

"Home," Cissy whispered, her wide blue eyes filled with yearning.

"Home." Emily nodded. She stopped pacing and sat on the floor, leaning her head against Cissy's arm as she continued. "Do you remember what that feels like? No more endless travelling from Paris to Brussels to Scotland to Wales to Cornwall to Bath under false identities and false names. Aren't you as tired of this lifestyle as I am? Never belonging, only pretending to belong. Never quite at home. Never really getting close to people. Only pretending to be. And with it, the constant unease, the perpetual fear of being exposed. Think of it: it can finally come to an end, this awful life of pretence and dissimulation. If you marry the Duke, we can finally have a home. And Meadowview Cottage can be ours. Forever."

Cissy shook her head firmly. "Not true. Meadowview

Cottage is located on Ashbourne Estate, so it'll belong to the Duke, even after marriage."

Emily pressed her hands together. "But you can ask him for it as a wedding gift. Meadowview Cottage can be yours. It can be our home again."

"The price is too high. Marry that devil?" Cissy shuddered. "He has no conscience and a heart harder than stone."

"True. But think of what you would gain."

"Other than material possessions, I can't think of anything I would gain from such a union."

Emily stood and stared out of the window, watching the sun set orange in the distance beyond the fields.

"Revenge," she whispered. "Revenge for Papa. Revenge for us." She let the words sink in. Then she added quietly, "It would be the perfect revenge. The perfect opportunity. Everything we've lost—restored. He won't know what hit him. He won't suspect our true identities—until it's far too late. This will be our final, grand deception. Our grand finale, if you will." She whirled around to look at Cissy, a gleam in her eyes. "Don't you think that alone is worth the endeavour?"

Cissy looked at her doubtfully. "Revenge? How unlike you to even mention the word. It doesn't sound like something we could ever achieve successfully. Not with a man like him."

Emily tried to stifle a grin, but it did not escape Cissy's watchful eyes. She brushed a stray thread from her skirt. "What? I know that look on your face. You've done something. Tell me!"

Emily picked invisible specks of dust from her sleeve.

"I may have seen his hat sitting on a chair, quite unattended. It's a ghastly one, with peacock feathers this high." She lifted a hand to indicate the height. "Fashion like that should be forbidden, I tell you. And I may have seen a pair of scissors lying on the bar... " She looked at Cissy with wide, innocent eyes.

"You didn't!" Cissy gasped. "Emily. He's a duke! You don't do these things with impunity. What if you were caught?"

"But I didn't get caught," Emily replied smugly. "I just improved his hat a bit. It looks so much better without all that frippery."

Cissy put her hand over her mouth. "What did you do with the feathers?"

She blinked innocently at the ceiling. "A handful of peacock feathers now decorate the pigsty."

The look of comic horror that crossed Cissy's face caused Emily to burst into laughter. She took her sister in her arms. "Don't worry, sister. I won't get caught. This is just a silly, childish prank." She pulled away and gave her a more sober look. "What I was talking about before wasn't such petty revenge. I mean righting a wrong. The wrong that was done to Papa and to us."

There was a tense silence in the room; only the ticking of the clock on the mantelpiece was heard.

Emily smiled sadly. "But I won't force you to do this, Cissy, if you don't want to. You're right. A lifetime of marriage to a devil like him is indeed too high a price to pay for one small moment of petty triumph. I don't want you to live an unhappy life. But, oh, for a moment, allow me to dream." She sighed. Then she gestured to the half-unpacked trunk on the floor. "Otherwise, let us pack up and go back to Scotland. We can be Ladies Annabelle and Honey Hepplewhite again, and convince a lonely old lady living alone in her big house that we are her long-lost great-grandnieces. We'll look after her, treat her well, and be the family she needs. In return, she will give us food and a temporary home. That's all we need, isn't it? It has worked like a charm every time. How many times have we done this? Three, four times?"

"Five times," Cissy whispered. "We were Lady MacCullen's granddaughters until she died. Then we moved to Brussels, where we were the nieces of Colonel Billington, until he died at the Battle of Waterloo. Then we were Miss Marianne Stephenson's cousins, fresh from India. Dear old Mr Sylvester Johnson's granddaughters, until, alas, he too died. And finally, Lady Henrietta Hepplewhite's great-nieces in Bath... " Her voice choked with tears.

Parting with Lady Henrietta had hurt the most. She'd been a kind, frail lady, and they'd had a truly affectionate relationship. They'd lived peacefully in her townhouse in Bath for the last three years, not taking part in any social life aside from going to the theatre now and then and taking the waters at the Pump Room. Their life with Lady Henrietta had been the closest thing to a home they'd had since Papa died.

"My girls, you are a blessing in my life," she'd often told them. "You are the light in the life of an old woman like me. What would I do without you?"

They'd been so happy. Then, out of the blue, a real cousin, a certain Lord John Hepplewhite, had appeared and begun to question their presence in his aunt's house. His interrogation began over tea.

"The daughters of which of the Hepplewhite sons did you say you are, exactly?" He'd looked at them with suspicious, narrowed eyes, a lock of yellow hair falling into his high forehead.

"George, of course," Emily had said with aplomb. It was a safe choice, since every second man was called George these days.

"George." His eyes had been cold. "I find that odd, because as far as I know, Uncle George died of smallpox when he was ten."

Emily waved her hand airily. "Of course he did. What I meant to say, of course, was that our father was Uncle George's brother. His name was... "

"These are Edmund's girls, John. I told you," Lady Henrietta cut in, her usually quiet, frail voice unusually firm. "There's no doubt about it. Now, instead of interrogating my girls and ruining our tea time with your rude behaviour, which I find most unpleasant for it spoils my appetite entirely, let us change the subject. Did you see Kemble's latest performance at Covent Garden in London? Tell me all about it."

But Lord John remained suspicious. When, shortly before his departure, he said he was going to London to investigate the matter and find out the exact whereabouts of his Uncle Edmund and his two supposed daughters, Emily knew with a heavy heart that their time with Lady Henrietta had come to a resounding and final end.

They had no choice but to pack their bags quietly

and disappear from Lady Henrietta's life before she discovered the truth.

For the truth was that she and her sister Cecily were not ladies at all.

They were impostors.

They were born as simply Miss Emily and Miss Cecily White, the daughters of a modest village school-master and a Berkshire lace maker, poorer even than beggars in Piccadilly.

No one had ever doubted their false identities. It was, Emily reasoned, because Cissy was so very beautiful. One look at her and people were dazzled. A creature like Cissy could pass for the Queen of England herself if she set her mind to it. Anyone would believe her in a heartbeat.

They had yet to test that.

Emily was growing weary of it all. So very weary!

No one had ever questioned their name and back-ground. No one had questioned their heritage. No one had ever asked if her father was really a duke or a marquis or an earl.

Until that accursed Lord John Hepplewhite had come along and upended their lives. They'd packed up and fled, boarding the next coach, which happened to be bound for London.

Cissy had cried the entire trip from Bath to Newbury. "Who will remind her to take her pills every morning? Who will take her for walks and make sure she doesn't trip over the cobbles? Who will finish reading *Northanger Abbey* to her?" she sobbed into the hand-kerchief.

Emily had simply answered with a heartfelt sigh.

They'd been on the road ever since. When they passed through Berkshire, so close to Ashbourne Estate, Cissy's tears had dried as she stared at the familiar landscape.

"We really shouldn't be here," she'd whispered.

Emily had initially agreed.

But fate had other plans. When the coach pulled into a coaching inn, Cissy had slipped and twisted her ankle, leaving them no choice but to take a room until she recovered. Perhaps—just perhaps—Cissy's injury was a convenient excuse to linger a little longer in the place of their childhood. Still, they couldn't stay indefinitely. Room and board came at a steep price, and their funds were far from limitless.

"Revenge is tempting," Cissy finally admitted in a quiet voice. "Shocking, isn't it? That I'm actually saying that. But it is the truth. Besides, I am tired of this life. It is time for us to settle down. And marriage may well be the only option left to us. What is your plan?"

"The plan," Emily replied, her eyes glowing with a belligerent spark, "is to continue the charade for a little while longer and attend Wolferton's country house party. Once we're there, things will take care of themselves." Such was Emily's confidence in Cissy's charms. She would sweep him off his feet. She could sweep anyone off their feet. Even the Devil Duke himself.

Cissy made a weary gesture with one hand. "But how?"

"I've tried to win over his coachman, but he's proving uncooperative—a vexatious, odious creature." Emily's cheeks flushed as she remembered his insolent wink. How dare he? "It cannot be helped. You must go down to the taproom, where he will no doubt be dining. All he has to do is see you, and I have no doubt he'll extend an invitation on the spot. I'll have to assume the role of your sister, Lady Poppy Featherstone, as you'll need a chaperone."

"But if I approach him first, he'll think me forward, terribly ill-bred. If he's a stickler for appearances, and he might be, it'll ruin our chances before we even set foot in his house," Cissy countered.

Emily's eyes flashed with determination. "Then we'll have to make sure he approaches you first. Leave that part to me."

"What about my foot?" Cissy gestured to her swollen ankle, still propped up on the pillow.

Emily inspected the foot. "Has the swelling gone down?"

"It has. It has improved considerably. But it still hurts a bit when I try to walk."

"You will have to bear it for a little while longer. But you must leave the room. How else are you going to meet the Duke?"

With a grimace, Cissy struggled to her feet, leaning on Emily's arm for support. "It might put him off when he sees me limping across the room."

Emily narrowed her eyes. "We'll use that to our advantage. Trust me. We will catch that Duke, come what may."

Dear Fenn the Forest Fay,

You, too, have lost your mother? I did not know forest fays had mothers.

I am so very, very sorry that you lost her, too. I would give you a hug, if I could. Instead, I have included a pressed violet for you. (Violets are my favourite flower).

Very well. I shall think of another wish, then: I should very much like a ribbon. A coquelicot ribbon, to be precise. The length of a lady's forearm.

Most sincerely yours,
Little Wren

P.S. I have made a stack of stones in front of the tree. Every time you see the stones stacked, you will know there is a letter from me waiting for you. If you add a black stone on top, then I know you have answered.

Dear Little Wren,

Ribbons don't grow under brambles or bloom from trees. Who do you think I am? A haberdasher? I shall search the forest nonetheless—give me a fortnight.

Your servant,
Fenn the Forest Fay

P.S. What, pray tell, is 'coquelicot'? And why are you called Little Wren? Are you that noisy urchin who runs *ramshackle about the forest, barefoot, in that threadbare grey gown?*

P.P.S. Thank you for the pressed violet. I shall use it as a bookmark.

P.P.P.S Very clever of you to think of stacking the stones.

Chapter Three

JASPER SINCLAIR, DUKE OF WOLFERTON, RAISED HIS
glass with a languid hand. He did not see the interplay
between ruby and gold in the wineglass as the Madeira
caught the glimmers of the firelight from the hearth. His
gaze was far away and a steep furrow darkened his forehead. He was deep in thought.

The taproom had fallen silent the instant he entered.
His name and reputation had preceded him, as usual.
He'd become used to the reverent hush by now, the
furtive glances, the fawning and cringing. He had to
command the respect of his inferiors. It was expected,
demanded, all part of the game. But tonight it grated
more than usual. These were people who'd known him in
his salad days when he'd been green behind the ears, half
the man he was now.

Everything had changed the moment he'd inherited
the title, and people had never treated him the same
since. Now they feared him and treated him like a half
god. And they had reason to.

Maybe he shouldn't be so surprised about the people's reaction to him; after all, he hadn't shown his face in these premises for years. He owned many estates, and this was not one of his favourites.

It was insufferably tedious.

The innkeeper had stumbled forward, his eyes widening slightly as he took in his appearance. "Your Gr-Grace. It is an honour beyond words." He rubbed his sweating hands together nervously. "If you would follow me to your private room."

Wolferton had ignored him and sauntered towards a table in the corner, close to the fireplace. "Bring me your best wine," he ordered.

"At once, Your Grace. M-may I offer you my best bottle of Madeira? It is nearly fifty years old. Or would H-His Grace prefer my twenty-year-old port? Or claret?"

"Bring the Madeira."

"Y-yes, Your Grace. Immediately, Your Grace."

The innkeeper was true to his promise. The Madeira turned out to be excellent.

He drank one glass swiftly and poured himself a second.

Then he passed a weary hand over his face.

Why had he chosen to come here? And what was this strange, blue-devilled sentiment that had come over him?

It was because of all the memories; he concluded. Entirely useless things, which only served to remind him that somewhere in this idle body of his there might still be an organ called a heart, and with it the most shocking thing of all: feelings. And that was something he didn't want to examine too closely. He'd got through his life quite well without that useless organ. He'd prefer to forget that he had one altogether. And those blasted memories, may they be consigned to perdition. For look at what was happening now: he was getting all soft and sentimental and nostalgic.

Zounds. Was that a lump in his throat? And why did his eyes itch? He wasn't about to start bawling like an infant, was he? He blinked, put down the wine glass and pressed his thumbs to the area between his eyes, praying that this, too, would pass.

He poured himself a third glass.

He asked himself, not for the first time, what the deuce had possessed him to come to this god-forsaken part of the country. What was the point of chasing after a past that was long gone?

Was that what this was all about?

One last desperate attempt to find what he'd lost so long ago? Before the iron shackles of matrimony closed about him with finality.

He shuddered.

He had no answer to that, except that it must be sentimentality.

Blast it all.

The buzz of conversation in the room resumed around him, though a little more subdued than before, as if people were afraid to disturb him. A moment later, the door swung open and his companion strolled in.

Friendship was an odd thing, the Duke mused, as he watched his friend make his way through the taproom towards him. It was very rare and very precious. It was surprising who would step forward to be a true friend.

They were the most unlikely of people. He hadn't experienced it too often, but when he did, he felt a strange warmth in his heart. Like gratitude.

Blasted sentimentality!

"Ah, there you are," his friend said lightly, sinking into the seat opposite him. "Hiding in your corner, brooding as usual. Are you already regretting coming here?"

"Even if I did, it would be too late to change my mind. Besides, I have obligations to fulfil. My aunts are expecting me."

"Ah yes. Your venerable aunts. I must say, I am fairly quaking in my boots at the mere thought of them. I hear they're quite terrifying." He shuddered visibly.

The Duke's face softened infinitesimally. "They are the only family I have left. It would behove me to remain in their good graces."

His companion nodded. "Fair enough. Anything to keep your family happy." His face took on a mocking expression. "Including getting shackled and starting a nursery if they command you to." He grinned as he leaned forward. "I hear they've arranged a bridal show to present you with a selection of the prettiest damsels in the entire empire, served on a silver platter. All you have to do is choose. Convenient, I must say. And very practical. Think of the time you'll save." He picked up an empty wine glass on the table, lifted it and inspected it for cleanliness.

The Duke grimaced. "Where did you hear that?"

"Common knowledge, dear friend. Common knowledge." His companion poured himself a glass of Madeira and took a sip. "Hm. That's a delectable drop of goodness." He picked up the bottle and inspected the wax seal that hung from the neck of the bottle on a fine string. "Who would have known this shabby little inn offered something as exquisite as that? But back to the topic at hand. So yes, word has spread faster than a horse on the track at Newmarket that the Duke of Wolferton is in search of a bride. And that he will select her at Ashbourne House, of all places." He leaned forward. "The interest is unprecedented."

"Is it?" The Duke seemed indifferent. "How well informed you seem to be."

His companion waved his hand. "I speak to the servants, you know." He chuckled. "I have just had an interesting conversation with the kitchen maid. You will want to hear about it. It seems there's a Lady Lydia Featherstone living under this roof at the moment. A most exquisite creature. How did she put it? Ah, yes. She is, and I quote, 'more beautiful than Aurora'." He leaned back in his chair, pleased.

"Is she?" The Duke raised a brow, sipping his wine. "Have you actually seen her?"

"I have, indeed. Saw her looking out the window earlier. It's true what they say. She's a prime article, all right. I almost forgot my own name. Look at me, struck dumb with admiration at her beauty." He put his hand over his heart.

"Hm."

"Doesn't that move you at all? That in this very house resides such an Incomparable?"

"The name is unfamiliar."

"Featherstone? I believe there is an earl in Northumberland with that name, is there not? If she's the daughter, you ought to show a little more interest, for she would be quite eligible, considering the fact that you are doomed to get yourself shackled. Especially when the ton consists of—by your words, I quote— 'pasty-faced, insipid-looking debutantes'. Especially when they hound you to death, those ambitious mamas and fortune hunters. If you must marry, you might as well choose an Aphrodite."

"Aurora," the Duke murmured. "Or was it Athena?" He pondered on the matter for a while. "It could have been Artemis. Or a mixture of all three."

His companion's shoulders shook with amusement. "Egad, you are an indifferent creature. I marvel at your cold-bloodedness, for nothing moves you. But that is who you are, Wolferton. It is what distinguishes you from all the others." He finished his wine. "What are you going to do now?"

A slight smile played about the Duke's lips. "Invite her to the party, of course."

His companion blinked. "Who?"

"Aurora." He finished his wine and set it down on the table, adding, softly, "And her maid."

Dear Fenn,

Coquelicot is French, you know. It means a bright poppy red, though my favourite colour is violet. Sadly, violet does not suit my hair, so perhaps coquelicot is the better choice after all.

Yes, that noisy little urchin you may have heard is indeed me. Though I might be poor, I am learning French! Papa says that, though we are poorer than church mice, we are rich in the treasures of the mind. When I am not reading, practising arithmetic, or reciting my French lessons, I roam the forest and sing. They call me Little Wren because, they say, I sing like one.

Yours truly,
Little Wren

My dear Little Wren,

I have enclosed your coquelicot ribbon. You cannot imagine the trouble I went through to procure it! But for you, it was worth every effort. May it bring you great joy.

Your humble forest fay,
Fenn

My dearest Fenn,

Thank you, thank you, thank you—a thousand thanks for the most beautiful ribbon I have ever seen! I feel as though I might fly with happiness! Never have I owned anything so fine.

I have been twirling and singing all day, and now everyone thinks me quite mad. Perhaps I am mad—mad with joy!

Yours most gratefully,

Little Wren

P.S. How might I show my gratitude? Is there a wish I might grant you in return, my dear forest fay?

My dear Little Wren,

That such a small scrap of fabric could bring so much happiness leaves me utterly astonished! Still, I am glad beyond words that you enjoy it so.

Your obedient servant,

Fenn

P.S. I do have one wish, Little Wren. Sing for me— only for me.

Chapter Four

In the end, it turned out to be far easier than they thought.

Emily helped Cissy into a simple, dark blue dress. It was the only formal dress they had. Cissy's light blonde hair was tied back in a loose bun.

"You look like an angel, as always." Emily tugged at the lace fichu and stepped back in satisfaction.

Cissy embodied all the ideals of beauty currently in fashion. She was tall, elegant as a reed, fair-haired with fine, pale skin, rose-petal lips and had cornflower blue eyes in an oval, Madonna-like face. She looked as if she had stepped out of one of Thomas Gainsborough's paintings, all elegance and charm.

Emily, on the other hand, had fine, mousy brown hair that refused to curl or stay in place, and regular brown eyes. Her curvaceous figure, which would have been celebrated in the previous century when tiny waists and wide, generous hips were the ideal of beauty, was at a disadvantage in the current fashion. The high-waisted empire dresses hung around her like a tent, too loose around her waist and too tight around her hips. She perpetually looked like she was increasing. It was very frustrating indeed.

Emily did not consider herself wholly unattractive; not at all. She was pretty enough, with full, generous lips, a slightly upturned nose and a chin full of character, and good teeth, white and strong. But next to Cissy and her dazzling beauty, Emily seemed quite insignificant. No one ever gave her a second glance, least of all the gentlemen. She was often dismissed as a companion at best, or a lady's maid at worst.

That's why she had slipped easily into the role of the maid when she had met the coachman. She'd also discovered that it was easier to obtain information as a maid than as Lady Poppy Featherstone. Not to mention that by being a maid, she solved a major problem: that of clothing.

Between the two of them, they only had one good dress, and even that one wasn't at the height of fashion. So it was easier for Emily to put on her simple cotton dress and pretend to be the maid, while Cissy was the lady. This solved the wardrobe conundrum.

But now that Emily, too, was impersonating a lady, how were they to solve that?

No matter.

Emily always came up with some story or other. In her mind, she was already busy constructing an elaborate backstory. Despite being the daughter of an earl, they were impoverished because their father had gambled away their dowry and the current earl wanted nothing to do with them...

From then on, it was better to stay as close to the truth as possible. With only a handful of gold coins and a ball gown between them, they were forced to travel from relative to relative...

Ah, that sounded good!

She told the story to Cissy, who agreed. "Yes, but we ought to add a kindly old aunt with whom we lived for the past three years, to give our story credibility. Besides, it's true. And you know, the closer we stick to the truth, the less likely we are to slip up and get caught in our own deception."

Emily winced. "You make it sound like we're liars and scoundrels."

Cissy looked at Emily with a sad but resigned expression. "But that's exactly what we are, Emmy. Liars."

Emily shifted uncomfortably. "You make it sound like we're black-hearted sinners. We're not quite as bad as all that. We just like to bend the truth a little. It's not like we do it deliberately to take advantage of people, to hurt them."

"Do we not?" There was a strange look in Cissy's eyes. "You don't think we took advantage of Aunt Henrietta? Or Grandfather Sylvester? When they fed us and gave us a home and even pin money? None of it was really meant to be ours. And who's to say they weren't hurt when we left?"

Emily swallowed painfully. She didn't want to dwell on the subject.

"And now we add revenge to our long list of sins."
Cissy sighed.

"Would you rather not? You don't have to, you
know." Emily paused to adjust the skirt around her.

Cissy stared at the mirror, her face pale. Then she
shook her head. "I don't like it. But I'll do it. For you,
Emmy." She turned and there was a wildly determined
look on her face. "I will do it for you alone. So you can
finally have a home."

Emily's eyes filled with tears. "Oh, Cissy," she choked
out. She felt a surge of love for her sister who would do
anything to make her happy.

"Let's go and do this." Cissy limped to the door.

Emily brushed the tears from her cheeks and rushed
to help her out into the corridor and down the narrow
stairs. Leaning on Emily's arm, Cissy limped down a few
steps and paused as the door to the taproom opened.

An elegant vision appeared, pausing in the doorway.
He opened his pocket watch. "I dare say we shall make
the last stretch before dinner easily," he said to someone
behind him in a nasal, arrogant drawl.

A deep, male voice, no doubt the coachman's, grumbled in reply.

It couldn't be. He was already leaving! They were too
late.

Emily's mind worked feverishly.

If they let him get away, they'd miss the opportunity
of a lifetime. Emily couldn't let that happen.

But how did one approach a duke when one was A. a
woman and B. a stranger?

Deuced etiquette!

There was only one thing to do.

She turned to Cissy with a pleading look on her face. "Forgive me, dearest sister. But you must trust me. This is truly for your own good."

Then Emily closed her eyes for a millisecond, took a deep breath and gave Cissy a firm push between her shoulder blades. "Your Grace!" she called.

Wolferton looked up as Cissy flew towards him with a shriek.

If he catches her, they'll be married, Emily thought. If he doesn't... well, best not to think about it.

For a moment it looked like the latter, as Wolferton just stood there, gaping. Just as Emily was about to rush forward to save her poor sister from a most ungraceful landing, Wolferton, thank heavens, finally activated his wits, opened his arms and caught her.

And very elegantly, too. Cecily fell into his arms with a soft gasp and looked up at him with wide, innocent eyes.

Wolferton looked down at her, visibly stunned, as if this beautiful vision had somehow fallen from the heavens into his life.

At least that was the effect Emily had been aiming for.

"By Jove," he murmured. It was unclear whether his breathlessness was due to Cissy's dramatic arrival or her undeniable beauty.

So far, so good.

"Lydia!" Emily exclaimed, as if she'd only just become aware of the situation. "Are you hurt?"

"N-no." Cissy made a few feeble movements in his

arms, causing Wolferton to tighten his grip, still speechless.

"Just... my ankle... "

Emily stomped down the stairs, sounding and undoubtedly looking like a herd of elephants, quite a contrast to Cissy, who always managed to look graceful even when tumbling down the stairs.

"Your Grace, you are a hero. You saved my sister from certain death." She clasped her hands and opened her eyes wide, hoping to look convincingly grateful.

"I did? I suppose I did." The Duke did not seem to know what to do with the bundle in his arms.

"This is Lady Lydia Featherstone, and I am her sister, Lady Poppy Featherstone." They'd agreed on new names, with new identities.

The Duke carefully placed Cissy on the bottom step, where she stretched out her leg and stifled a small moan that sounded thoroughly convincing.

Emily suppressed a pang of guilt. "My sister has twisted her ankle quite badly."

"Dear me." Just as Emily had hoped, the Duke seemed incapable of looking anywhere but at Cissy. Emily was confident that he wouldn't notice her thread-bare dress. If anyone was capable of turning the Devil Duke's head, it was her.

Cissy gave him a weak, helpless smile and murmured sweetly, "Thank you for catching me, Your Grace. You saved my life."

"You're... welcome. Glad to be of service."

Emily fussed over Cissy. "She won't be able to walk for at least a few days." She gave the Duke a pleading look. "What is to be done? The innkeeper mentioned that our room is needed as the inn is overbooked, but travelling is quite impossible in her condition. We're in a fix."

"What is to be done, indeed?" echoed the Duke, still staring at Cissy, who was sitting on the stairs looking up at him with doe-like eyes.

"Of course, if alternative accommodation could be found, that would be helpful," Emily suggested pointedly.

"Indeed. But where?"

The man appeared to be somewhat slow. Emily's patience was wearing thin. "Perhaps, Your Grace, you could assist us in this matter... ?"

The Duke didn't answer, seemingly lost in Cissy's gaze.

"Your estate isn't far from here, is it?" Emily prompted. "I hear it's only two hours by coach... " *If he doesn't understand now, he's beyond hope.*

At last a glimmer of understanding appeared in his eyes. "Oh! Yes, of course. One can't possibly leave a lady in such distress. I will see what can be arranged."

Emily nodded in satisfaction.

But then, to her astonishment, he simply bowed briefly, muttering, "I must go—most urgent business," and, before either of them could utter another word, he strode to the door, picking up his hat on the way.

"Egad! What happened to my hat?" —was the last thing they heard as the door slammed shut.

Cissy and Emily stared after him.

"Well," Emily said slowly, "that didn't go quite as planned. You were supposed to bowl him over and he was supposed to invite us to his house party at Ashbourne Estate. And then you were supposed to live happily ever after."

"That was Wolferton?" Cissy gasped. "How is that possible? He didn't look or act anything like I'd imagined."

"He's a wolf in sheep's clothing," Emily explained as she helped her sister to her feet. "Don't be fooled by his appearance. It's all part of the game. Anyway, he didn't take the bait. Were we too obvious? There was a moment after he caught you when I thought it would work out nicely, as he seemed to be immediately smitten, but then instead of inviting us to Ashbourne House, he just walked away." Emily huffed in frustration. "Annoying man! At least we tried."

"It's for the best, Emily." Cissy stared at the closed door through which the Duke had disappeared. "I must admit he took me by surprise. He didn't seem quite as fearful as I'd expected. Do you think much of it is just rumour? All this talk about him being a devil, I mean. If I hadn't known his personality from our own experience, I would have thought him a decent sort of man."

Emily leaned her weary head against the wall panelling. "Not that it matters either way, for our bird has flown."

"I dare say he must be used to women trying to catch him. He probably saw through our ruse immediately and decided to flee. Despite everything, I'd rather not be married to a man like him." Cissy leaned on her arm as she walked back up the stairs.

"It was worth the effort, but they say Wolferton is a

notoriously difficult catch. If only we had a sponsor to take us along... but if it can't be helped, it can't be helped." She sighed. "Oh fie. Our plan has failed. That leaves us with Plan B."

"Which is?"

"Scotland."

Cissy nodded and sighed deeply. "Scotland. It's for the best, I suppose."

Later that evening, after the sisters had snuffed out the lights and retired to bed, someone banged on the door.

Cissy slept on. An entire regiment of Wellington's armies could be marching through her bedroom and she wouldn't notice. Emily bolted upright, nearly tumbling out of bed.

"Who is it?" She scrambled out of bed and opened the door.

The innkeeper's wife peered at her, holding up a lantern.

"A carriage has arrived at this late hour for Ladies Lydia and Poppy Featherstone," she announced in a gruff voice. "Ye should've said ye were a lady when ye arrived," she added. "Would've given ye a better room, m'lady."

Emily blinked at her sleepily. "A carriage? What do you mean? The mail coach to Scotland? It leaves that early?"

"No," the woman growled. "The Duke of Wolferton's carriage. He sent it himself. Ye'd better hurry. A man like Wolferton doesn't like to be kept waiting."

With her heart pounding, Emily sat beside her sister in the well-sprung carriage as it sped through the darkened countryside. She couldn't be sure if the coachman was the same cloaked figure she'd glimpsed earlier—the rude, gruff, vexatious man she'd met in the inn's courtyard. The coachman had mumbled a greeting as they entered the coach before taking his seat, but she hadn't seen his face.

"This can't be happening," Cecily stammered, clutching Emily's hand. "Are we truly on our way to Ashbourne House? In the Duke's carriage? As Lady Poppy and Lydia Featherstone? Everything is happening too fast. Emily. I'm terrified!"

Emily clung to her hand. She too felt queasy. Even though she had orchestrated this very situation, she couldn't quite believe it was really happening. They were entering the wolf's lair. "Yes," she murmured. "I can hardly believe it myself." Somehow her plan had worked. The Duke, moved by a sense of noblesse oblige, had been persuaded by the story of Cecily's twisted ankle and, true to form, had sent his carriage to bring them to his home so that she could recover. It didn't fit the picture of the notorious Devil Duke she had painted in her mind, but she wasn't entirely surprised. Men invariably responded to Cecily with chivalry—every single time.

As the coach slowed and approached the village, the sisters fell silent. Fascinated, they looked out of the window, watching the warm lights of the cottages flicker. At the edge of the village, just beyond the shadow of the church, stood a solitary cottage, dark and silent.

"There it is," Emily whispered, her voice barely audible. "Meadowview Cottage."

They craned their necks to catch a last glimpse of the

darkened cottage as the coach turned and rumbled through the massive stone gates.

Home.

"I'll do as you say." Cecily's voice was barely audible over the steady clatter of wheels on the cobbled drive. "I'll marry him. We'll get our home back."

"Good." Emily nodded, her tone firm. "I will do everything in my power to make this match happen."

As they rode down the grand avenue lined with ancient oaks, Ashbourne House loomed into view, impressive, and proud, and cold.

Dearest Fenn,

This morning, I ran through the forest singing my favourite song as loudly as I could—just for you! Did you hear it? Did you like it?

If you wish, I shall sing for you every day. My songs will be yours alone.

Yours truly,
Little Wren

Dear Little Wren,

I did indeed hear you, and your voice is as sweet and lovely as your namesake. You truly do sing like a wren.

Because your song pleased me greatly, I grant you leave to make another wish. Choose wisely.

Your most obedient servant,
Fenn

My dearest Forest Fay Fenn,

Truly? Another wish? Very well... If, by some chance, as you wander the wild forest paths, you happen to stumble upon a ribbon—a velvet one, in the colour amaranthine, please think of my sister, Cissy. She would love it dearly.

Sofi Laporte

Yours most humbly,
Little Wren

Chapter Five

"Repeat that. Who did you say has arrived?" Lady Dalrymple, not usually hard of hearing, grabbed her sister's ear trumpet and pressed it to her ear. As the only one of the Duke's three great-aunts to have married, she had worn black since the death of Lord Dalrymple over twenty years ago. She had a proud forehead and an eagle nose, and sharp, grey eyes.

"The Ladies Lydia Featherstone and Lady Poppy Featherstone," repeated the housekeeper, Mrs Smith. "Invited personally by His Grace."

"Never heard of them." Lady Dalrymple frowned. "Jane, have you ever heard the name Featherstone?"

Lady Jane tilted her head thoughtfully. Lady Jane's face was severe and masculine. Her dress was also dark, plain and practical without any sort of adornment. "Featherstone, you say? Featherstone, Featherstone... " She narrowed her eyes in concentration, then shook her head. "No. Doesn't ring a bell. Mabel?"

Her other sister, Lady Mabel, shook her head.

Mabel, the smallest of the three, was clad in a simple, black gown. Though never married, she kept her sister company even in mourning.

"How very peculiar," Araminta mused. "The dear boy never invites anyone to his house parties. He abhors them. We had to coax him endlessly to agree to this one. And you are certain he invited them himself?" She gasped and put her hand to her heart. "Do you think it could be... " She leaned forward, her voice dropping to a low whisper. "Could he have developed a tendre for one of the ladies? At last?" She clasped her hands together in delight.

Jane sniffed. "Unlikely. Our 'dear boy' has built up quite a reputation with the ladies, but he'd never seriously take up with one, let alone develop a tendre for one. They call him the Devil Duke for a reason, you know."

Araminta sighed. "I wonder what happened to turn his heart to stone. He used to be such a sensitive, trusting boy."

"A woman happened," Mabel murmured, almost to herself. "Or rather, a girl. A long, long time ago."

"What did you say, Mabel? Speak up," Araminta said impatiently. "Surely some woman broke his heart. She must have been a cruel, cold-hearted sort of creature to break a man like that."

"Or sweet and innocent," Mabel added quietly. But neither sister listened.

Araminta turned to the housekeeper. "The ladies have arrived? Are they settled in?"

Mrs Smith nodded. "Yes, ma'am. The Duke gave

personal instructions for the Green and Blue Suites to be prepared."

"The finest rooms. How intriguing." Jane crossed her arms.

"Lady Lydia Featherstone injured her ankle in a fall at the inn," Mrs Smith informed her. "She fell down the stairs. The doctor has already been summoned."

Araminta raised an eyebrow. "Goodness. She fell down the stairs?"

"Yes, my lady. I was informed that the Duke caught her and prevented further harm."

Araminta dropped her quizzing glass. "How uncharacteristically chivalrous of him."

"Chivalrous, bah," Jane sniffed. "It's clear as daylight. He fell prey to a fortune hunter. I didn't think he was that green behind the ears."

"Or it was love," Mabel, always the passionate romantic, suggested gently.

Jane heard that and cut in. "Fiddlesticks, Mabel. Wolferton and love are as unlikely a combination as Prinny and frugality, or King George and sanity— extremely unlikely, to be sure. Well, it cannot be helped. One must wait until morning before one's curiosity can be satisfied. Pray, has Wolferton settled in, yet?"

"He has," a deep voice interjected as the Duke strode into the room. The maids and housekeeper fell to a curtsy. "Your Grace."

"My dear boy." Araminta dropped her embroidery and rose from her chair. "My dear, dear boy."

The Duke embraced each of his aunts in turn and

placed a kiss on their cheeks. "Aunt Mabel. Aunt Jane. Aunt Araminta."

"What a surprise, Jasper. We weren't expecting you until tomorrow afternoon." Jane patted his arm, looking fondly up into his face.

"We made excellent time, testing the new horses I bought at Tattersall's. Worth every penny, it turns out."

"You take after your father in that respect." Araminta touched his cheek. "Always the sportsman."

The Duke gave her a wintry smile. "I wouldn't know, would I? Having hardly known the man."

Jane shot Araminta a warning glance. "No, you wouldn't, of course, since your parents preferred to live in separate households. It was a thoughtless remark. Never mind. We were wondering about the two ladies who have arrived. Featherstone. It's not a name any of us recognise."

The Duke moved to the sideboard and poured himself a glass of cordial. "I daresay you wouldn't."

"But who are they?" Araminta pressed.

He shrugged. "More meat for the marriage mart? To broaden my options? That's the whole point of this farce of a party, is it not? You've invited the most eligible ladies in the ton so that I may choose a suitable breeding cow?"

"Jasper!" Araminta and Jane exclaimed simultaneously, thoroughly scandalised.

"What does it matter who they are? I am to be married, am I not?" He took a sip, nonchalant. "So the exalted Wolferton line doesn't die out with me, having been in existence since when—William the Conqueror? Thought I might expand the choices a little before I allow

52

myself to get snared in the parson's mousetrap. It's a life-long sentence, after all."

Araminta wrung her hands. "Yes, but you go about it in such a cold-blooded manner. Choosing a wife isn't quite the same as choosing a pair of boots."

"It's not?" He sat down, crossed his legs and inspected his boots, an exquisite pair made by London's finest bootmaker, Hoby's.

"It is not!" his aunts chorused.

"I fail to see why not. One inspects the boots, selects a pair that's pleasing, tries them on, and if they're comfortable, decides to purchase them and wear them out. Ideally, they will last a lifetime, although that may be optimistic. What is more realistic is that sooner or later one will have to replace those boots with a newer pair."

"It is highly improper of you to say such a thing, and furthermore, it is an entirely unrealistic comparison," Araminta scolded him in a sharp voice.

"You are quite right, Aunt. A more realistic comparison would be to have several pairs of boots, and to change them as one sees fit... "

Araminta shrieked, Jane covered her face with both hands, and Mabel turned pale and sank into a chair.

"Jasper!"

The Duke laughed. "Why not? We're being realistic, aren't we?"

Jane pointed her finger at him. "You really are a devil."

He chuckled darkly. "A glass of cordial, my ladies?" He lifted the decanter on the table in front of him.

Only Mabel accepted a glass.

"Oh, my nerves," Araminta groaned, fanning herself. "Surely, you are jesting. You cannot truly mean anything you've just said."

"I think he means it," Mabel commented thoughtfully, between sips of cherry cordial.

The Duke cast her a quick, fond smile. "Before I forget: Chippendale has arrived with me."

"Did he bring a sister?"

"No."

"Well, then... " Araminta dismissed him with a wave. "Hamish is here with his sister. Lord and Lady Willowthorpe and their daughters are to arrive later. The rest of the guests arrive tomorrow. Then, of course, there are the two ladies you invited."

Wolferton finished his glass and set it down with a dry smile. "Let the boot inspection begin."

A FOOTMAN HAD CARRIED Cissy to her room.

She had protested at first, but a sharp pinch from Emily silenced her. Reluctantly, she allowed herself to be lifted by a footman and carried up the grand staircase. Her eyes widened as she took in the opulence of the mansion.

How often had Emily seen the house from afar, an imposing structure overlooking the lake? Yet this was the first time she'd set foot inside. It was nothing like the sad, abandoned shell she remembered from her childhood. The house had undergone significant renovations and was brimming with treasures: oil paintings, marble busts and thick, expensive Persian and Aubusson carpets that softened each step. Polished tables held vases over-flowing with flowers, and gilded mirrors reflected every flicker of light, amplifying the splendour.

Upon their arrival, the housekeeper, Mrs Smith, stepped forward to greet them. She was tall and severe, dressed in an immaculate grey gown, with a jingling set of keys dangling from her waist.

"His Grace regrets he is unable to greet you personally," she said, her voice clipped but polite. "He is attending to business. He will be pleased to welcome you tomorrow, along with the other guests." With that, she led them down a series of corridors to their chambers.

Emily tried to maintain an air of nonchalance. After all, as Lady Poppy Featherstone, she was used to visiting great houses. Still, she couldn't help but stifle a small gasp of delight as Mrs Smith opened the door to her room. The room was a vision in velvet blue, with violets arranged in porcelain vases, filling the air with a sweet, delightful fragrance. Cissy's adjoining room was identical but decorated in a rich forest green, from the canopy bed to the drapes and wallpaper.

Once the maids had departed, the sisters looked at each other and then Cecily clasped her hands together with sparkling eyes. "Emily, this place is magical! If I could, I would twirl and dance around the room."

"I'll do it for you." Emily stretched out her arms and spun around in place. "Whee!" She collapsed onto the massive bed, giggling.

Some time later, dinner was brought to Cissy's room. A footman set the table with a damask tablecloth, silver cutlery and crystal glasses. "Potage aux champignons, filet de sole à la meunière, accompanied by haricots verts and pommes duchesse, a selection of cheeses and for pudding crème brûlée and petits fours," he announced in impeccable French. Then he bowed and retreated.

"I trust everything is in order and that dinner will be to your liking." The housekeeper watched the proceedings with eagle eyes. "Let us know if your tastes change and you prefer something else. You will be accommodated."

Emily glanced at the table. "Dinner seems quite acceptable, thank you."

"His Grace has ordered a physician to see you in the morning," the housekeeper added.

"That is hardly necessary," Cissy began, embarrassed, but Emily interrupted.

"This is most kind of His Grace. Please give our sincere gratitude for his thoughtfulness."

Once Mrs Smith had left, the girls stared at the beautifully laid table.

"I've never seen anything like it. Not even at Aunt Henrietta's, and you know how she liked to feast," Cissy stammered.

"I behold food, Cissy." Emily said. "That's all that matters. But this certainly tops anything I have ever seen. If this is how they feed individual guests, imagine a dukely banquet?"

Cissy's eyes widened. "It would be positively sublime!"

Emily nodded and sank into her chair. "I confess, I'm beginning to feel a little intimidated."

"We can do this. Yes, we certainly can." Cissy sat down across from her and ate with determination.

Emily sighed contentedly after a spoonful of soup, but quickly remembered something. "The code word. Remember, if one of us says it, the other must come to the rescue immediately, no matter what the circumstances."

"'Bubble and squeak'," Cissy said with a grin. "But, Emmy, can't we think of something better? Last time, in the Pump Room in Bath, when I was surrounded by admirers and feeling terribly anxious, it took me ages to remember what it was, and then I couldn't fit it into a sentence that made sense."

"I remember." Emily snorted. "You said, 'The taste of the mineral water reminds me of 'bubble and squeak.'" She clapped a hand over her mouth to stifle her laughter.

Cissy groaned. "It took me over half an hour to think of that!"

"But it worked, didn't it? Like a knight in shining armour, I whisked you away from that dreadful lot." Emily shook her head. "If only the gentlemen had been a decade younger. There was no suitable man for you among them, alas. Although I did have hopes for Mr Matthews."

Mr Edward Matthews, a man in his late thirties, dressed in plain brown, possessed an unassuming appearance and a gentle demeanour that quietly set him apart from others. It seemed initially to Emily that he couldn't hold a candle to the other suitors who had vied for her sister's attention.

But there had been something different about him. He'd appeared clearly infatuated. Of course, that was nothing unusual; most, if not all, gentlemen were. What was different, almost startling, was that for the first time Cissy seemed to be responding.

From the heart.

And that was a first, if ever there was one.

Except, Mr Matthews had disappeared without a trace. One day he was there—attentive and sincere—and the next he was gone. No letter. No goodbye. Nothing. It was as if the earth had swallowed him up.

Cissy put down her fork, her cheeks flushed. "I'm sure Mr Matthews is long married by now. With a child or two."

Emily tilted her head, considering her words. "That would be quite a feat, considering it's only been six months since we last saw him. But who knows? Maybe he had a secret family hidden away somewhere." She paused, her eyebrows knitting together. "Though I doubt it. He seemed sincere. With you, I mean."

Cissy pushed her plate away. "Let's not talk about Mr Matthews. He's in the past. Nothing can be done about it. I'm to marry the Duke, remember?"

Emily nodded slowly. "Yes. That is the plan. Surely you can do so much better than a simple barrister."

But a thread of unease tugged at her. Cissy's outward composure was impeccable, but she was eating her crème brûlée with far too much concentration, as if completely unaffected by the subject at hand.

"Wolferton," Emily said suddenly, breaking the silence.

Cissy looked up questioningly.

"He will make you happy," she declared firmly. "I

will see to it personally. If he doesn't, I will unleash my wrath upon him."

"Oh, intriguing! And how will you achieve this, dear sister? Challenge him to a duel? "

"Now there's an idea." Emily tapped her finger against her lips, pretending to think deeply.

"You don't even know how pistols work."

"Then we'll use swords."

"You've never touched one in your life."

Emily held up the butter knife. "I'll use this. A most fearsome weapon indeed."

"Terrifying!"

"Precisely." Emily nodded. "He won't know what hit him."

"A knitting needle might be more effective," Cissy said with a grin.

"An embroidery needle."

"A toothpick!"

"Imagine duelling with toothpicks! Didn't we try that once?" Emily laughed at the memory. "We caused such a commotion that Papa came in, enquiring whether the house was collapsing."

The sisters burst into laughter, their mirth echoing through the room.

Dear Little Wren,

Amaranthine? Coquelicot? What fanciful names you dream up! Next you will ask for stockings the shade of pomona green.

Sincerely,

Fenn

Dear Fenn,

Oh! Could you find me stockings the colour of pomona green? Truly?

Most gratefully,

Little Wren.

My dear Little Wren.

What will you give me in return?

Your obedient servant,

Fenn

Chapter Six

The physician came the next morning and prescribed a poultice for Cissy's foot, advising three days of rest.

"No standing, no walking and certainly no dancing during this time," he instructed.

This meant that Cissy would have to remain in her room, unable to socialise. But Cissy took it in her stride. "It's quite acceptable to me," she declared. "I'll sit by the window and admire the view of the park."

The view from the window was magnificent: a lake with a fountain in front of them, beyond which stretched the parkland and woods. "I will read, embroider and enjoy the wonderful food Mrs Smith brings me."

Emily, however, was far from finding it acceptable. How could she bring about a match between Cissy and the Duke if her sister was shutting herself away? "That won't do. Perhaps we could ask the footman to carry you down to the drawing room so that you can at least meet the guests, even if you remain seated?"

Cissy shook her head. "No, Emily. I'd rather not have people standing around looking down at me while I'm sitting. The situation is unnerving enough. Let me stay here until my ankle heals somewhat. But you must meet the other guests." She leaned forward. "Especially him."

Him. Emily's brow darkened.

She would have to set aside her personal feelings of antipathy if she was to orchestrate this match. She'd loathed the faceless image of the Duke before she'd actually met him. It was easy to dislike a faceless person. Now that she knew what he looked like, a silly popinjay no less, she found that her degree of loathing had diminished somewhat.

Now she only felt contempt for him. He was clearly a nincompoop with far too much power.

Emily reminded herself to focus on the goal, for nothing else mattered. But how was she to catch a duke? Especially when it was for her sister, not herself.

"Lady Dalrymple, Lady Mabel and Lady Jane are presently resting and would like the honour of welcoming you at nuncheon," Mrs Smith informed them.

"And His Grace?" Emily enquired, surprised that no one was there to greet them.

"His Grace is currently engaged with some pressing business and begs to be excused," the housekeeper replied.

Very well, then. That meant they had the entire morning to themselves.

"I'd like to rest as well, if you don't mind," Cissy said with a repressed a yawn. "To prepare myself mentally for what's to come."

Leaving Cissy to rest in the room, Emily decided to venture outside to take the air and to consider their next move.

It was a beautiful autumn day. The birds were chirping in the trees as Emily walked lightly along the path that culminated in the wide avenue that led out of the park.

Her heart beat with excitement as the little village appeared. The cottages, with their crooked walls and roofs, nestled around the Norman church. And somewhat farther off stood a little cottage whose walls were covered with green ivy, overlooking the valley beneath, where the sheep grazed on the meadow.

Meadowview Cottage. It was clearly unoccupied. Cobwebs hung from the corners, the paint was peeling from the door and window sills, the thatched roof was thin and worn, moss was growing in the cracks, and the walls, originally whitewashed, were now dull and grey, streaked with soot and grime. The garden was overgrown with brambles.

Emily's heart tightened.

She stopped outside of the stone wall, twisting her hands together, ready to burst into tears.

So this was what had happened to her beloved home. It stood lonely and abandoned, and no one cared for it at all. She wondered for one moment whether she should try to go inside, then changed her mind. Through the windows she could see that the cottage was empty. There would be nothing left of their life there, no reminder of her parents and her childhood.

After a while, she walked on, head bowed, until she

reached a neighbouring cottage farther down the road. Years ago, Mr and Mrs Kent lived there, an elderly couple. It was likely that they had died long ago. Her steps slowed as she debated whether to knock on the door. The door opened, and a woman came out carrying a basket of laundry, which she hung on a clothesline in the garden. She did not recognise the woman. She must be a new tenant. "Good morning," Emily called.

The woman shaded her eyes as she looked at Emily. "Good morning," she replied. "Can I help you?" She looked at Emily curiously.

Emily clutched her shawl. "I was just taking a walk in the area and happened to pass by. I saw that the cottage next to yours is uninhabited. May I ask who used to live there?"

"It used to be the schoolmaster's cottage." The woman bent down to hang up the sheets as she spoke. "Mr Bentley lived here for about ten years, until he left. No one's been living there since."

Mr Bentley. The name was unfamiliar. A schoolmaster. Of course he would be. Meadowview Cottage had traditionally been occupied by the village schoolmaster, which was why her father had lived there.

"Has this always been the schoolmaster's cottage?" she asked, feigning ignorance. "Forgive my curiosity. I am a guest at Ashbourne House."

"Are you, indeed? I hear His Grace is holding a grand house party there these days." She studied Emily, no doubt taking in her cashmere shawl and simple cotton dress and wondering who she was. "But to answer your question, yes, it has always been the schoolmaster's house, as far as I know. I moved here only three years ago."

Emily nodded. "And the previous school master? Before Mr Bentley? Do you know anything about him?"

The woman pulled out a shirt and paused, giving her a sharp look. "Why do you want to know?"

"No particular reason. I was just curious," Emily stammered, taken aback by the sudden suspicion on the woman's face.

"All I know is hearsay," the woman continued. "Mr White, who lived here before Mr Bentley, was a favourite, loved by the children and the village elders alike. He left suddenly one day, out of the blue. No one knows why. Rumour has it that he died unexpectedly, leaving behind two young daughters." She paused, frowning. "Nobody knows what happened to them. Or if they do know, they refuse to talk about it. Poor things. First, they lost their mother, then their father. Then the girls themselves vanished. For a long time, no one would move into the cottage, saying it must be cursed. His Grace had a devil of a time finding another schoolmaster. After Mr Bentley, no one was interested in moving in, as you can clearly see."

Emily found she had an odd lump in her throat that she couldn't swallow down no matter how hard she tried.

"They say they were beautiful girls, both of them, and intelligent. I daresay if they survived, they must be grown up and long married by now. But one can't help but wonder what happened to them." The woman went to hang up her washing.

Emily stood in silence. "Thank you for thinking of

them," she whispered. She bid the woman goodbye and continued on her way, furtively wiping her cheek as an errant tear found its way down.

Life had continued. But against all odds, they had not been entirely forgotten. She found some solace in that thought.

And what about Mr and Mrs Timms at the bakery? Their apprentice, John, had always slipped them bits of leftover bread when he could. They were long gone, too.

Her thoughts turned to the children of the tenant farmers—poor families who could barely afford the meagre tuition her father had charged. They sometimes paid with firewood or food they could barely spare, and her father, soft-hearted to a fault, had often refused even that.

Those children must be grown now. Perhaps some had stayed, still eking out a hard life on the Duke's land. Or perhaps they had left to seek their fortunes in London, dreaming of something better than the relentless toil of tenant farming.

Emily and Cissy knew only too well what life was like on the Duke's land. They had lived it themselves.

Her gaze wandered over the stately gardens of the park, where manicured hedges and flowerbeds gave way to the wilder, more unkempt woodland. Beyond the lake, wilderness reigned. She followed the path around the lake and entered the forest.

Oh, how familiar this place was! How much she had missed it. The foliage closed around her like the embrace of a long-lost friend.

Throughout her childhood, Ashbourne House had

been uninhabited. The previous Duke of Wolferton had favoured another, more lavish estate and never once visited. Ashbourne House had been closed, with only a handful of servants to maintain the estate. It had been safe to enter and roam the park and grounds, which had fallen into disrepair. Emily and Cissy had wandered through these woods, picking wild strawberries and elderberries, swimming in the lake, skipping across the stream and climbing the trees. It had been their own little kingdom. They'd believed in woodland fays and forest sprites. Emily had read stories about them to little Cissy as they lay on the moss under the trees. She had sung songs at the top of her voice, knowing no one would hear. Yes, they had been poor. But what a carefree childhood it had been!

The forest was so vast that it bordered the neighbouring estate. A narrow stone wall marked the boundary between Ashbourne Estate and Silvervale Valley, which belonged to Lord Hamish. Between the two estates lay a stretch of land—a sort of no man's land—untended by either side and left well alone. And there, in that forgotten patch of wilderness, was a magical place that belonged to her alone. Not even Cissy knew about it.

In the heart of a clearing stood an ancient oak tree. When one lifted the ivy that hung like a heavy curtain from its overhanging branches, a hole in the hollow of the trunk was revealed, which must have been once the home of owls.

With some determination, Emily parted the ivy and reached inside. It was empty.

Of course it was.

She hadn't expected anything to be there, really.

Not after all this time. How long had it been? Ten years? Longer?

She brushed the hair from her face with a tired movement.

He had long forgotten her.

A feeling of abandonment and betrayal washed over her. A feeling so old that it had become a part of her.

She stared at the tree, lost in thought. He'd granted many of her wishes over the years, Fenn, her forest fay.

It had begun so innocently. She'd read about forest sprites, and that they were benevolent, magical creatures who granted wishes when they wanted to. One summer afternoon, in a playful moment when her imagination had taken over, she'd written him a letter.

DEAR FOREST FAY,
Will you grant me a wish?
Yours sincerely,
Little Wren.

LITTLE WREN, that was what her father had called her. "You sing like a wren, in a voice as sweet and lovely. Just like your mother." Her mother had loved to sing. But she could hardly remember her, for she had died far too young.

She'd been so surprised when, a fortnight later, she'd reached into the hole again and found a letter! A sheet of parchment folded into a small rectangle.

She'd unfolded it, her hands trembling with excitement.

Yes.

He'd written the word in a scrawl of black ink. Nothing more.

Emily had jumped up and down with excitement. She'd run home and written another letter.

I wish Mama to be alive again.

The next day, promptly, she found an answer:

I can't bring people back from the dead.

With hammering heart, she'd stared at his signature.

Fenn.

He'd told her to wish for something else, and since she couldn't think of anything better, she'd wished for a ribbon. And a fortnight later she'd found a roll of the most beautiful red velvet ribbon. It had been so beautiful that she had been afraid to wear it, and instead she had kept it in a box under her bed, where she kept all her treasures.

Thus it had begun, her unlikely friendship with a forest fay, and their ensuing correspondence had lasted four magical, lovely years.

She'd told him all her wishes and dreams. Most of them had been girlish, childish wishes. A trinket. A sweetmeat. A book. A small bouquet of violets. Another roll of pink ribbon for her sister. More often than not, he gave her things that she'd never even wished for, like a pair of leather boots and silken stockings, which had been the best present she'd ever received in her entire life.

He'd left each item in the hole in the tree for her to find.

Once she'd pulled out a pouch of gold coins, which

she'd steadfastly refused to take. That refusal had nearly led to a quarrel, for he'd been very offended by her rejection.

If you are hungry, take the money and buy some food. If not for yourself, then for your father and little sister, he'd written.

This was after she'd confessed in a letter that she often went to bed hungry and dreamed of hot crumpets all night.

The next day, she'd found a plate of warm crumpets wrapped in a tea towel in the tree, along with the bag of coins. She ate the crumpets, saving one for her sister and father, but left the coins behind.

Fenn hadn't taken it well. He'd threatened to break off their correspondence.

If you do not accept my gift, you will break the magic and I shall disappear forever.

That had frightened her into submission, for she could not bear the thought of losing Fenn.

She reluctantly handed the pouch to her father, who opened it to reveal five gold coins.

He looked at her with concern. "You really do not know who gave you this?"

She shook her head.

Her father frowned, then sighed. "Whether gift or alms, someone wishes you well." He put the coins back in the bag and handed it to her. "It must be an anonymous donor from the parish." He hung his head. "I am ashamed that I cannot provide for my daughters as they deserve."

They led a poor but happy life, the schoolmaster and his two daughters. Emily walked around barefoot all day in a simple blue cotton dress that had been mended many times. Never before had she been made to feel poor; on the contrary, she'd always thought of herself as rich, for her father had given his daughters plenty of love and freedom.

"What do I do with these?" The pouch in her hand felt heavy.

Her father bent his head. "Do what you like. It's yours."

She'd kept it safe, not using the coins until years later, when they had to leave Meadowview Cottage.

Over all those years, they must have exchanged hundreds of letters. They had become more than correspondents. They had become friends, soulmates, almost. She had told him everything, baring her heart in a way she could with no one else. She had shared her dreams, her hopes, her fears, her wishes. Oh, how many wishes! He knew them all. He had listened patiently, offering solace and advice. He had been her only true friend, the one secret she kept from the world. Not even Cissy had known.

HE WAS the only one who understood her, who comforted her, who made her laugh.

An intangible fairy with whom she communicated only through paper. A forest fay who granted her even the most unlikely of wishes. Sometimes the replies were irregular, delayed by weeks, even months. He'd granted all her wishes. He'd always replied.

Except for that single, one time when she had needed

him most—that terrible winter when everything changed, when her childhood ended, and when her life and dreams shattered.

Emily stared at the tree bitterly.

In the end, he, too, had failed her.

In the end, it was just that: an ordinary tree with an empty hole, without magic. There had never been any magic.

Only illusion and childish dreams that, sooner or later, had to come to an end.

Maybe it was the natural course of things. Everyone had to grow up, after all.

With a weary sigh, Emily turned and headed back to the house.

My dearest Forest Fay,

As a thank you I have drawn you a picture of my family, which I shall give you in return for my wish. There is Papa, me and Cissy. Have I told you yet that Papa is a schoolmaster in the village school? Cissy is three years younger than me. We are very happy, living in Meadowview Cottage. I have to go to school every day, which I like very much, since Papa teaches there. Do forest fays go to school, too?

Yours Truly,
Little Wren

My dear Little Wren,

I was most pleased by your drawing. It wasn't half bad. I shall hang it up in my faerie cave and look at it every day. We don't have school, alas. We forest fays live a very solitary life... but your letters give me pleasure. Tell me more about your world—it makes me forget my own troubles.

Your obedient servant,
Fenn

P.S. I have enclosed the ribbon for your sister in 'amaranthine' and stockings for you—in pomona green.

Chapter Seven

It was almost midday when Emily returned to the house. She had to make haste and get changed for nuncheon. Not that her wardrobe offered much variety, but she could hardly appear as she was, with a mud-stained hem, nettles clinging to her shawl and twigs in her hair. She would have to borrow Cissy's lemon-yellow dress, which looked splendid on Cissy and gave her a golden glow. Unfortunately, the same colour gave Emily the complexion of a turnip.

Still, appearances had to be kept up. She would put on the dress, become Lady Poppy Featherstone, meet Lady Dalrymple, Ladies Jane and Mabel—and the Duke. Instead of hurling the tea in his face, she would feign a gracious smile as she thanked him nicely for his hospitality, only imagining that she was throwing the tea over his neatly tied cravat and throwing crumpets at his silly coiffure.

Wait, no. Not the crumpets. Those she would eat, with relish.

Emily grimaced. The prospect of the social obligations that awaited her filled her with dread. It wasn't that she disliked being in society; on the contrary. She often found it amusing. But she did mind not being able to be herself.

Yes, that was it.

With all the identities she'd assumed in the past, she hardly knew who she was.

What had happened to Little Wren? The wild, carefree girl who'd once skipped barefoot through the woods, singing at the top of her lungs and believing in fairies.

She was buried somewhere deep down, smothered under layers of silk and damask, lost amidst all the pretence.

But most of all, what grated was having to behave prettily towards her arch-nemesis, the very man she loathed, and not being able to tell him the truth of who she really was.

That, more than anything, was what galled her the most.

Her brow furrowed as she thought about everything he'd done to them, everything she held him responsible for, and the blight he'd been on their lives.

She rubbed her nose absently. It left her more than perplexed. There was *that* Wolferton, the threatening, faceless, ominous presence of her imagination that had hung over her like a dark cloud, bringing ruin and misery.

And then there was *this* Wolferton.

Wolferton, the fashionable dandy who'd been startlingly kind and unexpectedly thoughtful. He'd saved her sister from harm. Although, to be fair, the incident had been staged. Anyone, surely, would make an effort to catch someone like Cissy if they'd looked up and seen her plummeting towards them out of nowhere. Who wouldn't? Even the most degenerate duke had done so, proving her point. Still, she couldn't read too much into it, for it could have been simple self-preservation. After all, who would want to be crushed like a pancake on the floor? Of course, to prevent that terrible fate, he had to catch her.

Nevertheless, he'd behaved like a proverbial gentleman afterwards. He'd understood their plight at the inn and, after some prodding, had invited them to his house. He'd sent a carriage. He'd given them fine guest rooms, surely some of the finest in the house. He'd given them excellent food. He'd called the doctor for Cissy.

She couldn't make sense of him.

Should they truly proceed with this mad scheme?

And if so, how was she to orchestrate the match?

Past experience told her that Cissy would offer no help in the matter. Her sister was content to be passive, exerting the least amount of effort, while Emily did all the work, sometimes quite literally pushing her into the arms of a man.

Though perhaps the groundwork had already been laid since he appeared to be smitten already. But then again, that might not mean anything. Everyone who laid eyes on Cissy was smitten, unless they happened to be cucumbers.

There were those men, too, she supposed. Men with

the emotional depth of a cucumber: cool and watery and utterly bland.

Emily wrinkled her nose at the thought.

Emily liked most foods. Having lived in poverty for most of her childhood, she'd learned to appreciate every scrap. But cucumbers!

She made a face.

They were nearly as difficult to like as Wolferton himself.

Her stomach growled loudly. Zounds, all these food analogies were making her hungry.

"Watch where you're going," a voice shouted sharply.

She found herself grabbed, lifted into the air and set down as if she were a mere rag doll. By the time she realised what was happening, she had already been released.

Gasping, she looked up, meeting a pair of sharp amber eyes between strands of dark hair that fell into his forehead, belonging to a man who was standing close. So close she could smell his scent of leather, sandalwood and —mint?

"Meggie Blythe," a deep voice drawled. "Lady Lydia Featherstone's maid. So we meet again. Are you always in the habit of walking where you ought not?"

For a moment she couldn't manage anything more coherent than a breathless, "You!"

She looked around. She was standing in front of the stables. The coach house was buzzing with activity, preparing for the guests who were about to arrive. Two stableboys ran to fetch buckets of oats and water for the horses, while the groom brushed and saddled them.

"See that creature over there?" He pointed past her with his whip.

She turned, shading her eyes from the sunlight. She took a moment to gather her thoughts. "I can't be sure. Is it a bear? No, maybe a wolf?" She pressed a hand to her heart in mock alarm. "Don't say—it's a lion! I am most grateful to you, sir, for saving me from death at the hands of such a ferocious animal." She made a mock curtsy.

The coachman stared at her as if she'd lost her mind. Then the corners of his mouth twitched.

"You almost walked into the horse being shod. He doesn't like strangers, and he certainly doesn't like being shod. He tends to kick. Especially damsels who are afraid of horses." As if on cue, the horse, held by two stable hands, whinnied and kicked with its hind legs.

Emily jumped back. By all the saints, he was right. She hated horses. The wretched creatures were everywhere. They trampled around, smelled, left gigantic piles of manure wherever they went, splashed her with mud, were ferociously tall, impossible to mount, and, once she'd succeeded, invariably tried to throw her off again. If Emily were more honest, she'd admit that she didn't hate horses. She feared them.

But wait. How did the coachman know?

"How did you know I don't like horses?" she asked, her brow furrowed.

His lids drooped, veiling his expression. "Your entire bearing attests to it when you are near them. The way you creep around them. I noticed it at the inn. Your mere presence makes them nervous."

Had he been watching her? He was very observant, that coachman.

"And I don't know about lions," he added, "but if one of those hind legs had touched your head, you might have found your brains dashed out of that pretty skull of yours."

He reached out and plucked something off her back and then her head.

Unnerved, she turned.

He held out his hand, holding the nettles that had been clinging to her dress. "Scampering through the forest?"

It must be evident. The hem of her dress was torn, her boots were muddy and her back was covered in nettles.

She drew herself up with dignity. "I was taking a walk."

"You were woolgathering."

He made it sound like a crime.

"I was thinking," she corrected him.

His lips twitched. "No doubt, a maid like you has much to think about."

She sniffed. "Of course. More than a coachman might."

"Let me guess. I know the nature of your thoughts: You've been 'thinking' about how to lure His Grace into marriage with your mistress." A vague sneer crossed his face, so quickly she thought she'd imagined it. "I should congratulate you, for your schemes have borne fruit. I don't know how you did it, but you certainly managed to wangle an invitation from His Grace. That is no small feat. It is almost admirable how you have achieved it."

Her face flushed. "You're right. His Grace deserves to be fooled and trapped by my schemes. But it is my lady that I am most concerned about. Not him. I couldn't care less about the man."

He raised an eyebrow. "You do not like him. Yet you want him to marry your lady. How is that?"

She shrugged. "I have my reasons. But you are right, I find the man loathsome and detestable beyond words."

He looked at her curiously. "Do you care to tell me why?"

"No. It is none of your concern. Now, if you will excuse me. My lady is waiting for me."

She tried to get past him, but he blocked her path. He suddenly dropped to one knee in front of her, as if he were about to propose marriage.

"Wha-what are you doing?" she stammered, out of her depth.

"It is perilous to walk around with loose shoelaces, especially in the stables," he muttered, tugging at the lace and retying them tightly. "They're torn too. You dragged them through the mud. There." He gave them a final tug, but did not get up immediately.

Emily had frozen into a statue. What on earth was he staring at? Why was the hand still around her ankle? It was large and warm, covering almost the whole of her foot. And she didn't think her feet were that small.

"You've got holes in your shoes," he said softly, and there was an undertone in his voice that she couldn't quite make out.

Her cheeks burned. She pulled her foot away. "Yes, well, it should be common knowledge that maids aren't exactly affluent. If I could buy a new pair of boots every week with my paltry wages, I would. Not that I really need them. I prefer to go barefoot whenever I can."

Now why on earth she'd blurted that out? The only excuse she had was that, for some strange reason, he made her nervous. He stood and hovered over her, far too close for her comfort. She could feel the heat radiating from his body.

Her heart pounded loudly in her ears.

She took a step back.

His head was slightly tilted, his gaze held hers, captivating, unfathomable. The silence between them was thick, charged. He opened his lips to speak. Her gaze fell on his lips.

"Are you, really?" he said.

"Am I what?" She was entirely out of her wits.

"A maid. Meggie Blythe." He seemed to enjoy uttering the name. "The servants here speak of Lady Lydia and a certain Lady Poppy Featherstone arriving without a maid. Both ladies were assigned one of the housemaids. And when I asked the servants about a Meggie Blythe, no one seemed to know who she was. It was as if she never existed." He looked at her thoughtfully through narrowed eyes. "Strange, don't you think?"

Her eyes flew to his face.

He'd caught her.

How vexing! Switching identities made everything so complicated. She'd been careless; normally she never made that kind of mistake.

84

His lips curved into a slow smile. "Or perhaps you are who you say you are, a servant pretending to be a lady? Lady Poppy Featherstone. Dare I suggest that Lady Lydia is no real lady either?" He leaned forward.

She inhaled sharply. "Of course she is a lady. As am I." She lifted her chin. "You have it all wrong. I only pretended to be a maid to get the information I wanted from you."

"Indeed." His lazy gaze swept over her clothes once more. "A lady who wears boots with holes in them and a simple, threadbare dress."

"We are impoverished." She lifted her chin, trying to hide her discomfort behind a show of defiance. "It is not a crime. Our father gambled away our dowries. Our father is an earl. Which is why my sister—and I, of course, too—must marry well. As befits our station." Emily was lying through her teeth, but the man was no fool.

"I don't think so," he said in a soft voice. "I think you are both impostors."

Emily knew when a battle had been lost. She threw up her hands. "And if we are? What's it to you?"

Seeing the sneer on his face, she stepped closer and grabbed his arm. "Don't tell anyone," she begged him. "We're from the same class. We ought to stick together."

He scratched the back of his head. "Certainly. I won't breathe a word."

She let out a sigh of relief.

"For a price, of course." A devilish gleam flickered in his eyes.

She froze. "What do you mean?"

"Exactly what you understood."

"I don't have any money. I just told you we're poor."

"I'm not asking for money... but for favours."

Her eyes widened, and she backed away. "Oh no. No-no-no. You fiend!" She should have known he would abuse this in the crudest way possible. A pang of disappointment shot through her, bitter and sharp. While travelling with her sister, they'd encountered many men more than willing to exploit vulnerable women in exchange for 'favours'. She'd hoped, foolishly it seemed, that he'd be different.

"Dash it all. Not like that!" An unexpected crimson blush crept up his cheeks. "You've misunderstood me entirely. Good heavens, who do you think I am?"

She folded her arms and narrowed her eyes. "A fiend?"

He groaned in exasperation. "It would never occur to me... how could you even think... I meant favours of a different kind."

She stiffened. "I have no idea what else you could possibly mean."

He threw up his hands in frustration. "Wishes. I meant favours in the form of wishes."

Her head tilted. "Wishes?"

"Yes." He thought for a moment. "My wishes. Help me with my chores. Bring me food. Things like that."

"In other words, be your personal slave." She pursed her lips thoughtfully. She shook her head. "No, thank you."

"Very well." He shrugged. "I will go inside and inform His Grace that he has been grossly deceived, that his hospitality has been abused, and that he is harbouring a pair of fortune-hunting impostors under his own roof." He leaned in. "Do you know what happens to impostors?"

Emily swallowed. "No. Wha-what happens to them?"

"They are thrown into the Tower," he whispered. "According to the law, impersonating an aristocrat is punishable by death. Hanging, I think." He thought for a moment. "It could also be beheading. Historically, we seem to have an affinity for the latter. Our henchmen have had much practice. To have deceived a peer of the realm is no small matter. Either way, it's not nice." He rubbed his neck.

Emily paled.

"But I'm sure, scheming little maid that you are, you'll find a way out and get away with it." He pushed his hat further back, shoved his hands into his pockets and strolled away, whistling.

"Hey you," Emily called after him. "Coachman. I don't even know your name."

He stopped and turned. "My name's George."

"George who?"

"Just George."

She took a deep breath. "Very well, 'Just George'. I'll do as you say. You won't say a word about this, and I'll, I'll —" She swallowed painfully. "I'll help you with your, er, chores."

A slow grin spread across his face. "Excellent. Tomorrow morning. Here, outside the stables."

"To do what?"

"Help me muck out the stables."

Without another word, he turned and walked towards the stables.

Emily stared after him.

What on earth had that been all about?

This man saw far too much.

And that was dangerous.

Oh Goodness! Oh Heavens!

I have never in my life held such a fine pair of stockings! Real silk! In pomona green! Thank you ever so much. They are far too lovely to wear—I dare not! Instead, I shall keep them safe, staring at them in awe and touching them now and then, like a treasure too precious to use.

Thank you also for the ribbon for Cissy. I told Papa they were a gift from someone in the parish. I hope you do not mind, for I fear Papa does not believe in forest fays and might frown upon me accepting presents from strangers, even magical ones.

But then, are we truly strangers any more? After all our letters, I feel as though we are something quite different.

Your most grateful, yet confused,
Little Wren

My dear Little Wren,

Confused? You? Surely not! After all these letters, I feel I know you better than many who live in this forest. Strangers we are not—of that, I am certain.

As for the stockings, they are meant to be worn, not hoarded like some miser's coin! Put them on, or I shall be most cross. And trust me, you do not want to incur the wrath of a forest fay.

Yours, most sincerely,
Fenn

Chapter Eight

Emily washed quickly and changed, swapping her woollen walking dress for a more elegant afternoon dress, and her holed, worn-out boots for a pair of thin slippers. There was nothing wrong with her current pair of boots. Sure, the laces were torn; the leather was dented and maybe even had a hole in it, and she'd had the soles replaced countless times, but they were as comfortable and practical as any old pair of boots could be. Besides, these boots had been given to her once, a gift from her forest fay, and her heart was more attached to them than it should be.

No one ought to run around barefoot, Fenn had written when she'd found that pair of boots in the tree hole, together with his missive. Least of all you.

She hadn't even wanted boots. But her fingers had run reverently over the soft leather. She'd never owned boots as beautiful as those.

She'd had them resoled several times and replaced the old laces with new ones.

That coachman! She would never be able to wear her walking boots again without remembering the feeling of his hand on her ankle. The very memory of it sent a rush of warmth up her cheeks and goosebumps down her arms. He was blackmailing her in the most outrageous way, that scoundrel. She knew, of course, that he'd exaggerated. She and Cissy had done no harm to anyone with their deception. They committed neither fraud nor forgery, nor was there any financial gain involved. Death penalty, indeed! The worst that could happen to them was social ostracism and the complete ruin of any hope of a stable, secure future.

On reflection, she realised that his threats had been more teasing than serious, meant to provoke her. Still, they had frightened her. Words like debtor's prison, Marshalsea, and transportation had cast a long shadow upon her childhood. She'd grown up fearing them. They weren't abstract horrors, but real ones—threats the Duke's steward had made to her father when he couldn't pay the rent. And those threats hadn't just been empty words.

Now she'd have to help muck out the stables and do whatever other chores he deemed necessary.

Wishes, really! She huffed. She was done with wishes.

But as long as George's so-called favours were limited to such work, she'd be happy to do it, provided George didn't betray her to the Duke.

The maid jolted her out of her thoughts by informing her that Cissy was in the Chinese drawing room upstairs and that she was expected there.

Emily paused in the doorway, took a deep breath and entered the room.

Cissy was reclining on a sofa, a blanket wrapped around her legs, her hands neatly folded in her lap. Around her were three figures, one in black, one in brown and the third in grey: three elderly ladies, all looking up and raising their quizzing glasses at her at the same time.

Macbeth's hags, shot through Emily's mind. Then she remembered her manners.

She bowed her head and curtsied.

"And you must be Lady Poppy Featherstone. The sister," said the hag who sat closest to Cissy, a frightening creature with a nose as sharp as a hawk's. "I am Lady Dalrymple. This is my sister, Lady Jane, and Lady Mabel Sinclair." She nodded to the other two ladies, one with a horse's face who looked at her briskly, and another who gave her a quick, shy, almost apologetic look. She was the only one to get up and offer her a seat.

Emily thanked her and took the chair opposite her sister.

"I daresay he hasn't welcomed you yet, disobliging boy that he is," Araminta said without beating about the bush.

Emily and Cissy exchanged glances. "Do you mean His Grace?" Emily inquired. "If so, no, we have not yet had the pleasure of meeting him here."

"They say he saved you from an accident."

"He did indeed, my lady. My sister would have been seriously injured if His Grace had not been there. There is no telling what would have happened. She might have broken her neck and died. He is such a gentleman." Emily was not ashamed to exaggerate. She lowered her eyes, pleated her skirt under her fingers and hoped to give a convincing impression of being grateful.

"Good for him. And for you too, of course." Lady Dalrymple turned to Cissy, inspecting her thoroughly through her quizzing glass. "It wouldn't have been right if you'd really broken your neck. I must say, you are most pleasing to the eye."

Cissy dropped her eyes demurely and blushed. "Thank you, my lady."

"He's a busy man. I was hoping this house party would distract him a little, for he needs it. He works far too much."

Emily thought of the dandified figure who had been mincing through the courtyard. No doubt his work consisted of choosing the right waistcoat and tying his cravat. Hard work indeed.

"He's a nice boy. But he's not exactly—how shall I put it?" Araminta turned to Jane.

Jane raised an eyebrow. "Affable? Good-natured? Companionable? I'm not sure which word you're looking for."

"Sociable, it was," Araminta sniffed. "But I daresay the other words apply to him as well."

"Wolferton and sociable, indeed," Jane pursed her lips and shook her head. "He is as sociable as a hermit, despite the fact that every female is setting his cap on him—"

Araminta interrupted with a loud harrumph.

"Be that as it may." Jane sniffed. "It is time for this to end. He must settle down."

Emily and Cissy exchanged another speaking glance.

Emily brushed away a stray thread from her skirt. "Rumour has it he is quite popular with the ladies," she said in a tranquil voice. "One would think that is somewhat of a contradiction to his antisocial personality."

"You mean he's a rake?" Jane interjected bluntly.

Cissy gasped, then covered her mouth with her hand.

Emily bit her lower lip to suppress a grin. These ladies, they were something. She was finding the whole situation rather amusing. It was quite clear to her they had already nominated Cissy as a prospect for the Duke. They had eyes only for her. Little did they know they were playing into her hands. Who would have thought that they would be her allies? She would use this to her advantage.

"Nonsense. It is, as you say, merely a rumour," Araminta put in hastily.

"Of course," Emily agreed. "One should not listen to rumours. Ever."

"Yet it is perfectly true," Mabel murmured between sips of tea, but no one heeded her except Emily, who gave her a startled look.

Araminta drowned out her comment with a loud remark. "But we are forgetting our manners. How on earth did we end up on such an unpleasant topic of conversation? Lady Lydia." She nodded at Cissy, then turned to Emily. "Lady Poppy. We are very pleased to have you both here. Tell us about yourselves. Lady Lydia, how is it we did not have the honour of making your acquaintance in London? Did you not attend the Season?"

The three ladies looked at Cissy, who took her time sipping her tea with a calm demeanour, then set her cup down before answering.

Emily looked at Cissy sharply. Even though they'd agreed on a background story, they hadn't yet spun out the details. Creativity wasn't exactly Cissy's forte. That was more Emily's domain. She opened her mouth to spin a colourful tale of life on the continent, harrowing escapes during the wars and a near brush with Napoleon, when Cissy suddenly spoke up.

"We haven't attended the Season because we've been staying with our aunt in Bath these past three years. She is a rather reclusive lady with poor eyesight. Before that we lived with an uncle in Brussels and before that with our grandmother in Scotland. Our father died unexpectedly when Poppy was seventeen and I was fourteen."

The ladies uttered soft sounds of sympathy.

Emily managed a strained smile. Cissy had told them the truth. It may have been a clever move to avoid being caught in a lie, but it also left her feeling uncomfortably exposed.

"How unfortunate," Jane chimed in. "He couldn't have been very old?"

"He wasn't." Cissy took an emotionally charged pause. "He died of lung fever."

Mabel sighed softly.

"Orphans. That would explain why you have this innocent, otherworldly quality about you, so unlike most other ladies." Araminta gave a satisfied nod.

Emily had a sneaking suspicion that somehow they'd passed a very important test. Or at least Cissy had. As for herself, it seemed irrelevant what she said or did. She didn't matter. For the first time in her life, Emily was glad.

"We'll leave you to rest now," Araminta rose and motioned for her sisters to do the same. "We won't be expecting you for supper, though Lady Poppy may join us?" She gave Emily a questioning look.

Emily folded her hands. "Thank you, but I would like to keep my sister company tonight. If she gets enough rest today, the doctor says she will be presentable tomorrow."

Araminta nodded. "It would be most agreeable if you could both join us tomorrow. Wolferton is an excessively busy man, but he will be there, no doubt."

"Unless he tries to make himself scarce again," Mabel murmured.

"We could instruct one of the footmen to help you downstairs. It will not do for all the ladies to be present, but you, Lady Lydia—and, of course, Lady Poppy," she added as an afterthought, "to be absent. That would not do."

With an imperial nod, Araminta motioned to her sisters, and the three left.

"She will press the poor man to attend tomorrow night, come what may. I almost feel sorry for him. Did you also get the impression that the 'poor man' is being browbeaten straight to the altar?"

Cissy nodded vigorously. "Most dreadfully tyrannised by his own aunts."

"The poor man must be positively put out, having to

parade before these pernickety ladies who pester him with such persistence," Emily mused.

"He's peeved and plagued," Cissy agreed with mock gravity.

"Practically panic-stricken." Emily added, warming to the game.

"Piqued and petrified."

"Perishingly p-p... panoramic?" Emily faltered, then wrinkled her nose. "Oh dear, that's just nonsense, isn't it?"

They exchanged a look and burst into laughter.

Dear Fenn,

I was wondering—what do forest fays do all day, aside from granting wishes to us feeble humans? Do you flit from tree to tree with the birds? Can you change your shape, like the fairytales say? What is your favourite colour? Your favourite food?

As for me, I adore violets. But I already told you that. Did you know they can be eaten? I've heard candied violets are sweet, though terrible for one's teeth. I should love to try them someday. My favourite colour is purple (and coquelicot). My favourite food is crumpets.

I am deathly afraid of horses—a horse bit me on the shoulder once, and I haven't liked them since. Do you have fears, too?

Sincerely yours,
Little Wren

P.S. I made you some mittens! They aren't perfect—I unpicked an old scarf of Papa's to make them, and the wool is a bit scratchy. But they're warm, I hope. Tell me you like them?

My dear Little Wren,

Thank you for the mittens! They are a bit small, so I must fold my fingers to wear them, but they are warm, and when the winter winds bite, I walk through the forest with your mittens on and my thoughts are of you.

To answer your questions: my favourite colour is moss green. My favourite food is mince pie, and I despise turnips—they are ghastly things. And yes, I do have a fear: the dark. Even forest fays are not immune to shadows.

Sincerely,

Fenn

P.S. Because your letter made me smile, I'll grant you another wish. What will you wish for this time?

Chapter Nine

As luck would have it, Emily ran straight into the peeved, plagued and panic-stricken Duke as soon as she left the drawing room to fetch a book for Cissy.

He paused at the top of the stairs, ready to descend. He was dressed in a dark green coat and breeches with gleaming Hessians, a frothy cravat at his neck and a riding whip in a gloved hand. For a morning ride, he was dressed rather extravagantly, Emily thought. But what would she know, it might be the newest fashion to do so?

Emily struggled with an intense feeling of antipathy. The man was the embodiment of everything she loathed and despised. Yet she had to ignore those feelings and feign grace, even gratitude towards him. She schooled her features.

"Your Grace."

He turned, lifting an eyebrow upon seeing her. He glanced over his shoulder as if searching for someone, then made a brief bow.

"Lady Poppy, is it?" He raised a haughty eyebrow.

She was aware that she had to be on her best behaviour, regardless of her actual feelings towards the Duke. So she inclined her head. "I wanted to thank you for your kindness to my sister and for your hospitality."

He waved her away. "Your sister, Lady Lydia, is she well?" He glanced down the corridor to see if she was there.

"Her foot is badly sprained. The doctor has prescribed rest. She is recuperating in the Chinese drawing room today. We hope her ankle will have healed sufficiently by tomorrow for her to join us."

"I hope she is not in too much pain," the Duke responded politely.

"She can't move, unfortunately." The cogs in Emily's brain set in motion. "She does, however, require some reading material and has asked me to procure a book for her." Emily hesitated visibly. "I'm not sure where the library is. It would be forward of me to explore the house alone in the hope of finding it... " Her voice trailed off. She looked at him expectantly.

Fortunately, the Duke had his wits about him this morning. "I'll be happy to get Lady Lydia a book or two from the library," he offered immediately.

Emily gave him a bright smile. "Oh, could you, indeed? I am sure my sister would like that. She gets terribly bored just sitting around doing nothing."

"One must find a remedy for that, surely."

"She reads everything," Emily said, "preferably romances and novels by Radcliffe, Austen and Burney."

"Romance novels." He nodded. "I like to read them myself. I'll see what I can find." He smiled, looking younger, more boyish, and there was an eagerness in his manner that was not entirely unappealing.

A touch of confusion came over Emily. Who was he? She found it difficult to reconcile the man in front of her with the choleric despot in her mind.

She clasped her hands together. "Oh, would you? How kind of you. Deliver these to her yourself," she instructed, as if he were a footman and not a duke.

"It will be my pleasure." With a quick bow, he left.

Emily looked after him.

This brief attempt at matchmaking had gone better than expected. It was a good move to get him together with Cissy as soon as possible, before the other ladies sank their claws into him.

For a fleeting second, Emily deigned to feel sorry for him.

Then she shook herself. Was she out of her mind?

He was Wolferton.

A man she most heartily disliked.

He was about to become her brother-in-law, if it was the last thing she ever did, so she'd better work on overcoming that feeling of antipathy.

MOST OF THE remaining guests arrived that afternoon.

Cissy remained in her room, resting her injured foot, while Emily took on welcoming the new arrivals. Cissy would join the company tomorrow, provided the doctor agreed and her foot improved.

Among the arrivals were Lord and Lady Willowthorpe and their three daughters, all fresh out of the schoolroom. The girls were dressed in pastel-coloured dresses and clung to each other, giggling and looking around with wide-eyed excitement, as if they expected the Duke to jump out of every corner. Each time the door opened, and he did not appear, their faces would drop in unison, only to rise again in anticipation moments later. It was very amusing to watch.

Then there was Lady Blakely and her daughter, Miss Cowley, who carried themselves with an air of haughty superiority. Mother and daughter barely acknowledged Emily, holding out their hands as if expecting her to kiss them. Awkwardly, Emily shook their hands instead, aware of their arched brows and slightly disapproving expressions.

Last to arrive were Lord Hamish and his sister, Miss Ingleton. Lord Hamish appeared to belong to the Duke's set, the dandy set, with shirt points so high that Emily wondered how he managed to turn his head. Yet his cheerful demeanour and sharp humour made him seem less affected than others of his ilk.

"Has His Grace already fled the scene and hidden away in his hermit's cave?" he joked as he looked around, a mischievous smile on his face. "Or should I say wolf's lair? Seems more fitting, doesn't it?"

He leaned closer to Emily and whispered behind his hand, "Do wolves even live in caves?"

Fighting back a smile, Emily replied, "I believe they live in dens, my lord, though I can't say for certain." Lord Hamish radiated good cheer. Emily liked him very much and wished he could be a suitable candidate for Cissy instead of the Duke. Unfortunately, he was already married. Lady Hamish had stayed at home as she was expecting a baby. Their estate was only a stone's throw from Ashbourne House, as Hamish explained.

"Neighbours with Wolferton, imagine that. I have spent my whole life in the area, yet we never actually met until we both sat next to each other at White's Club in London, picking up the same newspaper. Like Wolferton, I spent my childhood growing up elsewhere," he explained. "It's a shame, really, because this is the most beautiful countryside. I will make sure my children grow up here."

After the introductions, the guests were shown to their rooms, and Emily took the opportunity to retire.

She'd received a message from Cissy asking to speak to her urgently, but when she knocked on her door she found her asleep. She returned to her own room, ready to turn in for the night.

Yet sleep wouldn't come.

Emily tossed and turned until, with a sigh, she lit the candle again.

She could ring for the maid and ask for some milk.

Her hand on the bell, she hesitated. Better to let the poor thing sleep and go down to the kitchen herself. A walk might calm her restlessness.

She put on a pair of slippers, picked up a candle, and ventured into the corridor.

The house was silent, but the kitchen was bustling with activity.

The cook was preparing for the next day, chopping, slicing, pickling, stirring and frying. Scullery maids were washing dishes and scrubbing pots, and footmen were polishing silver. The smell of freshly baked bread filled the air, and her stomach made an unladylike growl.

"My lady!" The housekeeper, Mrs Smith, rose from the table where she was counting damask napkins with the help of a maid.

For a moment, the entire kitchen froze as everyone turned to look at her. A maid turned and stared at her with wide-eyed curiosity as she stirred her pot. The cook paused mid-slice, frowning and holding his knife in the air. And a scullery maid dropped the pots into the sink with a loud clatter.

Emily raised her hand awkwardly. "How do you do?" She was clearly inconveniencing the servants with her presence.

Mrs Smith's expression didn't change as she raised an eyebrow. "Lady Poppy. Is the bell pull in your room not working?"

"It is working." She cleared her mind. "But there was no need to disturb Mary. Besides, I thought a walk might do me good."

Mrs Smith gestured for the staff to get on with their work. "How can I help you?"

Emily looked at her apologetically. "I was having trouble sleeping and wondered if I could have something warm to drink."

"Certainly." Mrs Smith nodded briskly. "I suffer from insomnia myself and have a special blend of tea that helps. It is a mixture of lavender and valerian. I will have it brought to your room."

"If you don't mind," Emily said with a sweet smile, "I'd rather drink it here. In your parlour."

The housekeeper pursed her lips briefly. "Certainly, my lady. If you would follow me."

Her parlour was surprisingly cosy, with a flower-patterned armchair in front of a fireplace, and a little table draped in lace. Small porcelain figurines lined the mantelpiece and lace doilies covered almost every surface.

Emily sat down on the sofa and watched as the housekeeper filled a kettle with water and placed it on the iron stove by the fireplace. She set the table with a simple blue and white tea service and a plate of short-bread. Emily was clearly interrupting the housekeeper's schedule, for surely she had more important things to do than entertain one of the house guests in her drawing room for a late-night tea party.

"You're very kind," Emily said as she poured the tea into Emily's cup, the aroma of lavender and valerian filling the air. It was soothing. "Have you worked here long?"

She placed a small porcelain bowl of honey in front of her. "Since the time of the old duke. Thirty-three years, if I remember correctly."

Emily spooned three spoonfuls of the golden liquid into her tea. "What was the old duke like?"

"As a person? I wouldn't know." Mrs Smith's tone was calm but clipped. "Inconceivable, is it not? I never spoke to him. All I ever had was a brief glimpse as he stepped out of his carriage outside the Covent Garden theatre. I was in London on a brief leave. Ironically, I saw him there, not here. He never visited Ashbourne House. He preferred Wolferstone Abbey. The estate is twice the size of this one." Mrs Smith had clearly warmed to the subject, as had Emily.

"And the present duke? He didn't live here either, did he?"

She shook her head. "Alas, no. Ashbourne House has been the summer residence of Lady Dalrymple and her sisters, Lady Jane and Lady Mabel, the last few years. His Grace rarely visits, though he has come more frequently in the last five years, but never for long."

"Why?"

Mrs Smith shrugged. "One can't be sure. I think he doesn't like this place. There was a dispute with the steward and His Grace was so angry that he dismissed the entire staff."

"The entire staff!" Emily's teacup paused mid-air. "Over a disagreement with the steward?"

Mrs Smith shrugged. "His Grace can be rather quick-tempered."

"They don't call him the Devil Duke for nothing," Emily muttered into her cup.

Mrs Smith didn't hear the comment, or chose to ignore it. "He demands absolute loyalty from his subordinates. Once he loses faith in people, they are dismissed. He is rather pernickety in this matter."

"Sounds like an absolutist monarch. Or a tyrant." She looked up at Mrs Smith. "But you—you stayed on, apparently. He must trust you very much."

"Indeed. I was one of the few exceptions." She took a sip from her cup.

Emily set her teacup down. "Thank you for the tea. I

think it's working already. I am beginning to feel rather tired."

Mrs Smith inclined her head as Emily rose to return to her room.

As she made her way back through the servants' hall, she noticed the Duke's valet handing a pile of garments to the laundry maid.

"These need to be pressed with haste," the valet instructed.

The maid nodded and took the garments, but her hands fumbled, and several pieces tumbled to the floor.

"Careless girl," the valet scolded. "These are His Grace's precious neckties."

Flustered, the maid bent quickly to retrieve the fallen items, her cheeks burning with embarrassment. However, as she hurried off, Emily spotted one tie that had been overlooked, lying in the shadowed corner near the door.

She stooped to pick it up, the smooth silk cool and luxurious against her fingertips. A thoughtful smile played on her lips as she examined the finely crafted fabric.

"His Grace's necktie. Hm," she murmured to herself, as a mischievous thought occurred to her.

Casting a quick glance around, Emily deftly slipped the tie into the folds of her skirt. A cheeky grin spread across her face as she turned and continued back to her room.

Dear Fenn,

I have made you candles so that you need not fear the dark anymore. Alas, they are not beeswax, for beeswax candles are far too costly, but simple tallow ones. Still, I worked dried flowers into them, so that perhaps you might think of me each time you light one.

Do you think they are pretty?

Affectionately yours,

Little Wren

Dear Little Wren,

The candles are lovely indeed, and they shall bring light to the darkest of nights. Thank you. But, Little Wren, you did not answer my question. I asked if you had a wish, and you left me waiting. Remember, it is the solemn duty of a forest fay to grant wishes.

So, tell me—what is it that your heart desires?

Yours,

Fenn

Chapter Ten

THE NEXT MORNING, EMILY DONNED HER SIMPLEST, most threadbare gown and put her old boots on. She tied her hair back with a handkerchief. She reasoned that when one had to muck out the stables, it was wise not to dress too nicely.

George was waiting for her at the stables.

Emily's steps faltered when she saw him. He leaned against the wooden wall of the stable, one boot propped up against it, his shirt sleeves rolled back to reveal muscular forearms, and his hands tucked into his pockets. He lifted his face to the sun, eyes closed, as if enjoying the morning rays on his skin.

He had a square chin, and with his dark hair slicked back from his forehead, he looked somehow younger, more vulnerable.

He looked every bit the rakish charmer he was.

Emily's heart fluttered.

Goodness, what had she been thinking? Rakish

charmer? Was she out of her mind? He was neither rakish nor a charmer. He'd been rude, domineering, obnoxious and annoying at every single one of their meetings. There had been nothing charming about him at all.

Except for the time he'd knelt in front of her to tie her shoelaces, as if she were a little child. Or the moment he'd grabbed her arms to stop her from running into a kicking horse, as if he truly cared about keeping her safe.

Yesterday, that teasing light had sparked in his eyes, even while he said those annoying things.

And now—he must have heard her approaching, because he turned to look in her direction. Was it her imagination, or did his eyes turn golden as they lit up? As if he were truly happy to see her.

Disturbed by her own thoughts, she greeted him with a grumble.

He stood up straight and took his hands out of his pockets.

"Lady Poppy." His lips curved into a smile, as if the sight of her amused him. Her eyes focused on his mouth. Those lips... Disturbed, she tugged at the handkerchief around her hair. "So, you have indeed come to help me clear out the stables." His eyes crinkled slightly, and one corner of his lips turned up more than the other when he smiled. She wondered what it sounded like when he laughed. Not the sarcastic bark she'd heard before, but a heartfelt, amused laugh. Irritated at having to ponder about such details, Emily was determined to be as rude to him as possible.

"Let's make this quick. I need to be back for nuncheon." She needed time to bathe, wash her hair and change her clothes, unless she wanted to scandalise her hosts by bringing back a whiff of the stables. Tea with horse manure. It wasn't a particularly appetising thought.

Emily grimaced.

"I see you're all eager and excited to help me." He pulled his hands out of his pockets. When he wasn't hunched over, he was quite tall. "Very well. Let's waste no time and get to work. Follow me." He led the way with long strides, and Emily had to run to keep up.

"Isn't the stable over there?" she said after a while, pointing in the direction of the stables. They'd gone the other way, towards the forest.

"We're almost there."

They walked in companionable silence for a while.

"How are things at the house?" He nodded towards Ashbourne House. "Any success with your matchmaking efforts?" He grinned, but his eyes remained on the path ahead.

Emily nodded. "It's going splendidly. His Grace has certainly taken an interest in Cis—I mean, Lady Annab— I mean, Lady Lydia." Dash it all if she wasn't getting all her names mixed up! She glanced sideways at George to see if he had noticed her faux pas, but he was busy bending aside a twig from a bush that was in his way.

His lips curved into a smile. "So he's interested, is he? That is amusing. What did you do to hasten their union?"

Emily told him how she had sent him on an errand that would lead him to her sister in the library, "Where, hopefully, they are busily falling in love as we speak".

"What a meddlesome busybody you are," he said with a chuckle.

Emily took it as a compliment. "I pride myself on my matchmaking skills." She lifted her chin. "They are unparalleled. In the past, I've successfully matched four couples, all of whom are now living happily ever after." Except she'd never been entirely successful with Cissy. Cissy, beautiful and admired as she was, never received any marriage proposals. It was rather perplexing. Gentlemen wanted to dance with her, walk with her, ride with her, and a painter even made her the subject of one of his paintings. Aunt Henrietta had thought it scandalous, but it had been an innocent affair, though the painter had never proposed. But in the end, none of these suitors ever came up to scratch. Not even Mr Matthews. None of them had ever popped the question.

If she had been unsuccessful in finding Cissy's match, she had been even more so when it came to her own future. But she was resigned to her fate as an old maid.

As if reading her mind, George said, "Except for your own happily ever after?"

Emily shrugged. "Lady Lydia's happiness comes first."

"Ah yes, of course. Forgive me for forgetting that you're a lady's maid."

Startled, she glanced at him, but his face showed no sign of teasing.

She found herself studying his features. He wasn't exactly a handsome man. He had a stern forehead and a sharper nose than she liked in men, but fine eyebrows and a strong chin. His lips were thin, and he rarely smiled, but when he did, a most incongruous dimple appeared in his left cheek. She found it disarmingly charming. His hair was thick, dark and long, setting off the brilliance of his amber eyes, framed by thick black eyelashes.

They emerged from the trees by the lake. Rays of morning sunlight danced on the water. The ducks glided calmly across the surface. The scene was picturesque and serene. She bent down to pick up some flat stones, but instead of throwing them into the water, she placed them into her reticule.

They reached the shore of the small yet charming lake that was part of the park.

Emily looked around, puzzled. "There are no stables here." She turned to George. "I don't see any horses either. There are ducks, though. What exactly do you want to do here?" She looked at him suspiciously.

George scrutinised the ground next to the lake. "The grass is still a bit damp," he muttered. "Better use this." He pointed to a log that lay by the shore.

"What do I do with the log?" Emily wrinkled her forehead. "I hope you don't want me to chop it up, because I'm terrible with an axe—" She interrupted herself, sniffing. There was no mistake. She knew that smell.

Her stomach growled. It was so loud she feared it would wake the ducks sleeping in the reeds. She put her hand to her stomach sheepishly.

George raised an eyebrow.

"I haven't had any breakfast, you see," she defended herself. "I know that smell." She sniffed again. It was coming from behind the log. "But how can it be? It smells like... "

George bent down and pulled out a basket.

"Crumpets!" Emily breathed.

There was nothing more wonderful in the world than a plate full of hot, steaming, crispy crumpets, wrapped in a tea towel to keep them warm.

"And not just any crumpets. These are cheese crumpets." He pulled out a plate and held it up to her. "I asked the cook to make some. That's no easy task, because Monsieur Henri is a proud French cook who looks down on simple English specialities like crumpets. It took some persuasion and bribery before he agreed to bake a batch."

Emily's mouth watered. They were her favourite. Then she put her hands on her hips and glared at him. "Let me think. You want me to do hard manual labour while you sit here on the grass like a pasha, eating my favourite food?" She groaned. "You really are a fiend."

And there it was, faster and more unexpectedly than she'd thought possible—a heartfelt laugh, deep and rumbling. She blinked at him, astonished.

"Come, sit down," he said. "But sit on that log, here, because the grass is still wet." He pointed to the tree.

Emily hesitated. "Really? What is the catch? What will you ask in return? Will you increase the number of favours—or rather wishes?"

"Sit." He commanded. "We will discuss the rest while we eat."

He didn't have to say it twice. He held the plate in front of her and Emily's resistance crumbled. She took a crumpet and bit into it, savouring the warm, buttery goodness mixed with the cheese. She rolled her eyes back in pleasure. "Hmmm." She could not say anything for a while.

He watched her, a small smile tugging at his lips. "That good, is it?"

Emily couldn't answer—her mouth was full of crumpets. She chewed enthusiastically. When she finally finished, she looked up with a sheepish grin. "Thank you. I suppose I was hungrier than I thought. I couldn't bear to go into that splendid breakfast room, where I'd have to sit all alone at that enormous table, served by an army of footmen. It would have been rather lonely." A thought struck her. "And perhaps worse: awkward. For who knows who might have joined me there?"

"Like His Grace. Terrible thought, breakfasting alone with the Duke." He picked up a crumpet and inspected it.

Emily shuddered. "Indeed."

"He wouldn't touch a crumpet, of course," George said as he popped the crumpet into his mouth.

"Never. Men like him live on horrible things like foie gras, oysters, escargots, roast pigeons and, horror of horrors, cucumbers!"

He looked at her, perplexed. "Cucumbers? What's wrong with cucumbers?"

"Everything that's wrong with this world," she grimaced. "They are God's only miscreation. I detest them."

He chuckled. "You dislike cucumbers? Who would have thought? I am not too fond of them myself, but I can think of other things I dislike more. Like turnips." He made a face. "Mashed turnips were the bane of my youth." He picked up a crumpet and handed it to her. "Here, have the last crumpet."

"I must savour this last crumpet," she said solemnly, "and eat it especially slowly." A shadow suddenly crossed her face. "It is the food of my childhood, you see. Simple, plain, everyday food. But how happy it made me, as a little girl, to be able to have some fresh from the griddle."

He looked at her, waiting for her to continue.

"Perhaps because it was so rare. Perhaps because of the memories I associate with it. It is the only memory I have of my mother. Her standing by the glowing coals of the hearth, the cast-iron griddle in one hand, pouring the dough on it with the other, and the sound of the batter sizzling, and the rich smell that would spread throughout the house." She sighed. "We never made them again at home, probably because they brought back memories of mother." She swallowed a lump in her throat. "So we rarely ate them, almost never."

He looked at her thoughtfully for a moment before speaking. "It appears you've had a difficult life." His voice was so low that at first she thought she'd imagined it. It startled her for a moment because his comment seemed out of context and she didn't know how to respond.

She met his gaze, and something in the depths of his eyes stopped her. If she didn't know better, she would have thought they looked almost... troubled. But no, they couldn't be. This made no sense at all. She shook her head as if to shake the thought from her mind.

"What gives you that impression?" she answered lightly. "Our mother may have died when we were

120

young, but our father adored us. I had a wonderful childhood. Do I give the impression that I was born on the streets, raised in the workhouse and condemned to a life of endless drudgery?"

He studied her closely. "Have you had such a life?"

She hesitated, then shrugged. "All maids have difficult lives." A sweeping, generalised statement seemed best, she decided. "From morning to night serving their betters, it's hardly a picnic. Though I suppose it's no more difficult than a coachman's life."

"Ah—yes, of course." He cleared his throat. "A very demanding life indeed. All that travelling."

"I mean it. It must be a challenge, working for that man."

"That man?"

"The tyrant. Nero."

He looked at her blankly.

"The Devil Duke," she added helpfully. "His reputation has spread far and wide. I pity anyone who has to work for him. Behind that handsome, fashionable façade lies a choleric temperament. They say that when he's not dismissing servants on a whim, they rarely last more than a fortnight. Except, of course, Mrs Smith. She must be an angel to have survived under that devil for so long. So how are you getting on under his iron rule?"

A deep frown appeared on his forehead. "Is that what they say?"

"Oh, yes." Emily brushed crumbs from her lap. "I suppose I shouldn't encourage a match between him and my sister, given his terrible personality. He doesn't look like it, mind you. I still don't understand how a man like that can look as delicate as a tulip. But then, I've always thought of him as a wolf in sheep's clothing. Or maybe the devil in a cravat. Lucifer in lace. It's all the same." She rose from the log and bent down to pick up a flat stone. He watched her in tense silence.

"Is that really how you see him?" he asked abruptly. "A devil?"

"Worse." Her expression darkened. "People born into power and wealth, who use those blessings to ruin innocent lives for no better reason than greed, deserve to be called worse than devils."

The wind teased a stray strand of hair across his forehead, shading his eyes. He dug his hands into his pockets.

"What happened?" he asked softly.

"Nothing in particular." She waved a dismissive hand, keeping her tone deliberately light. "Just the sort of stories you hear. In general, you know. Being a maid, you can't help but hear such stories. Evicting tenants from their homes, casting the elderly and infirm out in the dead of winter, leaving them to perish on the road, like animals. His Grace has a lot to answer for. He may wear a crisp white shirt, but his soul is blacker than tar."

His scowl deepened. "These are serious accusations. In all those years I've worked for His Grace, I've never seen any evidence of this. I would swear on my life that he would never do such things."

She gave a bitter laugh. "Then you don't know him as well as you think."

He shook his head. "I can't believe it."

"It's true." Her voice was icy now. "I hold him

responsible for all the evil that has befallen us. And worse."

"Worse?" His tone was wary.

Her gaze drifted to the lake, and a cool breeze teased another strand of hair across her face as she said softly, "He killed my father."

Dear Fenn,

I have so many wishes, I hardly know where to begin! I wish to see the opera at Covent Garden, the Royal Menagerie, and the entertainments at Astley's Amphitheatre.

I wish to be clever and wise.

And most of all, I wish to see the ocean.

Can you grant any of these?

Yours truly,

Little Wren

My dear Wren,

You ask for so much, Little Wren! But one thing at a time, for even a forest fay must have his limits.

For now, I shall grant only one of your wishes. Enclosed, you will find a sketch of the ocean by a man named Turner. They say he captures light as no other can, and he is often called 'the painter of light'. I hope it brings you joy.

Your humble servant,

Fenn

My dearest Fenn,

The picture is so beautiful! I have hung it in my room, and it is the first thing I see when I wake. Thank you from the depths of my heart!

I am not an artist like Turner, but I have made you a little bookmark as a small token of my gratitude. I hope you like it.

Yours truly,

Little Wren

Little Wren,

Your bookmark is most delightful, and I shall use it every day, thinking of you whenever I turn a page.

But there is something I have been wondering about. I have seen that you are still running about barefoot, even though you now have stockings. Pomona green silk stockings! Forgive me for asking, but... is it because you do not have any shoes?

Your servant,

Fenn

Chapter Eleven

He stared at her. "What has the Duke done to you to make you hate him so? If you're going to accuse a man of something like this, you'd better have a reason." His words were clipped.

She shook her head. There was bitterness in her voice. "I suppose this is the moment when I ought to tell you that I grew up on His Grace's land. What a coincidence, wouldn't you say? My father was the village schoolmaster. We were evicted in the middle of winter because he couldn't pay the rent. Father was ill, you see—too ill to work. Some of the villagers tried to collect the money and pay for us, but it wasn't enough."

She looked down at the lake, her expression hardening. "The steward came with his men in the dead of night and tossed us out like rubbish. He warned the villagers that anyone who dared to take us in would also face eviction. Per the Duke's orders." Her voice faltered for a moment, but she continued. "We didn't know where to go. Father was already feverish. He died that very same night on the road in the middle of a snowstorm."

She bent to pick up another stone, missing the look of horror that crossed his face. He passed a hand over his face, his voice a whisper. "Good God."

Emily didn't stop. "The vicar of a nearby village was kind enough to bury him, even though we weren't part of his parish. He and his wife took me and my sister in and gave us the shelter and hospitality we were denied here." Her eyes darkened as she looked across the lake. "So you see, I have every right to call him the demon that he is. Greed, power, money—whatever it is that drives him—he ruined three lives that winter. So yes, I have every right to call him every name under the sun. Including murderer."

He said nothing.

Realising how bitter she sounded, Emily forced a brittle laugh. "But don't worry, we survived, my sister and I." Her lips curled, but the movement felt hollow. "We managed to stay out of the workhouse. Barely. But we did." Her chest tightened, the familiar burn of old resentment rising. "His Grace will now pay bitterly for what he did to us."

There was an expression on his face that she couldn't interpret. "How?"

Emily raised an eyebrow as if it were obvious. "By marrying my sister. That's the least he can do."

He merely stared at her, his jaw tightening.

Emily tried to shake off the gravity of the conversation by forcing a lighter tone. "I suppose it is bad manners to speak ill of your employer. After all, he pays your wages. How did we end up talking about something as morose as my past? I'd rather you forgot everything I said."

She bent down and carefully balanced the stones she'd collected. She stepped back to inspect her handiwork. "A cairn. It's a tribute to the spirits of nature. Make a wish. Who knows, it might come true."

He hesitated, then bent down to pick up a stone and carefully placed it on top of the pile.

"He's not as bad as you think," he said in a clipped voice.

Emily tilted her head to study him. "The Devil Duke? You would defend him, of course, loyal retainer that you are. He's lucky to have you in his employ."

A sudden, cool breeze swept through and Emily wrapped her arms around herself, shivering. "We should return before our absence is noted."

He nodded firmly, and they turned back towards the path.

"George."

He looked at her, but his face was unreadable.

"Thank you." She gave him a shy smile.

He blinked. "For what?"

"For giving me crumpets instead of making me do hard labour in the stables. And—" Her voice softened. "I am sorry I misjudged you, thinking the worst of you, that you intended to blackmail me." She searched his face. "You will keep our secret, won't you? That I'm not a lady, I mean."

He held her gaze, his expression unreadable. Then he gave a brief nod.

"Thank you," she whispered. She felt a weight lifted from her shoulders.

His Grace was in a towering black mood.

He had refused to appear for luncheon, tea, or supper. A tray of roast beef had been sent back to the kitchen untouched, leaving the cook utterly devastated. "What a disgrace!" he moaned. "Never in all my years has anything like this 'appened to me. My career is ruined!"

"It's best to avoid His Grace altogether," the butler admonished the servants below stairs. "Approach him at your own peril. If you cannot avoid an encounter, turn to the wall, freeze and pretend to be a ceramic urn."

"What's set him off now?" a footman whispered to the valet.

"He dismissed his steward." The valet, Simonson, wiped his brow with a handkerchief.

"Again?"

He nodded curtly.

"It's the fourth this year."

Another nod.

"For what reason?"

"Incompetence. The books are in a shocking mess, and Johnson had made a minor miscalculation. Fatal. His Grace flew into a rage, asking if everyone was out to deceive him, and when poor Johnson admitted it was an inadvertent mistake, His Grace demanded to know if anyone in this country could still manage sums. Dismissed him on the spot with no references." Simonson leaned forward to add, "With that terrible, icy, quiet voice of his."

The footman shuddered. "The voice of nightmares."

"My sentiment exactly. The problem is, since no one else he trusts is left to do the work, I am now expected to help sort out the accounts." He sighed. "But my head for figures isn't any better than Johnson's. I fear I'm doomed to the same end."

"What about the secretary? Isn't that his domain?"

Simonson shrugged. "He's suddenly been sent to Oxfordshire on some errand, with the threat of dismissal if he doesn't perform his duties to His Grace's satisfaction. If you ask me, His Grace doesn't seem to trust that secretary all that much either."

"Poor sod. Well, after that shocking scandal a few years ago, who can blame His Grace?" another footman chimed in. "When he had to dismiss the entire old staff just because a single corrupt steward."

"I don't blame him, of course. It's why I have this job now, and I must say I've always found His Grace fair and reasonable to deal with," Simonson said, and the others nodded in agreement.

The cook, Monsieur Henri, shook his head decisively. "If you ask me, I'd put my hand in the fire that the real 'eart of the problem lies elsewhere."

Several of the other servants gathered around him. "What do you mean?"

"*Cherchez la femme!*"

"Eh?"

"That's French," Simonson translated. "It means 'the cause is a woman'. No doubt about it. He spent a whole evening staring gloomily into the empty fireplace, sighing and drinking a whole decanter of brandy. When he finished one decanter, he asked for another. The man was blue-devilled. "

"It's true," Netty, a red-haired housemaid, chimed in. "I went into the study, not seeing him at first, to light the fire in the fireplace. He almost bit my head off. I nearly burst into tears, for I was sure he'd dismiss me. Then, as I was about to leave the room to pack my things, he told me to stop. I was shaking in my boots, I tell you. But do you know what he did instead?"

"What?" All the maids leaned in to listen.

"He looked up, stared at me, and said, 'Netty'—he actually knew my name, can you believe it?—'Netty, you're a woman, aren't you?"

The housemaids gasped. "Good heavens!"

"I tell you, I almost fainted with shock. So I said, trembling in my shoes, 'I believe I am, Your Grace'. Then he said, 'Excellent. Tell me, Netty'—he said my name twice—'what is it that women like best when you need to get back in their good graces?' I swear he asked me that. So I said carefully, 'That depends on the woman, Your Grace.'"

"Excellent answer," the valet said, nodding in agreement. "Very diplomatic."

"His Grace didn't think so, though. He wasn't pleased at all and frowned at me. You know that terrible frown that makes him look like the devil himself?" She shuddered.

The others nodded in agreement.

"So I stuttered on, 'Ladies of the ton might be more

difficult to please than simple housemaids, Your Grace.'—Which he didn't like overly much, either. So I added, 'But at heart we're all the same: girls who appreciate a token of affection when it's given with sincerity.' Then he said, 'Token of affection. You mean the usual thing. Flowers, chocolates, jewellery and the like.' 'Yes,' I said, 'but it has to be sincere, from the heart. It does not have to be something material. Often a simple gesture or a word of apology is worth more than an expensive piece of jewellery.' And do you know what he did?"

"What?"

"He thanked me," Netty said triumphantly. "Very sincerely, too. He said he didn't mean to frighten me and sent me on my way. I tell you, I am shocked, absolutely shocked! I have never been so pleased in my life."

"Ooh!" said the housemaids in unison. "He must be in love!"

"I think so too," said the servant. "All the signs point in that direction. But who could she be?"

"I know!" The second footman snapped his fingers. "I know exactly who it is. There is only one lady in question."

A loud voice cleared its throat from behind the group. It was the butler. "If you are all done gossiping, may I suggest we return to our duties. Netty." The butler motioned to the maid with his finger. "You are to take a dozen red roses to Lady Lydia."

"That's the one!" one footman whispered to the other. "She's a goddess. And roses are for love. Shall we bet on it?"

"And violets for Lady Poppy," the butler added. "At once."

"Say, for how much longer do you want me to pretend to be you?" Chippendale crossed his legs and flicked an imaginary speck of dust from his immaculately polished Hessian boots. "I admit, it's been diverting to slip into your skin for a while, but it's becoming deuced tedious being 'Your Graced' the entire afternoon by Lady Lydia. Always makes me want to look over my shoulder to see whether you're looming over me. And let us not ignore the fact that by the time she rejoins the rest of the company—which should be now, for supper, her ankle having almost healed—the truth of our little charade will have been revealed, even though it was an honest misunderstanding to begin with and we never meant to deceive her on purpose. Her sister has mistaken us, and for some reason beyond my comprehension, you steadfastly refuse to set her straight."

Wolferton gave him a quick look. "Do you fancy her?"

Chippendale spluttered. "What, me? Lady Lydia? What on earth gives you that notion?"

"Your tendency to be rather protective of Lady Lydia. Or Cecily White, as she is really called." Wolferton pulled the cravat he'd been struggling to tie from his neck and threw it onto the growing pile of ties on the floor. "Remember, they are fortune-hunting impostors. Whatever face she shows you, don't fall for the mirage, however beguiling it may be."

Chippendale straightened in his chair. "Eh? Are you sure you're not speaking for yourself? You've fallen head over heels for this woman. I've never seen you in such a state." Chippendale shook his head in mock disbelief.

Wolferton opened his mouth to make a scathing retort, only to close it again as the door opened. His valet, Simonson, entered, carrying another starched and immaculately pressed tie. He did not move a muscle when he saw the pile of ruined ties on the floor.

Wolferton snatched up the offered tie and, with an impatient movement, threw it round his neck.

"One can hardly bear to look at this," Chippendale shuddered. "If you'd only allow me or your valet to help..." He threw up his hands in frustration. "You're doing it all wrong. You need to slip the broad end through the knot. That is, if you're going for the Oriental."

"I'm going for the Mathematical," Wolferton growled, tugging at the tie in frustration before tossing it aside with a muttered curse.

Chippendale sighed and rose. "Come here. I cannot in good conscience watch you slaughter another innocent, perfectly laundered tie. They've done nothing to deserve such cruel treatment." He picked up another fresh tie and approached the Duke.

Then he froze. "The deuce?" He leaned forward and squinted at it. "What's that? 'Peacock of Pomp'? What does that mean?"

"What are you talking about, man?" Wolferton snapped.

Chippendale pointed to the tie. "That's what it says. Is it a fashion statement? Blimey, if it is, I must hasten to have something similar embroidered on mine! It is quite a unique touch, I must say."

Wolferton stared at the skilful script embroidered on the silk. "Simonson!" he barked. "Explain this."

Simonson paled. "Good heavens. I don't have the faintest idea. How on earth did this happen? Who did this? I am completely baffled. A million pardons." Simonson looked as if he were about to cry.

Chippendale burst out into delighted laughter. "It seems that someone is playing a trick on you, old friend. I wonder who it could be? He or she must be an expert with a needle. It is quite a masterpiece. I'd wager a thousand guineas, it's a 'she'." He grinned delightedly at the Duke. "While there's nothing new about womenfolk chasing you, this is quite an original take. I wonder who she could be?" He took the cravat and read the inscription again. "But, my friend, she seems to bear a grudge, because that doesn't sound like a compliment at all, does it?"

"Nonsense," Wolferton tore the cravat from his hand. "I had it specially commissioned at, er, Weston's." He cleared his throat and attempted to tie it.

"So, so. Indeed, you did. A special commission at Weston's, of course. Here, let me." Chippendale took the cravat from him. "I didn't know they did such things. I must hurry and have something similar done to my cravats. What epithet do you think would fit?"

"Pompous fool," muttered Wolferton.

Chippendale chuckled. "Tell me, Simonson," he said, throwing one end of the tie over the other and tying it with sure, quick movements. "Is it my imagination, or does His Grace seem unusually nervous today?"

"It appears so, my lord," Simonson confirmed, earning a scowl from the Duke.

"Then I did not imagine it." Chippendale expertly tied the knot. "He will deny it until his deathbed, but we now have hard evidence that the cause must be a woman."

Wolferton snorted.

Simonson agreed. "No doubt His Grace's nervousness is due to all the ladies waiting for him downstairs," Simonson added loyally.

"True, true. The mere thought of the horde of ladies trying to drag you to the altar would make anyone nervous." He gave the tie a final tug and stepped back. "There. That looks good. The 'Peacock of Pomp' is on full display. What do you think, Simonson? He looks dashing, our duke, doesn't he?"

"He looks most splendid." Simonson wiped his glistening forehead with his handkerchief.

"What an excellent valet you have, Wolferton. If you ever need another job, you can come to me, Simonson," Chippendale said, patting him on the shoulder.

"Thank you, my lord, I shall bear that in mind," Simonson said as he made a hasty retreat to avoid the wrathful gaze of his employer.

Chippendale clapped Wolferton on the shoulder. "It's a pity you don't make more of an effort to preen yourself, because it suits you well, my friend. All dressed in the latest fashion, a veritable nonpareil. But I dare say you feel more at home in your stable boy's clothes than at the height of elegance."

Wolferton grimaced, but said nothing.

"Come, let us face the music. She won't eat you, my friend," he added *sotto voce* as they headed for the door.

"I wouldn't be so sure," muttered Wolferton darkly.

It was shockingly ill-mannered of His Grace, some of the guests whispered, to be so conspicuously absent; to invite them to his country party and then never show his face, leaving them to be entertained by his three elderly aunts.

Emily did not mind, for she found the aunts amusing. They'd clearly taken a liking to Cissy, after a footman had carried her into the blue drawing room, and fussed over her, which meant that Emily was unobserved and free to do whatever she wanted.

"To abandon one's guests is most discourteous," sniffed Lady Willowthorpe. Her three daughters, the Three Pastels, as Emily nicknamed them, sat side by side in pink, blue and green pastel dresses, looking equally disappointed.

"It's been three days since we arrived and he hasn't even made an appearance to greet us," Lady Blakely complained. "At this rate, a fortnight will pass and we will have to leave without even having seen His Grace."

"Wolferton is no doubt a busy man," Hamish put in. "He has three estates to manage, and I hear there has been trouble with his secretary. Or was it the steward? Or both. Either way, I think it speaks well for him that he takes his responsibilities seriously. You can't say that about everyone."

They'd been playing spillikins, cards, jackstraws and riddles since tea. Emily had been somewhat distracted, replaying in her mind the conversation she'd had with George.

After changing for dinner, they reassembled in the blue drawing room to await the gong for dinner.

Lord Hamish would lead her to the supper room. He stood before her, splendidly dressed in blue, with padded shoulders, chatting amiably. For the tenth time, at least, Emily thought it was a pity that the man was already married.

The door opened and His Grace entered—followed by George, the coachman.

"Wolferton. At last. I thought we'd never see your face while we lived under your roof," Lord Willowthorpe drawled.

Everyone stopped what they were doing and rose to greet the men, surrounding them.

Emily looked at George in surprise. What was he doing here? She was not normally a stickler for etiquette, but she found it rather odd that a coachman should mingle with the guests of the house. He was well dressed too; she noticed.

Gone were the baggy jacket and the stained leather breeches. He wore dark grey evening breeches that ended just below the knee, a dark tailcoat and a neatly tied cravat. His hair was fashionably styled, revealing a tall, proud forehead.

Emily looked at him uneasily. George cut a dapper

figure outside his coachman's outfit. Almost dashing, one might say. He looked very different from the coachman she'd known. In fact, he looked like a different person altogether. And he behaved differently too, playing with a quizzing glass in one hand as he nodded loftily at Lord Willowthorpe.

"Willowthorpe. Lady Willowthorpe. It is a pleasure." He said it in such a bored drawl that one could infer he meant the opposite.

Emily's jaw dropped.

Lady Willowthorpe led her three giggling daughters forward, and he merely raised an eyebrow at them, causing them to blush and giggle even more.

"Wolferton—" Lady Dalrymple rose and stepped forward "—it's about time. You have been shockingly neglectful of your guests. It is really quite unforgivable when we have such charming company. You have met Lady Poppy and Lady Lydia. Lady Lydia's ankle is healing nicely and we're all enriched by having her presence with us tonight."

It dawned on Emily that she'd made a terrible, terrible mistake as she met the Duke's amber eyes.

Dear Fenn,

You are right—I am ashamed to admit that I do not have any shoes. My feet grow so quickly, and Papa cannot afford to buy shoes for us all the time, for they are quite dear. Besides, Cissy needs them more than I do. Truly, it is no great hardship, for I rather enjoy running barefoot.

Your faithful barefoot friend,
Little Wren

Dear Little Wren,

This will not do.

Winter is fast approaching, and no one—least of all you—should be running about without shoes. I cannot bear the thought of you braving the cold with bare feet.

A little rain never hurt anyone, but that doesn't mean you must face every storm unprepared.

Enclosed is a pair of boots. Please wear them.

Your faithful Forest Fay,
Fenn

My dearest, dearest Forest Fay,

Oh, Fenn!

The boots! They are the most beautiful thing I have

ever seen! How can I possibly accept such a gift? It seems far too generous. Yet, I cannot stop staring at them. I am quite in love with them already.

And my pomona green stockings—how splendid they look with the boots! I vow I shall wear them every day, sleep in them, and never take them off!

Your friend forever,

Little Wren

P.S. I have enclosed a drawing for you as a thank you!

Chapter Twelve

"Your Gr-grace?" She opened and closed her mouth like a fish. When she finally managed to utter a few words, it sounded more like a helpless croak.

Wolferton merely raised an eyebrow, the corners of his lips curling up, as if he couldn't decide whether he was amused or not. "Lady Poppy Featherstone," he drawled, emphasising the word 'lady'. "It's a pleasure." He spoke as if they hadn't met that morning, walking side by side through the forest, stuffing their mouths with crumpets.

The words of that last conversation hung palpably between them.

Emily stared at him, pale, mouth half open.

His gaze pierced her very soul.

"But what is this? Is that some sort of writing on your cravat?" Lady Dalrymple pointed her quizzing glass at his neck.

"I'm told it's the latest fashion," the Duke replied with a lazy lilt, his words dripping with indifference as he never once broke eye contact with Emily, who had blushed a deep scarlet. "And as Chippendale says, one must always be fashionable, no matter how eccentric."

"Peacock of Pomp," Hamish read and laughed. "How charming. Is this some sort of joke?"

"If it is, it is entirely at my expense, Hamish." A flicker of a smile flitted across Wolferton's stern features, softening them. "It's good to have you and Miss Ingleton here." He leaned elegantly over Hamish's sister's hand, all gentlemanly. "The last time I saw you, I think you were in your leading strings."

Miss Ingleton simpered.

As Wolferton continued to make the rounds, greeting everyone, Emily's brain began to steam and she could barely make sense of the flood of conflicting emotions that were washing over her.

Betrayal. Humiliation. Anger. All moulded together in a hot, tight ball that settled in the pit of her stomach, where it festered.

George was the duke.

George was the duke.

Zounds. George was the duke!

The things she'd said to him!

The names she'd called him! She'd accused him of being a murderer, to his face. She'd told him her whole sad story.

That would explain why he'd behaved so strangely.

But why had he done it? Why had he pretended to be a coachman? Why had he deceived her like that?

Heavens above! A sickening feeling shot through her.

Speaking of deception. It was the other way around, too: he knew she was deceiving him right now.

He knew she wasn't Lady Poppy!

He knew she was a liar and an impostor, here under false pretences to trick him into marrying Cissy. He knew everything.

He could expose her publicly at any moment and ruin any present and future plans she and Cissy had. If he wished, he could ruin them so thoroughly that they would never be seen in society again. It would be a scandal beyond anything she'd ever imagined.

Her heart began to pound painfully and her hands grew hot.

Emily looked at Cissy in panic.

Cissy, however, remained calm. She folded her hands neatly in her lap and smiled up at him. "Please forgive me for not rising, Your Grace. Although my ankle is healing, the doctor has told me not to put any weight on it yet to prevent a relapse. My sister and I are truly grateful for your kind hospitality."

Her speech was very beautiful. She seemed completely calm. Emily gaped at her. Cissy had known! But how? Why? Why hadn't she told her? Why wasn't she worried?

And look at him! He actually smiled at her. It was an authentic smile, not the sneer he'd given her. "Lady Lydia. It is a pleasure to have you here. Please make yourself at home and stay as long as you like."

Emily, who'd been speechless before, was now struck dumb.

He was a devil indeed.

The dandy, who turned out to be Lord Chippendale, whom she had mistaken for the Duke, stepped forward with a beam. "Excellent words, Wolferton. I must say, for a first house party, you've outdone yourself with such lovely guests." He reached out to kiss Cissy's hand. "It will be my pleasure to escort you to the dining room." He looked deep into her eyes.

Cissy blushed. "That won't be necessary, my lord. I have a footman who will assist me."

Lord Hamish joined them, and now Cissy was surrounded by the most eligible bachelors in the country.

Not unusual, Emily had to admit, but a little annoying, yes.

Cissy smiled serenely.

"Cucumbers," Emily said stupidly.

She'd said it a bit too loudly. Heads turned, and she flushed painfully.

Admittedly, she didn't know why she'd said it. It must have been in response to something her dinner partner, Lord Hamish, had said to her, but for the life of her she couldn't remember what he had just said.

Not with coachman George—sorry, His Grace—staring at her so awfully as if he were about to pounce on her at any moment. She toyed with her boeuf aux champignons, wondering what he'd do to her if he had the chance.

Throw her in the dungeon, perhaps.

Which was nonsense. As far as she knew, Ashbourne House had no dungeons; it wasn't a medieval castle.

There was a priest's hole somewhere, though, of that much she was certain. Rumour had it that a previous duke had hidden his priests there during the Reformation. She couldn't quite remember how the story turned out, but she wouldn't be surprised if it ended with that duke forgetting the priest. There would merely be a skeleton left to tell the tale. Poor priest. Hopefully the current duke hadn't entertained a similar notion and decided to test the priest hole— with her.

Emily swallowed.

Of course that was all nonsense, but by Hera's petticoats, what was she to do? She was hot and uncomfortable and it felt like a million ants were crawling all over her body.

There, again! Their eyes had met anew. He was most definitely staring across the entire length of the supper table, over magnificent candelabras and an entire wretched swan gracing its middle, stuffed with apples and oranges amidst an elaborate arrangement of flowers and fondant. It was quite barbaric, and Emily would have lost her appetite, if she'd had any to begin with.

She tore her eyes away hastily and chewed and chewed on her beef, which seemed to have turned into a piece of leather and was growing in her mouth. She swallowed, and it almost stuck in her throat. Coughing, she took a sip of wine.

That didn't help either, because she needed to keep a clear head. The more wine she drank, the more dizzy she became. And the more nonsense she talked.

Which was no doubt why she'd blurted out something as inane as 'cucumbers' when Hamish asked her what she thought of the scenery in this area.

The corners of Hamish's mouth twitched. "Cucumbers. Not exactly a staple crop for most farmers as they are extremely difficult to grow. I'd know, I'm a bit of a gardener myself."

Emily blinked at him.

"Interesting how you associate the countryside with cucumbers," he mused.

Emily's eyes wandered to Wolferton, and she seemed to detect a faint sneer crossing his face, but it was so quick that she might have imagined it.

She sat up straight as if stung by an adder. "I was merely expressing my relief at the fact that this climate is such that growing such vegetables as cucumbers must be extremely difficult."

"You most definitely don't seem to like cucumbers," Hamish remarked.

"I detest them," Emily said, glaring at the Duke.

By the time they were served pudding—which took a good while, as they were served five courses over several hours, including the excellent syllabub that Emily would have usually enjoyed, but could not in that moment—the indignation in her grew as the realisation finally set in that there were two sides to the knife.

Certainly, he knew she was an impostor.

But he, too, had posed as someone other than he really was.

He too had deceived her.

He'd mocked her.

He'd made a fool of her.

He'd betrayed her.

He'd played with her.

Emily was not usually slow-witted, but this realisation took its time sinking in. When it did, a hot wave of anger rolled through her, and she gripped her spoon until her knuckles were white.

Lord Hamish, her dining companion, didn't seem to notice. He was happily talking about hunting. "Pheasants are such peculiar birds—they would rather run for cover than fly, only taking to the air as a last resort. My dogs are excellent at flushing them out."

"Indeed," Emily replied mechanically, spooning the syllabub into her mouth without tasting it.

"I average six brace a season."

"Hm."

"That's not such an impressive number when you think about it," Hamish added cheerfully. "After all, a brace is only one male and one female. Did you know that Wolferton once shot nearly a hundred in a single week?"

"Wolferton?" Emily's head snapped up. Her eyes met his at the head of the table. He was leaning back in his chair, a finger idly tracing the rim of his wineglass, his eyes fixed on her, dark with an emotion she could not identify. Was it desire? Irritation? Suspicion?

A shiver ran up her spine, down her arms and into her fingers.

Shaking, she tore her eyes away and took a sip of wine.

"Not to belittle the prowess of our esteemed host, Hamish," Lord Willowthorpe interjected with a grin, "but rumour has it that King George shot 300 in a week at Windsor."

"He didn't," Wolferton replied, his voice steady. "The best he did was 150. And for the record, I shot 100 brace. That's 200 fowls."

"That's an awful lot of fowl to eat," Emily muttered. She turned to Hamish. "Imagine the amount of fowl pie, fowl stew, fowl soup—not to mention braised fowl, roast fowl, boiled fowl—you'd have to consume with that number. I'd start dreaming about fowl."

Hamish grinned. "You don't sound overly fond of fowl in addition to cucumbers."

"I'm not." Emily dipped her spoon into the syllabub, splashing cream onto the tablecloth. She dabbed at the stain with her napkin. "I don't like to eat anything with feathers. Especially when you think it's chicken, and it turns out to be partridge. It masquerades as something other than what it is." She shot an icy glance at the head of the table. A muscle in Wolferton's face twitched, betraying that he'd heard her.

Hamish chuckled. "Yet you've just finished an entire second course of pheasant without complaint. I think I even handed you the plate for a second helping."

Emily's spoon stopped in mid-air. "Did I?" she asked weakly, her cheeks warming. She hadn't tasted a bite. She'd been too busy thinking dark thoughts about the Duke.

"Must we discuss the hunt at the table?" Lady Jane interjected with a sharp look. "With the ladies present, no less?"

"Yes, let's talk about the ball instead. There is to be a

ball here, is there not, Your Grace?" Miss Pastel Pink turned to the Duke. Somehow, she sounded even more girlish than she was.

Emily, for the life of her, could not remember her name.

"Oh yes, a ball, please," the other ladies chimed in, clapping their hands.

Cissy and Emily exchanged glances. A ball would be a problem as neither of them owned a ball gown. They had simply not expected there to be such an occasion. Not to mention that their current finances would not have allowed them to buy such a dress, not to mention all the accessories such as shoes, gloves, fans, feathers, ribbons, laces...

Maybe we should just leave, flashed through Emily's mind. Perhaps that was the wisest course of action. This Duke was up to no good; he was far too dangerous, watching her every move with his hawk eyes, and Emily was on tenterhooks. Any minute now he could reveal that she was not Lady Poppy but plain Meggie Blythe, a lowly servant.

She shifted tensely in her chair.

"A ball might be just the thing," Lady Dalrymple chimed in. "Especially now that the ballroom has been redecorated. You can't imagine the state it was in. This house hasn't been lived in since my father bought it nearly fifty years ago. Unfortunately, he never took to it, nor did the old duke, Wolferton's father. My sisters and I have enjoyed spending a summer here now and then, for the air is excellent, as is the surrounding country-side. It would be the first time in well over a century that a ball would be held here. I would say it is about time."

They could leave first thing in the morning. Cissy's ankle was well enough and there was a coach to Scotland leaving from the inn. Walking there would be a problem. Emily was annoyed that the Duke was not the coachman, as that would have made their departure much easier. She could have simply asked him to do them a favour and drive them to the inn. George, the coachman, would certainly have done that. Not that that would have made any sense, because then they wouldn't have had to leave in the first place.

Emily sighed. Her mind was muddled, and she had difficulty thinking straight.

She looked up.

Why was he still staring at her with those narrow, calculating eyes? Like a cat watching a mouse, ready to pounce.

Perhaps she had a speck of syllabub on her nose. She rubbed it self-consciously, just in case.

Then she noticed something worse. Everyone else was staring at her, too.

A prickling heat climbed up her neck as silence fell over the table. She glanced helplessly at Hamish, who turned towards her with an amused twinkle in his eye.

"What?" she mouthed.

"His Grace has just announced that it is up to you whether there is a ball," he said, barely suppressing a grin.

Emily's head snapped back to the Duke. "Why on earth would that be?"

"Because," Lady Dalrymple interjected smoothly, "you were planning to depart in two days, weren't you? That would be prior to the ball. Yet without you, there won't be enough ladies to partner the gentlemen."

Emily's brow furrowed. "Forgive me, but by my count there are currently nine ladies to four gentlemen. That seems more than adequate."

"Not if you include the officers of the militia stationed nearby," the Duke said, his tone maddeningly calm. "All the officers would be invited, which would leave us with a surplus of gentlemen. I will only invite them if they are guaranteed dance partners. The decision is yours."

"Oh, stay Lady Poppy!" Miss Pastel Blue urged. "It would be so nice to have a ball."

Emily hesitated, her mind racing. It wasn't a good idea. They had no ballroom dresses, no experience of high society balls and far too many secrets to keep. The Duke was bound to expose them—and then there would be a scandal.

Cissy looked at her pleadingly. Hamish watched expectantly. And the Duke—confound him—looked as devilish as ever, with that faint, knowing smile playing about his lips.

Her head hurt. When would this infernal dinner party end?

"Oh, very well," she said irritably.

There was a sigh of relief around the table.

The Duke raised his wineglass and took a measured sip, his dark gaze lingering on her. For a moment, Emily thought she saw a flicker of relief in his eyes—but surely, it must be her imagination.

Dearest Little Wren,

Do take off and wash those stockings once in a while, lest they begin to reek. I am glad they bring you so much joy. As for your drawing—so this is what you think I look like? Horns, wings, and a tail? I am not sure whether to be flattered or insulted!

Sincerely,
Fenn

Dear Fenn,

Then tell me, what do you truly look like? Or better yet, let me see you! Just a glimpse?

Yes, that is exactly what I imagine you look like, and I see no reason to doubt it. But I must say, it isn't fair that you have seen me while I haven't seen you. I waited by the tree all day yesterday, hoping for just a peek, but alas, you did not come.

I missed supper for it—not that I missed much. It was only bread and tea, but still, I went to bed hungry. I am often hungry when I go to bed, and then I dream of hot crumpets the whole night.

Tell me, Fenn, what do forest fays eat? Surely something more magical than bread and tea?

Yours truly,
Little Wren

Chapter Thirteen

This evening was agony.

Would it never end?

They were playing speculation, a card game that involved gambling. Sitting at a small table with the Duke's three aunts and Chippendale, Emily could swear that Lady Mabel was cheating. Since her mind wasn't on the game, she'd already lost heavily, which she couldn't afford. She hoped that the aunts wouldn't call in their winnings, for if they did, she would find herself in dire straits.

At another table sat the Duke, surrounded by the remaining ladies who were fawning over him. Emily supposed that they were playing speculation as well; however, the ladies seemed to be focusing more on the game of flirtation than on anything else. Miss Cowley brushed his arm with her hand, no doubt quite accidentally, but the Duke was clearly an unwilling participant, for he scowled more than he smiled. This made the ladies work even harder. It would have been amusing if Emily hadn't been in so much turmoil to enjoy his discomfort.

She and the Duke, however, seemed to be playing another game entirely; one that was only known between the two. Emily called it the 'catch me looking at you' game, and it went like this: one person would stare across the room at the other when they thought the other person wasn't looking. When they were caught as the other person turned their head to meet their gaze, they would quickly look away, pretending it was a mere accident. And it went round and round. Every time their eyes met, quite by chance, a shock of lighting seemed to go through her entire system, leaving her shaken to the core.

It was most disconcerting.

"There, I have won." Lady Jane threw down her cards. "Lady Poppy. If you please?"

Look how he squirmed away from Miss Pastel Pink's touch, as she placed a hand on his other arm. Emily gripped the cards so tightly that they bent.

"Lady Poppy?"

Emily snapped to attention. "Yes, Lady Jane?"

She tore her eyes away and turned to the older lady, who was watching her with a slight ironic smile playing on her lips.

"I see that Wolferton needs another cup of tea, but is quite unable to extricate himself from his current situation. Would you be so kind as to pour him a cup and take it to him? The poor man must be parched."

"Why yes, of course." She stood up, glad to be able to do something, not noticing the three aunts exchanging speaking glances.

"He takes it strong, with a good dollop of milk and three lumps of sugar," Lady Dalrymple added.

The tea tray was set on the sideboard, with the teapot on a silver-plated heating element that kept the water warm. Emily lifted the teapot and poured the liquid into one of the porcelain cups. She lifted a small lump of sugar with silver tongs, but hesitated before adding it to the cup. Her gaze wandered to the crystal salt cellar that stood next to a tray of savoury refreshments. Quickly, without thinking, she put the tweezers down. Her finger slid into the salt cellar, took a pinch and dropped it into the Duke's tea. For good measure, she added three more. And a fourth, a big one. Then she added a dollop of milk and stirred with a silver spoon.

There. Done.

She must have lost her mind completely.

No question, it was childish and stupid. It wasn't even a proper revenge. Her only defence was that her fingers had done it of their own free will; there was no other logical explanation she could offer for what she had done. But oh, the feeling of satisfaction!

A grin crossed her face. She took the teacup and carried it over to His Grace.

Dear me, the rumours were not exaggerated when they said he was constantly plagued by women. He looked up, a pained expression on his face. Miss Cowley was almost sitting on his lap, and her parents both seemed to be looking at them with approval. Emily clucked her tongue.

"Some tea, Your Grace, would be good for your forti-tude," Emily murmured.

"Thank you." Their fingers brushed lightly, sending another tingle up her arm and down her spine. Their eyes met for a split second and Emily looked away, flushed. Rubbing her hand, she returned to the table with the three aunts, who had been watching the entire exchange with Argus eyes. Once again, the three aunts shared speaking glances.

Araminta snorted and said, "The poor boy does not seem to get a minute's peace."

Emily watched as 'the poor boy' lifted the cup and took a big gulp of his tea. His eyes widened. He spluttered and coughed.

Emily folded her hands serenely and savoured the sense of petty triumph that washed over her.

"Wolferton." Araminta spoke with some alarm, when the wheezing wouldn't cease. "I trust you are well?"

"A glass of water, if you please," he managed. A footman leapt forward to serve him a glass of water, which he drank thirstily.

"Thank you for the most excellent tea, although it tasted as if half the contents of the salt cellar had been poured into it. Quite by accident, no doubt." He glared at her.

"Dear me. I was sure I put three lumps of sugar in it, as your aunt requested." Emily replied serenely.

"A word with you, Lady Poppy," he said in a stern tone.

Emily looked up in alarm. Oh no, he wanted to talk to her privately, to scold her for almost poisoning him with salt. She had no desire whatsoever to find herself alone in his company.

She looked to Cissy for help, but she was busy playing another round of speculation with Lady Mabel.

"I have a strong appetite for some bubble and squeak," Emily announced loudly.

"Really? After such a sumptuous dinner?" said Lady Blakely with a raised eyebrow.

"For the life of me, I can't bring myself to even try that dish." Lady Willowthorpe shuddered.

But Cissy didn't hear.

The Duke rose from his chair.

"Really, bubble and squeak must be the best dish under the sun," Emily babbled wildly.

"Why is it called bubble and squeak, I wonder?" Chippendale asked. "It's a most peculiar name for a dish."

"Because when you stir the potatoes and cabbage in the pot, it squeaks," explained Miss Ingleton.

"I confess I haven't tried it yet," Lord Hamish put in.

"A formless substance made of potatoes and cabbages is neither very aesthetic nor pleasing to the senses," mused Lady Willowthorpe. "Especially if one does not like cabbage. What about you, Your Grace?"

The Duke, who had started to make his way across the room to their table, paused.

"Do you like cabbage?" Miss Ingleton insisted.

"Not particularly," he replied. Then he continued on his way towards her.

Emily panicked.

Araminta unwittingly came to her aid. "What do you think, Lady Lydia? Do you like bubble and squeak?"

Cissy dropped her cards and turned her head sharply towards Emily, who had also risen from her chair.

"Absolutely, she adores bubble and squeak." Emily was sweating by now.

"Quite right." Cissy rose. "If you'll excuse me, ladies, I will have to escort my sister to her room."

She took Emily by the arm and, with a charming smile, walked past the Duke, who'd come to a halt. "Your Grace." She curtsied, then led Emily out of the room.

She could feel the Duke's gaze pierce her shoulder blades.

"What's the matter, Emily? You look rather pale."

"You knew about the Duke and Chippendale." Emily's voice sounded accusing. "Why on earth didn't you warn me?"

"I tried to tell you earlier, but there wasn't an opportunity."

"A warning or a sign would have been welcome. Anything, really." Emily sat down heavily in the chair by the bed. "Good heavens, what an evening." The strain of the evening had taken hold of her and she felt exhausted to the marrow.

"I'm sorry, Emily. It must have been a shock. But you were gone most of the afternoon, and then the three aunts requested my company, and then I was introduced to the guests, and one thing led to another, and there was no time for a private conversation with you."

"How did you find out?"

"Chippendale told me this afternoon when you sent him to bring me a book. He confessed everything—said

162

he'd only played along out of loyalty to the Duke, but he'd got tired of it and decided to come clean. I was pleased with his honesty. He's a good man." She thought for a moment, a frown creasing her forehead. "And he seems convinced that the Duke is too, for they have been friends since Eton."

Emily rubbed her forehead. "Is that what this is? A schoolboy prank? Has he explained why they did it?"

"Apparently the Duke loathes being relentlessly pursued by every female, as Chippendale put it. This charade allows him to avoid unwanted attention, and Chippendale doesn't mind the pretence."

Emily groaned. "So what do we do now?"

"He doesn't know who we really are," Cissy said in a calm voice. "He doesn't know that we are Miss Cecily and Emily White, his former tenants, whom he evicted. That is to our advantage."

Emily squirmed uncomfortably. "I actually told him," she muttered, avoiding her eyes.

Cissy stared. "You did what?"

Emily cleared her throat. "I may have told him. Accidentally."

"What?" Cissy shrieked. "You told him?"

"I didn't know he was the Duke!" Emily jumped to her feet, wringing her hands. "It was an honest mistake. I thought he was the coachman at the inn." She groaned as she remembered their interactions. "I trusted him. I even thought he was nice. Nice!" She gave a short, bitter laugh that ended in a half-sob. The truth was, she'd thought he was much more than nice.

Cissy groaned again and slumped back in her chair.

"You've basically told our enemy to his face what we intend to do. That's not good."

Emily nodded glumly. "He knows our secrets. He knows we're up to no good. He knows we want revenge. He knows,"—Emily took a deep breath—"that I want him to marry you." Her shoulders slumped in defeat. "I'm sorry I ruined it. I think the best course of action is that we leave immediately. There's no point in staying." Emily jumped to her feet, pulled the trunk from under the bed and began to pile her clothes into it.

Cissy watched her, chewing her bottom lip thoughtfully. Then she said, "I can see now why he asked you that question at supper. The one about the ball. To ask you to stay for the ball. To stop you from running away."

"No doubt he wants to retaliate with his own form of punishment." Emily said darkly. "Heaven knows what he'll come up with."

"I don't think so," Cissy replied thoughtfully.

"I don't know why I didn't see it before. That arrogant way of his. The way he carries himself. No coachman walks like that. And the way he lifts his chin, like this—" she lifted her chin proudly "—and how he seems so haughty and above everybody, a loathsome man!" Emily talked herself into a rage. "And later, when we met again, he didn't correct the misunderstanding. I blurted out that I hated the Duke; and he seemed so concerned and sincerely worried and asked why, so I just told him." Her shoulders slumped. "Oh, Cissy! I liked him. I really did. George, I mean. The coachman. Not the Duke! I am such a fool." She banged her head against the wooden board of the bed several times.

"Perhaps it's for the best," Cissy mused. "For the truth to come out, I mean. The idea of being a duchess has always seemed rather... suffocating." She tilted her head, a mischievous twinkle in her eyes. "It seems your matchmaking skills have gone hopelessly awry, dear sister. Even if you poured every ounce of effort into it, I don't think you'd manage to pair me with the Duke now. He won't go for it. Haven't you noticed? His Grace had eyes only for you all evening."

Emily sat up stiffer than a pole. "Nonsense. He was trying to intimidate me, nothing more."

Cissy gave Emily a knowing smile. "It's fascinating. I wonder... Anyway, I've made up my mind. I want to go to the ball."

"How? With what dress? We have only one nice dress between us! And it certainly is not a ballgown." Emily laughed bitterly. "Unless you wear it for the first half and I wear it for the second? We could switch halfway through the evening." Emily gave up her frantic attempt at packing and collapsed on the bed next to Cissy.

Cissy's smile widened. "Perhaps Miss Ingleton will help us. She seemed quite nice and talked to me all evening about fashion. She boasted that she had brought three ball gowns because she couldn't decide which one to wear. I was able to tell her that my dress was ruined because when the maid took it out to hang, I tripped just as I was crossing the room with a cup of tea in my hand and the contents of the cup ended up on the dress. We're about the same size."

Emily looked at her with her head tilted. "I don't

know how you can be thinking about dresses right now. What about the Duke?" Her sigh came from the depths of her being. "He knows we're impostors. He could ruin us at any moment. A word from him carries so much more weight than from anyone else. I dare not risk it. There is too much at stake if we stay now."

"I don't think he'll do anything like that," Cissy said with a confidence Emily didn't feel.

"Why are you so sure he won't?"

Cissy smiled knowingly. "Because of what I saw in his eyes when he looked at you."

Emily shot to her feet. "There again! What on earth are you talking about? What did you see? There was nothing in his eyes at all. Nothing! Other than—" she sputtered, grasping for words "—a nasty smirk, if that!"

"He could hardly bear to tear his gaze away from you all evening. The expression in his eyes definitely changes when he turns them on you. They get all big and golden and melting, and his pupils double—"

"Fiddlesticks!" Emily stammered, sounding like Lady Araminta Dalrymple.

Cissy burst out laughing. "Oh, Emmy! You are so charming when you are embarrassed. I'd wager you have a better chance of becoming duchess than I do. Now, let me find Miss Ingleton to ask about the dresses."

Cissy left the room, leaving Emily behind, spluttering.

Dear Little Wren,

Do not wait for me beside the tree; it is a futile endeavour. I may not even currently reside in this forest, for I have many forests to tend to. You must forgive me if my replies are not always immediate—there is much work for a forest fay.

As for what I eat: flowers, sunshine, and the rays of the rainbow, like any true forest fay.

Your humble servant,

Fenn

Dear Fenn,

I do not understand. If you are not currently in the forest, then how are you delivering these letters?

Sincerely,

Little Wren

Dear Little Wren,

Ah, but I have minions, of course! Mortals of humble origin who scramble to do my bidding and deliver my letters. Which is why waiting by the tree is quite hopeless. The person you might glimpse delivering my letters is, in all likelihood, not me.

But enough of this. You have said you are hungry, and I cannot allow that. Eat what you find enclosed at once.

Faithfully yours,

Fenn

Chapter Fourteen

SHE WAS AVOIDING HIM.

He was fairly certain that this was the case, for she had, not once, that evening, made eye contact with him. Perhaps she felt guilty for having ruined his cravat—he fingered the embroidery on his cravat, for now that article of clothing had become his favourite—deliberately, no doubt motivated by a petty need for revenge. His valet had been horrified when he'd insisted on wearing it again this morning.

He suppressed a smirk.

Then she'd added salt to his tea instead of sugar, with such abundance that he'd thought he'd taken a sip of the Dead Sea. He'd never had such a horrible mouthful of salt in his life, and he'd almost spat it out all over Miss Cowley's bodice, only stopping himself at the last moment. His toes had curled up in his boots in the effort to swallow.

He'd spent the entire morning wondering what mischief she'd be up to today, but to his disappointment, she was sitting meekly with his aunts, eyes downcast, playing Whist and, to all appearances, losing spectacularly. He tried to catch her eye, but she stubbornly looked away, ignoring his presence.

Chippendale had spent the entire evening mercilessly roasting him after she'd fled the scene of yesterday's salt fiasco. He had taken every opportunity to pepper the conversation with references to salt—pointing out that it was a wonderful preservative and joking that the Duke, having been brined inside and out, would undoubtedly outlast them all.

He'd ordered a dish of bubble and squeak for today's nuncheon, which, his butler had informed him, had so horrified his chef that he'd almost handed in his resignation.

"Monsieur Henri finds it beneath his dignity to cook such a, er, mundane dish and begs you to reconsider today's menu. His argument is that it is considered a humble repast of the lowest of classes, which renders it quite unworthy of Your Grace's table, which should be graced with only the finest delicacies," the butler reported.

"Nonsense," Wolferton had replied. "Lady Poppy has a craving for that dish, so tell him I expect him to serve it today. Along with crumpets for tea," he added as an afterthought.

The butler looked at him unhappily. "I beg your pardon, but Monsieur Henri has threatened to resign if he is forced to cook food so far beneath him. If Your Grace could be moved to compromise, perhaps such a terrible event could be averted."

Under normal circumstances, he would have fired his cook without batting an eyelid, but the Duke was in a strange mood and the whole conversation amused him. "Compromise? How?"

"Have him prepare some of the most challenging French dishes to be served alongside bubble and squeak, Your Grace," the butler said earnestly. "Such as a lobster souffle, perhaps, and croquembouche—a towering confection of choux pastry filled with cream. My mouth waters just thinking about it, Your Grace. It is such a challenge to prepare that Monsieur Henri will be mollified and more than happy to throw in some bubble and squeak."

"Then let him, by all means," Wolferton agreed. The simple nuncheon they were eventually served had far surpassed any state banquet Prinny could ever offer in his Pavilion.

Stuffed full with bubble and squeak, lobster and pastry, the guests were now assembled in the drawing room for coffee and tea.

The ladies crowded around him as they had the day before, vying for his attention. He ignored them all, as he usually did, but interestingly this had the opposite effect as they renewed their efforts to get his attention. The lady with the pointy nose, Miss Cowley, went on and on about Lord knows what, and he threw in an occasional 'hm' and 'huh' which seemed to satisfy her; another girl in pastel pink had the audacity to tug on his sleeve and demand his attention. When he raised his quizzing glass to her, she blushed a deep red that clashed with her pink outfit. And another, in pastel green, no doubt inspired by Emily the day before, kept insisting on serving him drinks of all kinds, so that he had not only a cup of coffee on the table but also a cup of tea, a glass of liqueur, negus, and a glass of water.

He had an agreement with Chippendale that he would draw some of the ladies away from him, but that rogue was flirting outrageously with Lady Lydia and had no eyes for anyone else.

He studied the sister dispassionately. Emily wanted him to marry her. The girl—Cecily was her real name— was indeed uncommonly beautiful, and her manners were pretty. But there was a reserve about her, even as she flirted with Chippendale, a shell that kept everyone at a distance. The lady was clearly in no danger of losing her heart to him; he decided. Chippendale, the eternal bachelor, was in no danger of getting caught up in any kind of marital ambitions. And neither was he.

His eyes wandered back to Emily, watching as she leaned forward to throw a card, a strand of her hair escaping from her bun and falling across her cheek. His fingers itched to reach out and feel the downy softness of her cheek. As though she could read his thoughts, she tucked it behind her ear and began to chew on her lower lip.

He watched, fascinated.

Something stirred deep inside him.

It was an aching longing in the region of his heart.

A tender little flame he thought he'd long forgotten.

In the nick of time, he prevented his hand from moving to cover his heart. The surrounding ladies would have been beside themselves if they'd known that the

Devil Duke was suffering from a rather severe case of infatuation.

An infatuation that had lasted far too long for his liking.

Yes, that was it. It was utterly fleeting and meaningless, this feeling, this unbearable longing that had taken root in his heart. It was all too familiar.

Once upon a time, he'd thought it was love.

His hand trembled as he reached for his wineglass, which he downed in one gulp. Where had this absurd idea come from?

Love, indeed. He snorted. He'd long since outgrown fanciful notions of love and affection, although there had been a time when he'd believed in the sentiment, back in his salad days, when he'd been a moon-eyed romantic and green behind the ears. Surely it had been youthful infatuation, nothing more, back then—as it must be now.

Dash it all to hell and back. Hadn't he sworn to himself that he would never, ever, ever again allow himself to feel this way?

He scowled, and the pastel green girl's face sank, no doubt thinking it was in response to her shyly stammered question of whether he would like her to bring him another cup of coffee.

This was intolerable! He was bored out of his wits in this company of pastel petticoats. He would march to his aunts that very evening and beg them to put an end to it.

Only he knew what they would say. They'd only do that, they'd told him firmly already, if he chose one of them as his bride. Even his Aunt Mabel, usually so soft and gentle, had a resolute set to her mouth when it came to the matter and steadfastly refused to yield.

They wanted a bride?

Well, they would have one.

He narrowed his eyes to slits and his gaze wandered over the heads of the guests to Emily once more.

Just then she raised hers, and their eyes met.

Finally.

His breath caught.

How could just meeting her gaze make him feel like he was breathing in fresh air and drowning in a stormy sea at the same time?

There was a sombre expression on her face and a question in her beautiful brown eyes.

Then a look of determination crossed her features. She said a few words to his aunts, put the cards down, rose and made her way across the room to him.

Quite illogically, his pulse began to quicken. The grip on his glass tightened.

She stopped just outside the circle of women surrounding him. "May I have a moment of your time, Your Grace?" she said stiffly.

Heads turned, and more than one lady pulled a face.

He raised an eyebrow. "Certainly. If you will give us a moment." He looked pointedly at the ladies, who reluctantly withdrew. "Now, Lady Poppy." He deliberately emphasised the 'Lady' and watched in fascination as it caused her lips to purse for a moment. "How can I help you?"

She clasped her hands in front of her stomach. "I confess I was a little surprised to discover that George the coachman turned out to be the Duke of Wolferton. I hope you enjoyed your little charade." She lifted her chin proudly as if to indicate she did not care in the least.

So she finally wanted to talk about the elephant in the room. It was about time. He placed his glass on the mantelpiece and turned to face her.

"Ah. Yes. I did." He curled his lips into a smile. "It was amusing, in a way. It was entirely unplanned, though." He looked at her searchingly. "I was testing my new horses when you approached, mistaking me for my coachman. It was never my intention to deliberately deceive you."

"Yet you never corrected the misunderstanding when we met later outside the stables."

"Hm. No, I suppose I didn't."

"Why?" She tilted her head to the side, making her look like a confused little bird.

A soft smile played across his lips. "To keep you under my roof, perhaps?"

Her eyes widened. Then they narrowed. "You're full of contradictions, Your Grace."

She took a step forward and lowered her voice. To any onlooker it would have appeared as though she was flirting outrageously with him. "First, you have us evicted, now you want to keep us under your roof. There is no rhyme and reason to your behaviour at all, is there?"

Now he was in a quandary. What should he say? The truth? What exactly was the truth? He hardly knew it himself. That he'd planned this all along? He had, hadn't he? That he would keep her here until he was certain of one thing, and one thing only? It was probably not a good idea to reveal that. Not yet.

She continued to talk. "We are grateful for your hospitality, of course, but all things considered, I think it best for my sister and I to continue with our plans to travel to Scotland." She lifted her chin with stubborn determination.

"I don't think so," he said quietly.

She blinked. "What do you mean?"

He looked at her through hooded eyes. "You're not going anywhere."

Her heart beat in loud, heavy thumps. "Wh-why?"

"Because... " He wrestled with how to phrase it. "It's the right thing to do."

She knitted her brows and tilted her head. "Right thing to do?"

He huffed. "You look like a confused little bird when you do that."

Emily blinked. "Do I?"

"I want you to stay here as my guest," he continued. "You need not fear any exposure. I will not reveal your identity. You have my word."

"Why?"

The silence between them was heavy and charged. "Give me a chance to make amends," he said heavily. "Please."

Her eyes widened. Her lips parted, then closed again as if she were searching for words. It was clear she understood what he referred to.

Just at that moment, Miss Cowley returned to stand

beside him, placing her hand on his arm in a rather possessive manner.

He disliked the woman and resisted the urge to shake off her hand, but for the moment he was rather relieved that she had interrupted.

She looked from one to the other. "Such a weighty discussion, Your Grace? How fascinating. Careful now, or tongues might wag that you're about to be leg-shackled by a clever lady."

A flush of pink spread across Emily's cheeks. "Far from it," she stammered.

Why did this reaction irritate instead of relieve him?

Miss Cowley threw her a baleful glance. "I didn't think so, in truth." She turned to Jasper with a pout. "Perhaps a little dance could be arranged if we had some piano music?" Her eyes travelled to Emily. "Do you play the piano, Lady Poppy?"

"Indifferently." She shrugged.

"Surely your skill must be sufficient to play a few tunes for us to dance?" She smiled at him.

"Oh yes, let's dance," Lord Willowthorpe's daughters chimed in almost in unison.

"I don't think so," he exclaimed in alarm. The last thing he wanted was to prance about the stuffy drawing room, trapped with a gaggle of ladies eager to sink their claws into him. He'd be forced to dance with all of them, for if he danced with just one, it would be interpreted as a clear preference.

Not that it wasn't true.

But the one lady he preferred was staring daggers at

him at the moment, and a quick mental calculation told him that the chances of her accepting if he asked her to dance were zero. Maybe even less than that.

"Really, how churlish of you, Wolferton," Araminta exclaimed. "It would be nice to see the young people dance."

"Good decision," Chippendale murmured to himself. "We will be besieged by the ladies, there being only four of us men," he counted, "to eleven women. We would be well advised to save our enthusiasm for dancing for the ball later in the week, when we have some reinforcements," he said to the room.

Wolferton gave him a grateful look. "That's certainly an argument," he put in, "but my reason for declining is that I'm not in the mood for dancing." He nodded to Emily. "I'd rather hear Lady Poppy sing."

Heads turned and Emily squirmed at the attention.

"Oho. Yes. Now that's an idea." Araminta lifted her quizzing glass and pointed it at her. "Lady Poppy. If you please." Aunt Jane rose, took her hand and led her to the piano.

"I really, really don't want to sing," he heard Emily hiss at her.

"Fiddlesticks. Now, who will accompany you?"

In the end, it was Lady Lydia who sat down at the piano to accompany her.

Emily sang several folk songs and a more complicated one, pointedly avoiding looking in his direction.

Then she sang that song, that one song that made him want to cry like a little child.

It was a simple lullaby, a folk song that his mother had also sung to him. He was flooded with memories of a woman whose face he had long forgotten.

He reached for his wineglass again, if only to distract himself, but he did not drink. His fingers clenched the glass so tightly that it would undoubtedly break if he increased the pressure.

"I must say, you have a very fine voice," Lady Willowthorpe said grudgingly after she finished the song. "Exceptionally sweet and clear."

"Reminds me of that opera singer we heard the other night," Chippendale chimed in. "What was her name? The Italian one. Lady Poppy sings at least as well, if not better."

"Like a nightingale or a lark," said Mabel softly.

"Now, none of the rest of us dare sing, for our voices will be unflatteringly compared to yours," the pink Willowthorpe girl complained.

"Well. Now that we can't dance or sing, how about some parlour games?" Miss Ingleton put in.

"What a marvellous idea!" The ladies flocked to him again, surrounding him. "Shall we play The Game of Sighs, or even better, The Don't Laugh game? Oh, please, Your Grace."

Lady Lydia rose. "I beg you not to be offended if I excuse myself. I confess I'm rather tired and I'd rather not overexert myself while my foot is still healing," she explained to the room at large.

He didn't miss the quick look of gratitude that Emily shot her sister.

"I will accompany you," she announced. Of course, Emily had to escort her sister back to her room. Coward.

With a sinking feeling of disappointment, he watched her say goodbye and gracefully leave the room.

It would be a tediously long evening without her.

My dear Fenn,

Crumpets! And not just any crumpets, but cheese crumpets! They were still warm and smelled so heavenly, I could not help but eat one at once. The rest I shared with Cissy and Papa, who send their thanks as well.

Your ever-hungry Little Wren (who is most grateful to have been fed by a forest fay.)

P.S. I have returned your other gift to the tree hollow. While your generosity overwhelms me, I cannot possibly accept so much.

Little Wren,

I am quite offended that you rejected my gift. If you are hungry, you should take the money and buy food—not just for yourself but for your father and little sister. Do not let misplaced pride stand in the way of what is needed.

Your servant,
Fenn

Dear, dearest Fenn,

Please forgive me, but I cannot possibly accept money

from you, no matter how kindly it is offered. It feels wrong to always take while you give, and worse still when it is actual coin. It leaves me feeling indebted, as though I am the object of your pity—and I do not like that.

Yours humbly,
Little Wren

Little Wren,

You seem to forget who I am: Fenn, the Forest Fay. Do not test my patience. It is my solemn duty—and pleasure— to grant the wishes of lesser mortals. And it pleases me greatly to give you this pouch of coins. Accept it and use it wisely, to buy food for yourself and your family.

Yours,
Fenn

Dear Fenn,
I must refuse your gift.
Most humbly,
Little Wren

Emily,

If you refuse my gift, you will break the magic—and I shall vanish from your life forever.

Fenn

Chapter Fifteen

EMILY WAS EXHAUSTED. SHE HAD SPENT A SLEEPLESS night tossing and turning, her restless mind replaying every moment of her confrontation with the Duke. How she had, at first, avoided him, then barged into him like a battleship, outing his charade as coachman George, right there in front of everyone, in the middle of the drawing room. What was she thinking? It was sheer madness.

Amends, the Duke of Wolferton had said. He wanted her to stay on because he wanted to make amends. There had been a time when she'd assumed it'd be far easier for the Highlands to shift and relocate themselves to Cornwall rather than to hear Wolferton utter the word 'amends'.

It was shocking. It was unheard of. It was almost an apology. Probably the closest she'd ever get from him.

Of course, it was clear to her what must have transpired. He'd had them thrown out in the dead of winter, that was a fact. And, when she still thought he was coachman George, she'd as good as told him her story, and that she considered him responsible for her father's death. And now he realised the error of his ways and wanted to make amends.

Emily sat up straight in her bed and stared into the void.

But things were not that simple! She couldn't just let him make amends. She needed her revenge. She needed to stay the course. She couldn't afford to lose focus. What had become of her cold-hearted resolve to orchestrate a match between him and Cissy? She mustn't give up so easily.

Ah, how cynical she had grown over time.

Cynical enough to arrange a loveless marriage between her beloved sister and the man she despised most—all in the name of revenge.

But she would also secure them a home, she reminded herself. Stability. Security. Was that really so terrible?

And did she truly hate him?

She certainly didn't hate George.

Quite the opposite, in fact. She felt that telltale flush creep up her neck again. What was this feeling that came over her every time she met his gaze? It was as if she were drunk, even though she hadn't touched a drop of alcohol.

Her mind replayed his words, his gestures, the moments when he'd surprised her by being unexpectedly kind.

Wolferton and kind! It was outrageous to even admit it.

"Emily White, you are a fool." She dropped her face

into her hands with a loud groan. "You don't hate him at all."

There it was. She'd finally said it. The earth didn't shake, and the heavens didn't fall. She merely felt a pang of guilt gnaw at her. But she didn't hate him. She didn't even dislike him, not really. Oh, he was arrogant, obnoxious and far too used to getting his own way, but... there was something else.

Something that made her stomach turn when he met her gaze. Something that warmed her when his lips curved into one of those rare, fleeting smiles.

Something... something maddeningly, bewitchingly charming.

She fell back onto her bed, buried her face in the pillow and pounded it with her fists.

When she finally calmed down, exhausted from the physical effort of punishing the pillow, she drifted into a restless sleep. She dreamed of the Duke, his face twisted into a cruel grin as he threatened to drag her off to Newgate Prison. When she asked him why he was doing this, he replied: "Because you have the audacity to like me, Lady Poppy. Or should I say Meggie Blythe? Liar and fraud. Admit it!" He continued to drag her towards the prison, laughing maniacally all the while, a sound that lingered long after she awoke.

The next morning, Emily sat in the breakfast room, shuddering as she remembered the dream. She took another sip of her tea, burning her tongue.

She coughed and spluttered.

"Ah. Lady Poppy. Here you are." The three aunts sailed into the room and sat down beside her. Araminta to her right, Jane to her left, and Mabel across from her. Emily had a vague feeling that since last night she had somehow, inexplicably, acquired a special status. Was it because of her singing? Or because she'd added salt to the Duke's tea? Surely they couldn't have known? Or was it really, as Cissy had said, because of the strange look in the Duke's eyes? Had everyone really seen that? How humiliating! What had Cissy said? 'Golden and melting.' Emily shuddered again.

"You're not catching a cold, are you, Lady Poppy?" Jane put a hand to her brow. "You look rather pale, and you've shivered twice in the space of a minute."

Emily forced a smile. "I'm quite well, thank you. I'm not a morning person and just need some time to wake up, that's all."

"Just like Wolferton," Araminta observed with a nod, as if completely satisfied that the two of them had at least that in common. "He sleeps like the dead before noon, and nothing will wake him."

"Unless he goes hunting," Jane chimed in as she helped herself to a cheese crumpet. "Then he sleeps with his clothes on so he can get up before dawn."

Emily squirmed in her chair. She would rather not have known about Wolferton's sleeping habits. Now she couldn't get the image of the Duke out of her mind, sleeping in his big bed. With or without his clothes.

She fanned herself as the temperature in the room seemed to have risen inexplicably.

"You must make sure you get enough rest during the day, child," Araminta said now, patting her hand. "The next few days are likely to be exhausting. Tonight will be another evening of games, cards and the like. Then there is the ball. Ashbourne House will shine in all its splendour as never before. We have invited the whole neighbourhood, and I dare say people will come from as far away as London. The guest rooms are ready. It will be a most enjoyable affair."

"Indeed," Emily said, not knowing what else to say.

Jane put down her teacup. "We're expecting an announcement," she said with an air of satisfaction.

"Are you, now?" Emily said, distracted. "About what?"

The three aunts looked at each other, then back at her, pointedly.

Araminta kept patting her hand.

Mabel took her other hand. Emily looked from one to the other, completely mystified.

"Everything will be well," Mabel said in her soft voice. "You'll see." She kept patting her hand.

She didn't quite know why, but she felt comforted, and the feeling of nervousness that had covered her like an oilcloth fell away. Her eyes itched, and she swallowed the lump in her throat, but that might just have been a remnant of dry toast that had lodged itself there.

"Thank you," she whispered.

Dear Fenn,

I found your pouch on my pillow—truly! How did you manage to leave it there? Mrs Talbot, our neighbour, claims she saw a hooded figure sneaking about the house in the evening. Now that I think of it, I might have left my bedroom window open. Was that you—or one of your mysterious minions?

I asked Papa about it, and he believes the pouch is from someone in the parish. It still doesn't feel right, but he has allowed me to keep it, so thank you, Fenn. I shall save the coins for a time when we truly need them.

How can I ever repay you?

Yours most humbly,

Little Wren

Little Wren,

If you wish to repay me, then send me a lock of your hair.

Yours,

Fenn

O Most Honourable Forest Fay,

I have enclosed a lock of my hair, though I cannot

imagine why you would want it. It is hardly a proper lock —it does not curl and feels coarse as straw. Its colour is the dullest mouse-brown, entirely unremarkable. You should have asked for one of Cissy's golden locks instead. She is far lovelier than I. Sometimes I wish I were as beautiful as my sister. And no, that is not a wish I'd expect you to grant!

Nevertheless, here it is.

Yours truly,

Little Wren

Dear Little Wren,

Stop comparing yourself to your sister. To me, you are just as beautiful—if not more so. Look in the mirror, and you will see lovely brown eyes, warm and trusting, and lips shaped like Cupid's bow, ~~perfect for kissing.~~

Now, tell me—do you have any other wishes I might fulfil?

Yours always,

Fenn

Chapter Sixteen

"I'm tired of playing speculation. Let us play blind man's buff instead," Miss Cowley announced. All the guests were once again gathered in the blue drawing room for post-supper refreshments and entertainment. Emily had suffered through another meal during which she had been determined not to look at the Duke at all. He was air. He did not exist. One did not look at people who did not exist. So she had an absolutely marvellous time chatting to her table partner, who this time was Chippendale.

While he might not have been the biggest wit under the sun, he was sufficiently entertaining.

Much to her surprise, he'd made her laugh more than once. It was his self-aware mockery, she decided, as if he himself did not take himself too seriously. Somehow it made her warm to him.

How could she ever have mistaken him for Wolferton, even for a fraction of a second? He was altogether too nonchalant. She decided that if the Duke would not do,

Chippendale might be the perfect match for Cissy. She would try to throw the two together whenever possible.

"A new game is a splendid notion," Lord Hamish agreed. He and two other gentlemen were both hovering over Cissy, who managed to flirt charmingly with both of them, while Wolferton lounged as usual by the fireplace, looking forbidding and intimidating as ever. His scowl seemed to deepen every time Emily laughed at something Chippendale said.

"Let's draw for who's going to be the blind man," one of the girls said.

"That's not for me," Aunt Jane put in. "I'll sit this one out. Blind man has a tendency to get quite rowdy and wild."

"I'd rather not join in," Cissy said immediately. "My ankle is healing nicely and I wouldn't want to put it at risk. It is, after all, a fairly active game."

"Quite right," Chippendale chimed in. "Perhaps we should choose a quieter game, one that everyone can participate in. How about charades?"

"Famous," Hamish agreed. "Played in pairs, yes?" He immediately lifted a finger to summon a footman. "Fetch us some straw sticks, will you? One for each guest in this room." The footman did so immediately and Hamish proceeded to shorten two straws of the same size. Then he shuffled them and held them out to each person in turn.

"I would like to be paired with the Duke," Miss Cowley insisted.

"Don't all ladies," Araminta muttered.

"I'm afraid Lady Fortuna will have to decide that,"

Hamish laughed, holding out the straws to Miss Cowley, who pulled one.

"You can give me whatever's left," Emily said, not too enthusiastic about the prospect of playing charades.

"Wolferton, stop scowling at all and sundry and pick your straw." Hamish held the straws up to his nose. He chose one.

Everyone paired up. Miss Ingleton was paired with Hamish. "You'll have to be content with me, Miss Ingleton," he joked, and Cissy, to Emily's great satisfaction, was paired with Chippendale. She would have been quite content if her partner had been one of the aunts, perhaps Jane, for she enjoyed her wry humour. Instead, she looked into a pair of gleaming eyes that belonged to the Duke.

He held out his straw to hers: they were a match.

"Oh no!" Emily groaned.

Miss Ingleton, the self-proclaimed Mistress of Revels, decided to change the rules of this game of charades. "Instead of guessing the word based on a riddle or rhyme, let's try something different and guess the word by acting it out. The rule is that the actor does not speak at all. One person in each pair has to act out the word, and the other has to guess. The twist is that there is time pressure, as both pairs perform at the same time. The first person to guess the word wins."

"Excellent." Chippendale winked at Cissy. "We're sure to win this one."

It should be easy enough, Emily thought as Miss Ingleton showed her the note with the word. It was love.

When she gave the signal, Emily immediately

clasped her heart, rocked her body back and forth, and sighed.

Wolferton just stared at her, not understanding. "Indigestion?"

Emily groaned, shaking her head. Thinking that was part of the act, he immediately called out, "Pain. Judging by your grimace, it must definitely be pain, of the intense kind."

"No!" Emily glared at him.

He threw up his hands. "Help me. I'm at a complete loss. Anger? You're scowling. It must be anger."

"No! It's... " Emily clasped her heart again, repeating her first movement.

"No talking, Lady Poppy," Miss Ingleton warned her. The other couple, Chippendale and Cissy, were already on their third word, while Emily and the Duke couldn't seem to get past the first.

"A heart condition resulting from a woman's choleric temper." Wolferton threw up his hands.

The audience roared with laughter and chimed in with all sorts of unhelpful suggestions, despite Miss Ingleton's stern warnings to the contrary.

"Maybe it's heartburn," cried Hamish.

"Distemper of the stomach!" Lord Willowthorpe suggested with a chuckle.

"The ague!"

Emily gave up. "Love. It's love!" She turned to the Duke with a glare. "It wasn't hard to guess, Your Grace. Love pertains to the heart"—she thumped the left side of her chest—"but of course you wouldn't recognise where the organ is located, let alone its metaphorical significance." That came out harsher than intended. She did not know why she'd said it, but there it was.

He narrowed his eyes. "Metaphorical significance? Is that how you interpret love? With an agonised grimace, as if you're suffering through the seven gates of hell?"

"I didn't!" Emily protested. "I was acting out the state of falling in love." She repeated the motion of clutching her heart.

"Good Lord. Falling in love for you must be equivalent to having a canker in the mouth, the way you're grimacing."

Emily glared at him. "Says the man who knows nothing of the feeling."

"How well you seem to know what I do or do not know about love or other emotions." His voice had suddenly become dangerously quiet, a telltale sign of impending danger, something Emily missed as she continued to rant merrily at him, giving free rein to her frustration of the past few hours.

"Yes, that is certain. One thing I know: you have no heart at all." She put her hands on her hips. "You wouldn't know love if it was staring you in the face."

"Wouldn't I?" He took a step towards her, his eyes boring into hers. "What if the opposite is true, and the person simply does not see the truth in their heart? Through forgetfulness, stubbornness or a need to protect themselves from something they dare not admit?"

"No, I-you-that's—" Emily stammered. "I don't know what you're talking about." She stopped herself, blinked and looked around to find everyone staring at her.

The room had become so quiet you could hear a fly

crawling up the wall. Why was it suddenly so hot? She fanned herself with one hand and laughed, sounding shrill and artificial to her ears. "We have strayed from the topic." She cleared her throat. "It seems we've lost this round."

"You certainly have," Miss Ingleton said slowly. "And rather spectacularly too. I suggest we give another pair a chance. You may sit down."

"I must protest, Miss Ingleton," said the Duke. "Can we not consider this a warm-up round? As I have been assigned a partner who is spectacularly untalented at acting, as well as being unreasonably irritable and annoyingly quarrelsome, I would appreciate the chance to try again. This time with the roles reversed."

"It's a fair request, considering that the rules of the game are new to all of us," Chippendale suggested. "Besides, there is something amusing about seeing the two of them tear into each other like an old married couple... " He interrupted himself with a cough.

Emily placed her hands on her burning cheeks.

"Yes, give them another chance. Let's see if Wolferton can do better," Lord Willowthorpe commented with a grin.

Miss Ingleton thought for a moment. "Very well. I'll give each team new words." She picked up the pen and scribbled on small pieces of paper, handing one to Cissy and the other to Wolferton. "On my command, go!"

Wolferton read the paper and his eyebrow rose so high it almost disappeared into his hairline. "Miss Ingleton, you're a minx."

She giggled behind a hand.

"Other than that, it should be easy enough," he muttered. Turning to Emily, who was watching their exchange with a frown, he asked, "Ready?"

She lifted her chin. "I've been ready since the beginning of time."

A slow, wolf-like smile spread across his face. "Excellent."

He stepped up to her closely—rather too close, Emily thought—so close that she had to tilt her head to look up at him questioningly, and still he stepped closer, and just as she opened her lips to say, "What are you doing?" he swooped in on her, bending her backwards over one arm. His hand cradled her neck, while his other held her firmly by the waist.

Then his mouth crashed down on hers.

Emily didn't hear the women gasping, the men hooting and the aunts applauding enthusiastically. It all receded into the distance. Her thoughts scattered, her mind left her and her mind ceased to function altogether.

Her senses were filled entirely by the man, and her hands slowly crawled up to his neck and dug into his hair, pulling him closer. He obliged.

She sighed against his lips.

So this is what it feels like to be kissed, was the first dazed thought she was aware of when she regained the surface of consciousness. It really was the most wonderful experience to be kissed by Wolferton.

Wolferton! She was kissing Wolferton!

By all the saints—

At that moment, he released her.

They stared at each other for a charged moment.

"You-you kissed me," she said stupidly, her hand crawling to her swollen lips.

"Correct," he said hoarsely, then cleared his throat.

Hamish and Cissy stood beside them, watching with open mouths. Hamish applauded slowly. "Well done, Your Grace. I concede you have won this round. It took me a little too long to properly perform 'courtship', which was our word—though to be fair, we were rather distracted." He beamed at them.

Miss Cowley sulked. "That was rather over the top. Isn't it cheating to touch the other person?"

"I disagree, the rules never said we couldn't touch our partners," the Duke replied, tugging at his cravat.

"You're setting a high bar," Chippendale said cheerfully. "The rest of us will find it hard to surpass you. But, by Jove, I like the direction this game is taking. Can we be next?" He looked at Cissy and waggled both eyebrows, causing her to burst into a fit of giggles.

From that moment on, all inhibitions were gone, and the game took on a teasing, slightly naughty air, with lots of enthusiastic kissing being incorporated into even the most unlikely of scenarios. When Chippendale was given the word 'turnip', he creatively managed to incorporate kissing his partner into his performance. "You love turnip so much you have to kiss it," was his far-fetched explanation, after planting a kiss on his partner's rosy lips.

For the rest of the game, Emily was unable to concentrate. She wasn't functioning properly. She had cotton where her brain should be, and champagne in her veins instead of blood. Otherwise, she couldn't explain the state of drunkenness that had gripped her.

The Duke had retired to a corner, where he was leaning against the wall, watching his Aunt Mabel act out a drunkard with a slight smile on his lips. When he turned his head, their eyes met, and he held them for a moment too long.

And then he winked.

Emily almost fell out of her chair.

That was Coachman George, as he lived and breathed, not His Grace.

She rubbed her nose in confusion. George who was cheeky, arrogant, yet observant and unexpectedly kind.

Not at all the horrifying devil she'd made him out to be.

The truth was, Emily admitted to herself, she really didn't know him at all. She'd never given him a chance. She'd been dead set against him from the start, more than willing to see the worst in him. She'd avoided him like the plague because she was afraid—

... No, terrified, of discovering that maybe he wasn't the man she'd made him out to be.

He was an enigma, this duke.

And then, with a terrible jolt of clarity, it hit her—she had been fooling herself all along.

It wasn't that she didn't hate him.

It hadn't even been about liking him.

She had gone far, far beyond that.

It was hopeless, deep and completely out of her control.

She was well on her way to falling head over heels in love with him.

Dearest Fenn.
   I wish for a kiss.
   A real one.
   Yours ever,
   Little Wren

My dear Fenn,
   I changed my mind.
   It is not a kiss I want, but—love.
   Because that is more lasting.
   Humbly yours,
   Emmy

My dear Little Wren, my dearest Emmy,
   You already have that.
   I remain, always,
   Fenn.

Chapter Seventeen

"What are you doing, Lady Poppy? You just smeared strawberry jam on both sides of the toast," Lady Jane exclaimed at the breakfast table the next morning.

Emily stared at the toast in her hands, which was indeed thickly spread with red strawberry jam on both sides. A red glob dropped onto her plate, right on top of her scrambled eggs.

"Oh," she said weakly.

"You're woolgathering," Lady Araminta Dalrymple said, with a satisfied note in her voice. "Which is understandable, given the circumstances."

Emily should have asked what exactly was so understandable, and what circumstances she was talking about, but she was too busy stuffing her mouth with toast in a most unladylike manner to continue the conversation.

A look she couldn't interpret passed between the three aunts. Emily should have asked herself what that had been about, but she was too busy daydreaming.

Of course it wasn't love, she'd told herself for the

thousandth time that day; a feat considering it was still early in the morning. And the kiss hadn't really been a kiss. It had all been a game. Nothing more. But she'd spent another night tossing and turning, thinking about it. For heaven's sake, she had to stop thinking about his soft lips against hers, and how wonderful he had smelled, and how soft his thick hair had felt between her fingers...

And now, what was that? The man wasn't even here, and her heart was pounding harder than a drummer boy beating his drum on the battlefield. What was it about him that made the pulse in her neck flutter every time she merely even thought of him?

He was her enemy; she told herself for the thousand-and-first time that day. Surely the good Lord couldn't have meant it quite so literally when he said she should love her enemies. To the point of kissing him in public and, what's worse, wanting to kiss him again, quite fervently.

Besides: Love?

It was a ridiculous idea.

She stared at the eggs on her plate. One didn't fall in love like that. She knew that from experience, because it wasn't the first time she'd fallen in love with someone. No, a long, long time ago there had been someone she'd loved very much.

Look where that had got her.

It had been enough of an experience for her to learn that when she loved, it was long and deep and lasting. The charade they played the previous day hadn't been just an act. Love, to her, was painful indeed; it involved her whole being, her whole soul, her whole self. It had almost destroyed her when it had ended.

So the idea that she could fall in love with Wolferton —villain! devil! scoundrel!—was, indeed, most outrageous. It was a scandalous thought!

Her shoulders slumped, as she crumbled the toast between her fingers. Looking up, she wondered why the aunts looked so content.

"I would like to get some fresh air," she announced, pushing back the chair with a force that must have torn a hole in the expensive Aubusson carpet. "Will you excuse me? There is nothing like a brisk morning walk when you are feeling a little tired. Would anyone care to join me?"

"A splendid idea, child. Wipe that pallor from your cheeks. Walking is most beneficial to one's health," Lady Dalrymple agreed.

But no one seemed interested in joining her. Cissy said she did not want to take any strenuous walks yet, as she wanted to be able to dance at the ball, and preferred to rest. Miss Ingleton immediately said she would keep her company, and Miss Cowley said she had to prepare her wardrobe for the ball, while the three Pastels hatched a plan to get the housekeeper to show them the house, no doubt with the ulterior motive of 'accidentally' running into the Duke somewhere.

Very well, she would go alone then, Emily decided. It was what she preferred anyway, to be alone and stew in her own thoughts.

The morning mist still hung like a gossamer veil between the trees, and the crisp, chilly morning air had brought her to her senses.

It was so strange, on the one hand, how time passed, but on the other, how certain things seemed to stay the same. The smell of the trees, the way the birds chirped in the foliage. The feeling of peace that washed over her every time she stepped into the forest. She quickened her pace and immediately felt herself calming down.

She reached the trunk of the tree in the clearing, and she sat on it. Emily let out a loud moan and hid her hands in her face. "Emily, you goose! Of all the men, why did it have to be him?" What a treacherous heart she had!

He was a duke, and she was a schoolmaster's daughter. He was at the top of the social ladder, she at the bottom. They were worlds apart.

That was the ultimate truth.

"Emily White, why do you always choose the most unsuitable of men to love?" she groaned, and her words seemed to echo through the forest.

It wouldn't be the first time. Once, long ago, a wood sprite had swept her off her feet. A forest sprite, conjured from her imagination. Emily had fallen for him faster than one could say cheese crumpet.

It was strange, really, considering that Emily had never even met him. But she had lost her heart to him with astonishing ease. Stupid, perhaps, but she'd been so young, just a child. Could you blame a child for being swept away by the pretty words of a stranger?

She'd tried, oh how she'd tried, to discover his identity. Emily had waited for him for hours in the bushes, but he'd never come. Somehow he always managed to elude her.

Emily sighed, her chest tightening with a pang of something bittersweet.

Fairies and dukes. They were equally impossible to love.

She wasn't that little girl anymore—the one who believed in forest fairies and clung to dreams spun from ink and paper. But all that was in the deep past, long gone and buried.

The hole in the oak tree was empty, and it would always be empty.

It was time to let go.

The forest seemed to hold its breath, as if listening, the surrounding air impossibly still.

"Goodbye, Fenn," she whispered.

Emily turned and made her way back to the house, the faint rustle of leaves the only sound as the forest exhaled once more.

WHEN SHE RETURNED to her room, she found a pair of brand-new, shiny calfskin boots on the floor at the foot of her bed. They were the most beautiful pair of boots she'd ever seen, except for the pair Fenn had given her so long ago.

"Netty, who left these boots here?" she asked the maid.

Netty shrugged. "The truth is, I don't know, my lady. I had to step out for a moment and when I returned they were here."

"There was no note?"

"No, my lady. I found them as they are now, without a note."

Emily exhaled slowly. She turned to the boots in her hands. The leather was soft, and the inside lined with fur. They were perfection. And exactly her size. They'd clearly been made for her.

"Why don't you try them on, my lady?" the maid suggested.

"I'm not sure they're meant for me," Emily hesitated.

"Why else would they be here?"

True.

She unlaced the boots and slipped them on. They fit her like a second skin. They were made for hard walking outdoors and would keep out any moisture and cold.

"Perhaps you have an admirer," the maid suggested.

"It seems so," Emily said gruffly.

It seemed that George the coachman had been at work.

Wolferton, she corrected herself. Not George. Must remember that.

Now, he was giving her boots? She tipped up her toes to admire them.

What, exactly, she wondered, did it mean?

Fenn,

Oh.

Must you say such things in a letter? Can't you tell me while looking at me? Can't you say it in person?

It has been four years—four whole years since I first knew you. Can it truly be? Tell me who you are. We both know you are no magical creature but a being of flesh and blood, like me.

Come. Have the courage to meet me. Let us sit down together, share a cup of tea, and talk—not as mysteries to one another, but as true friends.

Will you meet me?

Emmy

My dearest Emmy,

Friends? That is not what I desire, nor what my heart yearns for. I crave so much more than friendship could ever offer.

And tea? It is but a pale substitute for the dreams that fill my mind whenever I think of you.

Yours in restless hope,

Fenn

Chapter Eighteen

On her way up to the library to pick up a book, she promptly ran into the Duke.

Her heart leapt and pounded as if a hundred blacksmiths were hammering at it.

"Thinking of the devil," she grumbled under her breath.

"Lady Poppy, well met." He paused mid stride. "A word, if I may?"

He led her into the library, with Emily trudging behind him in his wake.

"Please, sit down." He said formally, gesturing to the green sofa by the windows. Emily sat down and smoothed her skirt under her fingers.

The afternoon sun was pouring through the windows into the room, teasing her eyes. She blinked.

The Duke sat across from her.

Emily cleared her throat. "Thank you for the boots." She lifted her toes to reveal her new leather boots. "It's probably shamelessly improper of me to accept such a lavish gift from a gentleman, but as you saw, my old boots were, well, rather old." Not to mention that she had no financial means to buy new ones.

He gave a brief nod to acknowledge her gratitude. "I'm glad they fit."

"How did you know my shoe size?"

"I've got a good eye for these things." His gaze moved up her body and back to her face. There was heat in his eyes as he regarded her, and she shifted in her seat, her entire body began to tingle. "As for this being 'shamelessly improper,' that is a matter of interpretation." He crossed his legs.

"What do you mean?"

"Is it truly shamelessly improper for a gentleman to present shoes to a lady with whom he only has a fleeting acquaintance? Possibly."

Her fingers froze on the fabric of her skirt. "I would say it depends on the motivation behind his intention."

He smiled vaguely. "Correct."

Emily felt that their conversation was entering dangerous territory. Nevertheless, she took a deep breath. "So, what were your intentions?" She raised her chin. "Were they shamelessly improper?"

"My, you do tend to assume the worst of my personality," he murmured.

"How else am I to understand it?"

"A simple gift, given without expectation, condition, or demand?" His eyes were wide with innocence.

She narrowed her eyes suspiciously. "Truly?"

"Of course not." He smirked.

"I knew it!" Scallywag! Devil! Rogue! He had

214

intended all along to make a scandalous proposal in return for giving her the boots. Well, she would have none of it. She was going to take them off and throw them in his smug face. Emily bent down and untied the boots.

"How brave of you, Miss White," he said, a teasing note in his voice as he watched her remove the first boot. "But we've only just begun this conversation. No need to start removing... anything quite so soon."

Emily's fingers froze on the laces. His meaning sank in and a hot flush crept up her neck. "You misunderstand! I was m-merely taking the boots off to return them to you."

"Shame," he murmured. He leaned back and crossed his arms.

Emily stood up. "You're insufferable. I don't know why we're having this conversation." She stomped across the library to make a grand exit, in one stockinged foot, holding her boot in one hand.

"Emily." His voice was warm but commanding. It stopped her in her tracks. "Turn around." As if she lacked a mind of her own, she turned slowly. "Come back. Sit down," he suggested gently. She did.

She skewered him with a glare.

He regarded her sombrely. "I was merely teasing you. Keep the blasted boots and do whatever you want with them. Yes, even throw them at me if you must, which would be a shame since you seem to have a need for them. My giving you the boots is completely meaningless, except that I enjoyed doing it, and there really is no, er, scandalous proposition attached to them."

She tilted her head sideways as she considered his words.

That seemed to draw a smile from him. The dimple flashed and disappeared into his cheek as quickly as it had appeared. "I have a different proposition for you, which has nothing to do with these boots, I hasten to add, and which is why I asked for this meeting to begin with."

She tilted her head in the other direction. "What proposition?"

He began to fiddle with his quizzing glass. "I think we've already established that you're quite good at pretending. At the inn, you played the role of the maid Meggie Blythe, and here as Lady Poppy Featherstone. How many times have you done this?"

She looked at him wide-eyed. "Often. I've been Eliza Talbot, the Honourable Miss Marcellina Swinton, Evangeline Angus, Miss Suzanne Dornton and Lady Honey Hepplewhite."

"Good heavens."

Emily shrugged. "One gets used to it."

"I cannot fathom what it must be like to constantly change one's identity. I'd like to take advantage of your talent and make a suggestion." He stood up, clasped his hands behind back and rocked slightly on his heels.

She tilted her head inquisitively. "A proposition?"

"Yes. One that could benefit us both."

"I can hardly imagine what that might be."

"Become engaged to me."

Emily blinked. She must have misheard. "I beg your pardon?"

"An engagement," he repeated, utterly composed.

"To Cissy."

He shook his head. "No. To you."

Her jaw dropped.

"It's the most logical step," he explained patiently.

Logical? Logical?! Nothing about this man or this moment was even remotely logical.

He paced as she continued to watch him, momentarily speechless. "It would be entirely hypothetical, of course," he went on. "Another charade, but one that we would coordinate and play together. The advantages would be many: I would be freed from tedious evenings being pursued by ambitious ladies—" his face took on a hunted expression "—and I would no longer have to subject myself to their onslaught. By voluntarily removing myself from the marriage market, even if only by pretence, I hope to regain some semblance of peace in my life, at least temporarily. I intend to make some extended travels on the Continent, and until then I would be left in peace, and could appear in society without being hounded by females."

A steep furrow appeared on Emily's forehead. "Indeed, I can see how that would be an advantage—for you. What about me? How could I possibly benefit from such a masquerade? For if the engagement is to be a pretence, when it is finally dissolved you will come out unscathed, but it is always the lady's reputation that suffers, and what is worse, my sister's as well."

"You could take advantage of this engagement by trying to find a match for your sister.

My aunts will be happy to sponsor a Season for her. Afterwards, we can dissolve our engagement quietly.

Your name will not be affected, as Lady Poppy Feather-stone doesn't exist. As for your reputation, it will not matter nearly as much if word gets out that it was the lady—you—who broke off the engagement first. Unless you, too, are looking for a match, it is hardly an issue?" He looked at her inquisitively.

He was right. She had long since resigned herself to her status as a spinster, with no prospects at all.

She shook her head. "It might work for Cissy because what she can't offer in terms of class, she makes up in terms of beauty and grace. People are willing to overlook an ineligible background when it comes to her. But not for me. It's entirely impossible. Not after what happened to Papa." She lifted her chin belligerently.

"Ah. You're referring to the matter of me, er, killing your father." His face hardened. "I believe those were the words you used." He stopped pacing and stood in front of her. Emily had to crane her neck to meet his gaze, which was most exasperating. He looked forbidding, almost stern, and terribly intimidating. His proud, angular features could have belonged to a marble statue, his swept-back hair framing a face so severe it seemed carved from stone.

The word echoed unpleasantly through the library. When he said it, so directly, so matter-of-factly, it sounded almost absurd.

She lifted her head proudly. "Do you deny it? Do you deny that your steward had us evicted?"

His face looked cold and stony. "I do not deny it. Such orders were indeed given."

Emily exhaled loudly. He admitted it. She didn't

know what she'd expected. Maybe an explanation that it had all been a mistake. The flush of disappointment that rushed through her was so strong it brought tears to her eyes.

"I take full responsibility for the matter. Instructions were indeed given to evict all tenants who were in arrears with their rent. I understand how this must appear, for how could you possibly consider becoming engaged to the man who is responsible for your father's death, even if the relationship I am proposing is entirely hypothetical?" He played with his quizzing glass.

"Indeed," Emily said tonelessly. "It is entirely impossible. Even hypothetically."

His eyes were hooded. "What if I were to offer you a financial incentive to make this more palatable to you?"

"Financial incentive." She looked up, blinking. "You mean money? How much of a financial incentive would that be?"

He mentioned a figure that almost made Emily's eyes pop out of her head.

That would change everything, of course. It was a figure big enough to support them for a long time. If his aunts could sponsor a Season for Cissy on top of it, and Cissy could get respectably married as a result, it might be worth the endeavour. Might it not?

"You really are a devil, aren't you?" said Emily bitterly. For how could she ever say no?

She watched as his mouth twisted into a humourless smile.

"Well?"

"That's all very well," Emily said, fiddling with the

fringes of her shawl. "But I would like you to give me one more thing, irrespective of the financial deal regarding the fake engagement."

"I'm all ears."

She took a big breath. "Meadowview Cottage."

He arched an eyebrow upwards. "That old ramshackle cottage? It is entirely dilapidated. Are you certain this is what you want? A half-ruined house?"

"Yes. It is my home," she added softly. "I want a home that is all mine, where no one can come in the middle of the night and throw me out suddenly—" She interrupted herself and drew herself up. "If you meant what you said earlier, when we talked in the drawing room, that you wanted to make amends—if you meant that sincerely, then I want you to prove it. Give us the cottage in recompense. It won't undo anything that happened in the past. But it would be a symbolic gesture that we, Cissy and I, would appreciate, to have our home returned to us. If you give us the cottage, in addition to financial support, I will stop calling you a murderer. I'll accept it as the amends you spoke of." She cleared her throat. "And I'll do anything you want."

"Anything?" he asked in a low voice that made her skin crawl.

She held his gaze. "Anything."

She squirmed under his long, thoughtful look.

"Very well." He drew his lips into a vague smile. "It shall be yours. I'll have my secretary draw up the papers."

Emily could hardly believe it. Had she really just haggled like a fisherwoman—and won? And now was she to receive not only her beloved cottage but also a substantial sum of money that would give them security for the rest of their lives?

All she had to do was pretend to be engaged to him. Surely that couldn't be so difficult?

"What would it involve, such a fake engagement?" she enquired cautiously. More kissing? Her heart began to beat heavily.

His fingers kept playing with the quizzing glass. "It would mean, first and foremost, convincing those around us that this is an authentic relationship. That includes my aunts and your sister. They must not know about this arrangement."

"Then how do I explain to Cissy why we are to receive the cottage?"

He crossed his arms over his chest. "As you said: reparations. She doesn't need to know about the rest."

Emily chewed her lower lip.

"Secondly," he continued, "we would have to make it public and make an appearance in the social scene in London." He pulled a face. "Believe me, as unpleasant as it may be for you, it is a necessity. After all, every one of our appearances would have to be staged in such a way as to convince all onlookers that this engagement is indeed authentic."

Kissing. He definitely meant kissing.

"But why? Surely no one in your class would expect a love match. There shouldn't be any need to pretend that we... that we... " She gestured vaguely, her cheeks warming. "You know. That we're in love, I mean."

"Indeed." His expression remained unreadable.

She swallowed hard and looked away. That would be

the real challenge. She'd have to feign reluctance to like him when, in truth, she already did—far, far more than she was comfortable admitting, especially when she wasn't supposed to.

"Judging by the expression on your face, you don't seem too excited about the prospect." He peered at her. "The point is to convince my aunts. They don't want just any lady for me, you see. They have set their hearts on my engagement being a love match." He shrugged. "They are hopeless romantics. Even Aunt Jane, even though she professes to be the contrary. I want them to be happy."

"Oh." She rubbed her nose. "I don't know if we can convince them."

"Why not?" he said lightly. "You've already proven yourself to be an exceptional actress, and you seem to have enough experience pretending that feigning emotions should be child's play."

Although true, it stung. "Yes, but we never set out to deceive anyone for the sake of deception. We may have taken advantage of people, but our aim was never to maliciously deceive or hurt anyone. It was always for our own survival and protection."

"You must have had a difficult life if this was the only way to ensure your survival." There, again, that odd, soft look on his face, as though he genuinely cared.

She was taken aback by his sudden compassion. It was on the tip of her tongue to retort sharply, "And whose fault was it that we ended up in such a precarious situation in the first place?" but something stopped her. If she continued to point out his role in them losing their home, he might withdraw his offer. She had to admit, his offer was very, very tempting.

She'd never be a victim again, she'd vowed. Never again homeless and hungry.

Never again.

True, it wasn't the revenge she had planned when she started this venture. But it was a small triumph. Small, but delicious.

She pulled herself up. "Very well. I will pretend to be your betrothed, madly in love with you. God help my soul," she added in a mutter.

Dearest Fenn,

You have only to speak the word, and I am yours—always, and only ever yours. My heart has long belonged to you; I can no longer imagine a world where it does not.

Ever and always devoted,

Emmy

My dearest Love,

There is nothing I desire more in this world than to stand before you, to take your hand in mine, and to lose myself in the depths of your gaze. You are not merely my world—you are my every hope, my every dream, the very air I breathe.

Ever and always your devoted servant,

Fenn

Chapter Nineteen

EMILY WAS BACK IN HER ROOM, WONDERING IF IT had all been a dream. And if not, whether she was completely out of her mind. Pretending to be in a fake engagement with the Duke? Was she mad?

She'd just sold her soul.

But all she was to gain in return! Financial security. Meadowview Cottage. Her home! And Cissy didn't even have to marry the Duke. She realised now that it had been a short-sighted plan and that it would never have worked. A real marriage between them would have been impossible, given the difference in their status. Sooner or later, their deception would have been discovered—at the latest when it came to signing the marriage register. Their marriage would have been invalid and the scandal that would have ensued would have been unimaginable! Through this pretence, all this unpleasantness could be avoided. Cissy didn't have to ruin her life, and they still gained Meadowview Cottage. If she pretended to be the Duke's betrothed, it would only have to be for a while.

They would simply call off the engagement at the end of the Season. The Duke would go on his travels, and when he returned a few years later, all would be forgotten. Lady Poppy Featherstone would disappear, never to be seen again. She could finally go back to being ordinary Emily White and live happily ever after in her own little cottage.

It appeared to be a sound plan.

Then why was there this nagging feeling that it might be too good to be true?

"Let's announce the engagement at the ball," the Duke had suggested. Since it was as good a time as any to announce it, she'd agreed.

It was a mad plan, for sure.

Would his aunts be convinced? If not, what could they do? Certainly nothing that would have serious consequences for them—but if the Duke was to be believed, they would unleash their full arsenal and assail him with every eligible young lady in London.

Poor man! An involuntary grin escaped Emily.

But what about London? She and Cissy had avoided London until now, not wanting to risk running into someone they'd known under another identity. What if they did, and she was exposed in public? The scandal would be unimaginable, and it would certainly be uncomfortable for them and Cissy. But in that case, her engagement would simply end earlier than expected. She could still disappear and take a new name.

"What do you think, Emily?" Cissy turned in front of her. She wore a low-cut silk dress with small sleeves and playful flounces at the hem that allowed her to show off a trim ankle. "Isn't it pretty? The colour is dazzling and seems to change when the light hits it." She twirled. Indeed, the fabric did take on a slightly greenish hue as she turned.

Miss Ingleton had graciously agreed to lend Cissy one of her ball gowns, so that nothing would stand in the way of them attending the ball. "I shall be glad to help! And even better if someone gets to wear my blue dress, since I have fairly made up my mind to wear rose—it's ever so en vogue," she told Cissy the next day. "It will suit you most charmingly! And I have a peach dress for you, Lady Poppy," she'd added.

Emily was wearing that peach dress now, but to her it made no real difference what she wore. It flowed better than other dresses she'd worn, but her figure would never have the slender, long elegance of a classic column that was so in vogue these days. She looked more like a triangle.

"I have hips," she shrugged, as she turned in front of the mirror. "It is as it is and there is simply nothing one can do about it." Her hips were perfect for carrying babies, water buckets or turnip baskets. A farmer's wife would be delighted with them. Emily had long since made peace with the fact that she'd never embody a fashion ideal, and that was that.

"My lady looks right lovely. Shall I tell you a secret, m'lady?" the abigail whispered, her eyes glinting mischievously.

"By all means."

She leaned in close and whispered, "Men mostly like

women with a bit o' curve." She winked. "I'm sure His Grace does, too."

"Molly!" Emily squealed. She normally wasn't easily scandalised, but for some reason, she definitely was now. "I don't even want to know how you know that."

Emily put her hands on her hips. Then she glanced at Cissy, who was busy across the room with another maid, choosing ribbons, and had missed the whole exchange. "How do you know?" she whispered.

Molly laughed. "Lawks, m'lady, when His Grace was doing up the house, he told them to put all the Raphael paintings where folks could see them better and to take down all the old ones. Said he didn't like looking at those flat medieval folks and much preferred curvy women. His very words." She giggled.

Cissy turned to look at them. "What's so funny?"

Emily kept a straight face. "Nothing. There, we're ready. Let's go."

"You look particularly lovely tonight, Emily," her sister took her hand. "There's a glow about you that wasn't there before." She tilted her head to one side. "Don't you think so, Molly?"

"Oh, aye, quite, m'lady," Molly replied cheerfully.

HIS THREE AUNTS were in the middle of a lively debate when he strolled into Aunt Araminta's drawing room. He paused behind them as they sat on the sofa with their backs to him, listening to their debate.

Aunt Mabel, contrary to her normally shy nature, was arguing passionately. "I still say that love should be the deciding factor in choosing a bride. If we put too much emphasis on genealogy, we eliminate the majority of eligible ladies. The only thing that really matters is love."

"Be that as it may," Aunt Jane countered, "a bride cannot simply be a nobody. Family and breeding are paramount. Sentiment has never been the cornerstone of marriage among our kind, as you well know."

"Which is precisely why I never married," Aunt Mabel replied. "Politics, family name and business are poor substitutes for genuine affection. I know my position is unconventional, but I stand firmly by it."

Jane sniffed and lifted a finger. "If we disregard family altogether, we might as well open the floodgates. The noble name must be preserved."

"Indeed," Aunt Mabel shot back, her voice tinged with uncharacteristic sharpness, "but if we insist on the family name above all else, we narrow the field to only two families—neither of which has suitable ladies."

"Not to mention," she added, her eyes narrowing slightly, "the dangers of inbreeding. That is a very real problem in our circle. What do you think, Araminta? You have been unusually quiet on the subject."

Araminta, who had been embroidering as she listened to the debate in silence, cut the thread with a pair of scissors and put them aside before replying. "I think you are both right. Shocking, I know. I have always believed that the family name is the most important factor in choosing a bride. But a marriage without affection isn't quite right either. Just look at how Jasper's parents lived." She shook her head disapprovingly. "I wouldn't want that for Jasper. Not in a million years."

"I'm relieved you feel the same way." Mabel shot her a grateful look.

"But still, a complete nobody?" Jane pursed her lips. "It's too much of a risk."

"Why don't you let the boy have his say?" Mabel said.

"Has he made up his mind?" Jane asked.

"If he hasn't, he must be ignorant or blind or both," Araminta grumbled.

"He certainly has," Wolferton said from behind them.

"Jasper!" the three aunts said in unison as they turned.

"I hear you are busy discussing my marriage options." He sat down beside Aunt Mabel and took her hand in his. "I am certain you are keen to know on which pair of boots I have settled."

"Horrible metaphor, Jasper," Mabel said with a shudder.

Araminta raised her quizzing glass. "Well, who will it be? I would have put my money on Lady Lydia, with all her beauty and charm. But then Miss Cowley seemed the most determined to win the prize. That lady is a little too ambitious for me, I must confess."

"It's certainly not Miss Cowley," Jane agreed.

"No, there is only one lady you have ever had eyes for," Mabel interjected quietly. "I pray she is the one you have chosen."

Three pairs of eyes looked at him expectantly.

"Well, who shall it be?" Araminta barked as he hesitated.

To cover his sudden onslaught of bashfulness, he shrugged to feign nonchalance. "Aunt Mabel's right."

Mabel gripped his hand tightly. "I am? Of course I am," she said breathlessly.

"The only one you seem to eat up with your eyes every time she walks into a room. Don't think we haven't noticed," Jane sniffed.

"Well? A name, please," Araminta insisted. "Is it Lady Poppy Featherstone?"

He had no idea why he suddenly felt a hot blush creep up his neck; these were his three aunts, for heaven's sake. "Yes." He cleared his throat. "Lady Poppy it is."

"Excellent choice." Mabel beamed at him.

Araminta set aside her embroidery. "I'm glad you finally made a choice, of course, as I didn't think I'd live to see the day, but it does raise the question of who she is."

"Exactly," Jane said with a frown. "Her background is somewhat unclear. Featherstone is not a name we're familiar with. I couldn't find her in Debrett's. Are you sure she's not a fortune hunter?"

"I am certain. You have nothing to concern your-selves over," Jasper replied firmly. "Please trust me. My secretary in London is already looking into the matter. As far as I know, she comes from a distinguished and perfectly suitable family. There's nothing to worry about."

"Very well, Jasper," Araminta said, inclining her head. "That's all we need to know. We'll trust you in this matter. Now, about the betrothal—what are the plans?"

"I intend to announce it at the ball," Jasper said. "Until then, may I ask you to keep this to yourselves? I would prefer to break the news in person."

His aunts exchanged glances and nodded. "As you wish," Jane said.

THE OFFICERS of the garrison had already arrived, filling the ballroom with their scarlet uniforms. The music was playing and Emily was immediately approached by an officer as she entered the ballroom.

She danced a reel with him, which she found herself enjoying. Emily hadn't had much opportunity to dance in the past. She allowed herself to enjoy every minute of it now.

Wolferton did not dance. He stood at the entrance, greeting the guests. His aunts stood beside him, similarly dressed in stately grey silk. Lady Dalrymple wore a feathered turban, and Lady Jane a formal evening cap of lace, while Lady Mabel had nothing at all in her hair.

"Save the midnight waltz for me," he'd told her earlier. "We'll make the announcement immediately afterwards."

Emily's heart pounded in anticipation. When she wasn't dancing, her foot kept tapping the floor, which some gentlemen interpreted as a desire to dance, so they approached her and asked for her hand in the next dance. She always said yes, because it was worse to stand around and be a wallflower.

Cissy danced as well, but she limited herself to the

more measured, less vigorous dances, avoiding all the lively reels and taking breaks to rest between sets.

Emily watched her, wondering if she could set her up with someone else, now that the Duke was out of the picture.

Where was Chippendale? He was dancing with Miss Ingleton at the moment. Though he'd seemed infatuated with Cissy at first, he'd made no move to suggest his interest was more than fleeting admiration. Perhaps he needed a little help? A little push?

Cissy returned from her dance, heated. "It's quite hot in here," she fanned herself.

"Come, let's go out on the balcony and get some fresh air. I'm quite stifled myself." Emily took her arm and led her to the balcony doors.

"Are you well, Emily?" Cissy asked. "Your cheeks look almost feverish."

"Quite." The best was yet to come, but Cissy would find out sooner rather than later. "I've been dancing too much, I suppose. Aren't you a bit chilly out here?" She rubbed her arms. "I must confess, I am. Wait here, I'll be back with our scarves." Emily went inside to fetch her cashmere shawl from the back room.

On her way back, she saw that the dance had finished and Chippendale had returned with Miss Ingleton on his arm, laughing. He bowed and handed her back to Hamish, then strolled off towards the card room.

Emily intercepted him before he spent the next hour or so playing cards.

"My lord."

"Lady Poppy. Are you enjoying yourself?" He smiled pleasantly at her.

"I am, indeed. I was just out on the balcony with my sister. Only the night air got a bit chilly, so I went to fetch our shawls." She hesitated a little before continuing. "Would you mind taking them to my sister, as Lady Dalrymple requires my attention?"

It wasn't even a lie, for Lady Dalrymple had been waving at her for the last five minutes or so.

"Gladly," Chippendale said, taking the shawl from her arm.

Emily watched with satisfaction as he walked to the balcony where Cissy was waiting.

With any luck, there would be more than one engagement announced tonight. At least one of them might be a real one.

"You're positively glowing, child." Lady Dalrymple examined her through her quizzing glass.

"So is Wolferton," Lady Mabel murmured. All four heads turned towards the Duke, who was surrounded by a group of women, each no doubt expecting to be the next one chosen for a dance.

"He is beset by women," Lady Jane said with a frown. "It can't be good for him, all that vanity. It can't be good for anyone, really."

"I do disagree," Araminta countered. "Though he gives the impression of being somewhat annoyed, I doubt it will have any ill effect on his character. If anything, all this attention seems to leave him entirely unmoved."

"I quite agree," Mabel chimed in. "As the past has taught us, he doesn't give his heart away easily."

Emily perked up. "Indeed? He's fallen in love before?"

Mabel nodded. "Indeed. Had his heart broken. When he was but a young, green boy."

"So it was a while ago."

"Hasn't been the same since," Jane chimed in, direct and to the point, as always.

Emily blinked. "How odd. I mean, he must have pined for his lady for a long time if it took him so long to get over her. It is most unusual." Emily found it hard to believe that a man like the Duke could have had his heart broken in the first place. If he had a heart, it must be cold, hard and smooth, like marble, and completely unbreakable.

"She must have been quite a lady," Emily added quietly.

"We didn't meet her, but he told me about her. He always lit up when he did. She must have been a lovely little thing," Aunt Mabel said softly.

"What happened?" Emily's curiosity grew.

"I believe his father found out and put a stop to it. He hasn't been the same since."

"How sad," Emily whispered.

"Yes, but these are all Jane's conjectures, and it's all long in the past. Let us not speak of this any more. It isn't appropriate." Araminta said, bringing the conversation to an end.

It was midnight when the orchestra played the waltz. Wolferton walked over to Emily and bowed. She licked her lips nervously. Everyone's eyes were on them.

Emily put her hand in his before he led her to the dance floor.

She was surprised that he was a good dancer and that they danced well together. For someone who avoided it as a rule of thumb, he danced rather well.

When the dance ended, he stayed with her on the floor, holding her hand in a firm grip.

Her mouth had gone dry.

"If I could have your attention, please. I have an announcement to make," he said in a calm, clear voice.

Her stomach churned with nervousness.

"Hear, hear," Chippendale replied with a grin.

"I am pleased to announce that Lady Poppy Feather-stone and I have decided to become engaged." It was direct and to the point, no-nonsense and, in short, the most unromantic announcement she'd ever heard.

There was a collective gasp. Whether it was dismay or joy, Emily couldn't be sure. The three aunts looked pleased but not surprised.

Lady Dalrymple nodded. "We expected it, of course."

Miss Cowley's face grew longer and longer and she pouted.

Chippendale clapped, followed by the rest of the guests. "Is anyone really surprised? Well done, Wolferton."

Emily blinked. What did he mean? Was anyone really surprised? Was everyone expecting it? But why?

Her sister Cissy pushed through the crowd and threw her arms around her neck. "Oh, I'm so glad!" she whispered into her ear. "I can't say I'm surprised, though. But isn't this the best solution? A true love match, and look, it happened all on its own. I am so, so happy for you, sister dear!"

Emily hugged her back, with the strange feeling that people were far happier for her than they ought to be. The three aunts dabbed at their eyes with handkerchiefs. Chippendale and Hamish approached to pump the Duke's hand, and Miss Ingleton rushed forward to embrace her after Cissy had released her. Only the three pastel girls looked as if they were about to burst into tears, and Miss Cowley looked furious.

It's only a ruse, Emily felt compelled to call out. None of this is real! But seeing the joy on his aunts' faces made her feel both guilty and touched at the same time.

Her hand trembled in Wolferton's large one. He tightened his grip.

What on earth had they done?

As Emily stared at the aunts' delighted faces, she was struck by a startling clarity that left her breathless: a desire, a longing. If only it were real...

My dear Fenn,

I dreamed of you last night. You were laughing, and I was not alone. Then I woke to the grey morning, and the silence was unbearable.

Your sad Little Wren

Fenn?

It has been nearly a fortnight, and I have yet to hear from you. My previous letter remains unanswered.

Papa is unwell, but Cissy and I are as healthy as ever.

Is all well with you? Have you forgotten me?

Anxiously awaiting your reply,

Emmy

Chapter Twenty

THE ENGAGEMENT BROUGHT THE COUNTRY PARTY AT Ashbourne House to an abrupt end.

There was little reason for them to stay on, Lady Willowthorpe confided to Lady Blakely in no uncertain terms. What use was there in pursuing a quarry that was no longer part of the hunt? The grand prize had already been claimed, and it was time to move on to greener pastures. Therefore, Lord and Lady Willowthorpe and their three girls left early the next morning, followed soon after by Lady Blakely and her daughter.

Only Hamish and his sister remained, and Hamish said, as he stretched out his legs in his armchair in the morning room, "We're in no hurry to return, as we're living in the vicinity. We can pop home any time Wolferton decides to throw us out. Besides, I must confess I'm rather enjoying it now that everyone's gone. Aside from Chippendale, of course." He nodded at Chippendale, who was dozing in the armchair opposite him. It was midday, and they'd just finished luncheon.

"The idea is to go to London to introduce Lady Poppy to the ton before the official Season begins," Wolferton said, leaning against the fireplace.

Hamish nodded. "Very wise move. This way, you spare her the public spectacle, scrutiny and gossip of the spring Season, allowing for a more discreet introduction now."

"You will, of course, be staying with us at Grosvenor Square," Aunt Araminta told Emily. "Wolferton has his own bachelor abode at the Albany. Lady Lydia is coming with us too." She nodded to Cissy.

Emily and Cissy exchanged glances. London!

In all their years, they'd made sure to stay away from the city and its bustle of social activity, its balls, theatres, operas, musicals, galleries and museums. It had been a strategic move on their part to avoid running into familiar faces who might have known them under an alias in Brussels or Bath.

"We shall have to attend some minor social events," Lady Jane added, "dinner parties and perhaps even a small private ball, but nothing on the scale of the Season. Needless to say, we'll take you to the dressmaker, the milliner for new hats and the cordwainer for the finest shoes London has to offer. I've always said a proper duchess needs to have proper shoes to stand her ground. Of course, no ensemble is complete without gloves from the glove maker and perhaps a visit to the jeweller— although it may be time to bring out the Wolferton jewels. I am referring to your mother's garnet set, Jasper," she said to Wolferton, who was sitting in an armchair, reading a newspaper.

"I will have my secretary fetch them from the bank vault," Wolferton replied lazily, without lowering the paper.

Good heavens! It was all happening too fast. Emily's fingers clenched in her lap as she tried to catch his eye, but he merely turned the page, seemingly oblivious to her efforts to communicate with him.

It was only later, when he got up to meet his secretary, that she hurried after him and caught up with him in the corridor, tugging at his sleeve.

"There was never any discussion of me getting new clothes and jewellery," she hissed. "That wasn't a part of the agreement."

A faint crease appeared between his brows. "It was implied."

She dropped her hands. "Implied? How so?"

"It's part of playing the part." He shrugged. "If you are to be truly my affianced bride, then that is what would happen next. A duke's bride has to look the part. It is expected, so go along with it."

Emily shook her head vehemently. "But spending all this money on a sham relationship is not the right thing to do at all. It is a waste and downright indecent." Poverty had taught her all about the value of money and that it ought not to be spent lightly.

His sharp eyes studied her. "You misinterpret the situation and seem to forget that this isn't about you at all."

"Isn't it?" She crossed her arms.

"No. This is about my aunts and their delight at finally having a Wolferton bride to play with. This includes dressing you up like a doll and parading you about town. Humour them. Be true to your agreement and play along to the best of your ability. Be glad it's not during the Season. That is all I can say on the matter. I beg you to excuse me, for I have a pressing meeting with my secretary." With a curt nod, he climbed the stairs to the upper floor, leaving Emily to stare after him.

So it came that within the next few days, the three aunts, Cissy, the Duke, and Emily arrived in London at the Duke's townhouse in Grosvenor Square, and they were immediately whisked away into a whirlwind of activities that left Emily's head spinning.

In a single afternoon they visited Miss Blacklin, the dressmaker in Bond Street, Carter's for shoes in Jermyn Street, Jeffrey and Jones, a jeweller on the Strand, and Gunter's Tea Shop in Berkeley Square for ices, even though the weather was blustery and cold. Emily couldn't resist trying the pistachio and candied violet ice, which was a most unusual combination, though probably not as unusual as parmesan and pineapple, which Cissy had ordered.

"It's sweet and salty at the same time." Cissy licked her spoon with delight.

When they returned from shopping, Emily found a lovely bohemian crystal bowl on the dresser in her room.

Emily admired the dish, then lifted the lid to find it filled to the brim with candied violets. She slipped a petal into her mouth and sucked on it with delight.

"Candied violets! My favourite."

"His Grace ordered this especially for you, my lady," her abigail explained as she unpacked the boxes from her shopping trip. "The dish is to be kept filled at all times. And your room is to have fresh violets every day." She paused, wrinkling her forehead. "The housekeeper is at a loss as to where to find fresh violets at this time of year."

"What a romantic gesture," Cissy exclaimed, catching the maid's words. "To make sure you always have your favourite flowers and sweets! He is positively spoiling you. I wouldn't have thought the Duke capable of the slightest romantic inclination." Her tone was teasing.

The truth was, there was a part of Emily that was charmed by the Duke's actions. Candied violets! Emily popped another into her mouth and twisted her eyes in delight. How did he know they were her favourite sweet-meat? And the other day, when he'd come to take her for a ride in his curricle in Hyde Park, he'd also brought a small bouquet of violets, which he'd handed to her with a flourishing bow.

It wasn't so much the gesture that had touched her, but the smile on his face as he did so. Carefree, as if she were the centre of his world and he was truly happy to see her.

Almost as if he'd meant it.

Almost as if he'd been sincere.

Almost as if he was truly in love with her.

Of course, it had been a ruse, a gesture made only for the benefit of his aunts, for they had stood in the hall, watching.

Aware that she, too, was expected to play a part, she'd simpered and extended her hand to him to kiss.

He'd done so, then pulled her into the loop of his arm and planted a kiss on her cheek. It had been such an unexpectedly sweet gesture that she'd blinked at him in confusion. There it was again, that jolt of heat rushing through her veins, leaving her heart galloping like horses bolting with a carriage.

It left her breathless, confused, and vexed.

Then, the other day, he'd given her a most unusual gift: a roll of ribbons. He had done so in the presence of his aunts once again. Emily stared at the satin ribbon in her hands.

"Very well done, Jasper," Jane said approvingly. "A girl can never have too many ribbons. In red, too. It suits your complexion."

"It's not red, Aunt Jane," the Duke pointed out. "It has a most unusual name. What was it again? Something outlandish. Ah yes." He snapped his fingers. "Coquelicot."

Coquelicot ribbons.

In her entire life, she'd possessed only one strand of coquelicot ribbon. It had been the length of a lady's arm, enough for a small bonnet and a bow. She'd worn it until it faded to a washed out pale pink and had to be thrown away. She hadn't had a ribbon of that colour since.

Cissy had admired the ribbon. "How pretty. Almost makes me want to have a beau who gives me ribbons, too," she added teasingly.

"Thank you," Emily whispered to the Duke, who nodded.

He seemed to be in an excellent mood.

"It's a beautiful day today," he said as he held out his hand to help her into the carriage, followed by Cissy, who accompanied them as a chaperone. "Perfect for a visit to the Royal Menagerie."

Emily's face brightened. "I've always wanted to see the Menagerie."

"I know," the Duke replied, absent-mindedly.

Emily blinked at him with a puzzled frown as Cissy interrupted, chattering happily. "So have I! Can we visit Astley's Amphitheatre one day?"

"Certainly. The equestrian displays there are particularly fine," Wolferton agreed. "The horsemanship of the performers is excellent. There are even re-enactments of famous battles from the French wars."

"I don't know about the horses," Emily interjected, "because I'm not too fond of them. But I would like to see the pantomimes and the acrobatics. And the fireworks at Vauxhall."

"Unfortunately, Vauxhall Gardens is closed until May," the Duke said. "You'll have to wait until spring for me to take you there."

"Then let's go to the Opera House and hear some Rossini," Cissy suggested eagerly.

"Kean as Richard III at Drury Lane," said Emily.

"The mummies at the Egyptian Exhibition," Cissy countered quickly.

"A lecture by Coleridge at the Royal Institution," Emily shot back.

"Madame Tussaud's waxworks!"

"Sir Thomas Lawrence's portraits!"

"The Elgin Marbles!"

"Ascot!"

"Gentleman Jackson!" Emily retorted, as if watching Jackson in the boxing ring were a genteel pastime for ladies.

The girls looked at each other in silence for a second and then, as if on command, burst out laughing.

Wolferton leaned back, watching them, a gentle smile playing about his lips.

The carriage pulled up to the tower at the west entrance, and they dismounted.

The Duke paid the keeper a shilling for each of them to enter, and the man proceeded to explain in great detail what kind of animals were kept there and where they came from.

"I must say," Emily muttered to him after the keeper had finished his long lecture. "I thought it would be exciting to see these exotic beasts, but I am feeling my spirits somewhat dampened upon seeing them caged up like this. It's rather sad."

There were lions, tigers, bears and leopards, panthers and a lone, scraggy wolf.

"I can't help it," Emily said to Wolferton, "but the wolf reminds me of you. I wonder why that is?"

"Surely my hair is better combed than his?" Wolferton touched the back of his head.

"No, it's not the hair. It's in his eyes."

"You're right!" Cissy said, squinting through the bars of the cage. "He even has the same expression."

"What expression?" Wolferton narrowed his eyes at the animal.

"Yes, of disgruntled weariness," Emily pointed a finger at his face. "Just like now. Like the entire world, all and sundry, is boring beyond words."

"That's what my expression says?" The Duke looked put out.

"No." Cissy shook her head. "It's more like, 'Leave me alone, lest I bite you'."

Emily spluttered.

A lion paced restlessly in the den beside the wolf's.

"Poor thing," Emily whispered. "Do you think he remembers the days when he was free, roaming the jungle?"

"Unlikely," Wolferton said matter-of-factly. "The keeper just explained that most of the animals here were born in captivity."

"Still. They must feel they were born to a very different kind of life."

"Much like yourself," he murmured.

Emily shot him a quick look. Before she could ask him what he meant, Cissy pinched Emily's arm.

Emily stifled a cry of pain.

Cissy inhaled sharply. "Emily. We have to go. Now!"

Emily looked up, trying to find the source of Cissy's sudden reaction. Too late, she saw a group of people standing nearby, and one particular gentleman, standing slightly apart, frozen as he stared at them openly. After a moment, he dissociated himself from the group and stepped up to them.

"Good heavens," he exclaimed. "Lady Cecily Hepplewhite. Lady Honey?" His attention shifted to Emily. "And who is this you're with?"

Unaccustomed to being addressed so brazenly by strangers, the Duke arched a haughty eyebrow, ready to cut him.

Emily gasped, her hand flying to her mouth.

Cissy, however, paled.

It was Mr Edward Matthews.

The only gentleman Cissy had ever been in love with.

My dear Little Wren,

It takes me longer to reply because I have other forests to tend—not just this one. But know this: I dreamed of you too. And I have thought of you every single day since.

I cannot think of anything or anyone else.

Always your devoted,

Fenn

Dearest Fenn,

I yearn for you with a longing I scarcely understand. I think of you always, as if you were a part of me that I somehow lost before we even met. How is it possible to miss someone you've never seen, never touched? Yet, I do —I miss you so much it aches.

What are we to do? How can we continue like this, so far apart, yet so near in spirit? I am at a loss.

Yours, waiting, waiting—always waiting,

Emmy

Chapter Twenty-One

IT WAS EXACTLY THE KIND OF ENCOUNTER EMILY had always dreaded.

Here was Mr Edward Matthews, a man from their past life, someone they'd thought they'd never see again, appearing in the middle of the Royal Menagerie in London, addressing them in public with names they'd thought they'd long left behind.

It was enough to make one's hair stand on end.

Emily glanced around. Fortunately, no one seemed to have heard them, since the people in the other group were too far away to overhear their exchange.

She tugged at the Duke's sleeve, who looked at her with a frown.

"You are mistaken, sir," Cissy said as haughtily as she could, but two patches of frantic red on her cheeks belied her. "The name is Lady Lydia Featherstone."

"But how can that be? I am certain you are Lady Cecily Hepplewhite?" the man pressed.

"A mistake."

The Duke stepped in, not mincing words. "Who the devil are you?"

"I-I beg your pardon," Matthews stammered, his cheeks flushing. "The name is Matthews. Edward Matthews. I have an acquaintance with Lady Honey and Lady Annabelle from Bath. With whom do I have the honour of speaking?"

"Wolferton," the Duke drawled.

Matthews paled. It was obvious he knew the name.

"And this is my betrothed, Lady Poppy Featherstone." He nodded to Emily, then to Cissy. "Her sister, Lady Lydia Featherstone."

The man flushed painfully. "I beg your pardon," he stammered. "I must have made a mistake." With a last doubtful glance at Cissy, he retreated.

Emily grabbed the Duke's arm and pulled him away. "Let us go."

"Hepplewhite?" the Duke inquired once they were safely back in their carriage. "A manifestation of one of your former lives?"

"He was one of my sister's beaux," Emily explained.

"He was not." Cissy sat as stiff as a statue and averted her face. "He's no one. A man of no importance at all. I've already forgotten his name."

Emily waved an impatient hand. "We thought he would come up to scratch and ask for Cissy's hand, but he never did; he just disappeared one day." She bit her lower lip. "We think maybe he was intimidated by Aunt Henrietta and the Hepplewhite name." Which was ironic, of course, since it wasn't really theirs to begin with.

"Dastardly of him," the Duke remarked with a shrug. "Giving up at the first sign of an obstacle. A little rain never hurt anybody."

Emily looked at him with wide eyes. "Oh. Indeed." Something about his words tugged at the edges of her memory. It was a fleeting glimpse of something she couldn't quite place.

"It was so long ago," Cissy said, with a white, drawn face. "In another life. Let us not speak of it again." She lifted her chin with a forced smile. "What shall we do next? Astley's?"

Wolferton consulted his pocket watch. "I think we must return for tea. My aunts want to take us to the opera tonight."

"Famous," Cissy said, in a deflated voice.

Emily chewed her lip anxiously. One went to the opera to be seen, not to hear music. What if they met more people like poor Mr Matthews?

"I hope it's not a bad idea to go," Emily muttered. "I don't want any more encounters like the one we just had with Mr Matthews."

"Of course it's a bad idea," the Duke said cheerfully. "But if my aunts insist, what can one do? They are all too eager to show off their nephew's bride." He held her eyes, as if to remind her to keep her promise.

Her first opera visit was all she'd ever wanted it to be.

The music—Rossini's *Il Barbiere di Siviglia*—was divine. They had their own box, which gave them both privacy and publicity. Sitting in a box was like sitting in a shop window: one was on display for all London society to see. The ladies showed off their latest gowns and jewels, while the gentlemen paraded like peacocks in the gallery behind them. During the intermission, they received visitors who wanted to be introduced. Girls sold oranges in the pit and champagne in the refreshment room. The Duke sent a footman to bring the champagne directly to their box, so they did not have to mingle with the crowd.

When the music began, her fears were forgotten. Emily's heart soared with the music, for she had never heard anything so glorious, so divine. For once, she felt she was in the right place at the right time.

Wolferton, it seemed, was watching her more than the stage.

When her eyes teared up at Rosina's aria, he pulled out a handkerchief and handed it to her. Emily wiped her nose and handed the crumpled ball back to him, and he pocketed it without a word.

"It was wonderful." Emily chattered excitedly all the way home. "That music, that clear voice. I wish I could sing like that."

"But you can," Lady Dalrymple said with a sniff. "I daresay you can easily hold a candle to any of them."

"Nonsense," Emily said, blushing. She had been asked to sing for them every evening after dinner, and it had become a cherished part of their routine. His aunts listened with rapt delight, while Wolferton usually lounged in his armchair with his eyes closed, seemingly unmoved. Only a muscle twitching in his jaw indicated that the music might be affecting him more than he led on.

"I quite agree," Lady Mabel chimed in. "Your voice is much sweeter."

"Bellini sings beautifully," Lady Jane agreed. "But our Emily sings like a nightingale."

"Or a lark," Mabel suggested.

"A wren, more likely," the Duke said quietly. Then, seeing Emily's face, he raised an eyebrow. "What, my dear? You look as if you've seen a ghost."

"Nothing." She shook her head. "I haven't heard the word in a long time. It is what Papa used to call me," she added in a whisper.

Back at the townhouse, Emily rushed into her room, sat down at her desk and hastily took out a pen and paper. Her hand shook as she began to scribble.

Crumpets

Boots

Violets

Candied violets

The Royal Menagerie

The Opera House

Coquelicot ribbons

A little rain never hurt anybody

Wren

She stared at the list in disbelief. Her mouth went dry as a single thought took hold of her mind.

This couldn't be. Surely not.

Her forest fay had been a figment of her childhood imagination—or so she had always assumed when she was younger. Later, she'd realised he was just a boy, maybe the vicar's son, maybe the steward's son from the neighbouring estate, sharing her dreams and secrets through the hollow of a tree. Her attempts at discovering his identity had been unsuccessful, because Fenn had been uncooperative.

Her eyes scanned the words again. These phrases and gestures were so painfully familiar. These were not just the Duke's gifts or comments—they were details from her childhood letters. Letters she had exchanged with her forest fay, Fenn.

The crumpets, her favourite food, which she'd written about in her letters, describing the delight of their buttery warmth on cold mornings because they reminded her of her mother. The bouquets of violets, her favourite flowers, and the candied violets she had dreamed of eating as a child. The coquelicot ribbons, Fenn's first gift to her. The boots. The Royal Menagerie and the opera houses she'd longed to visit. Even the phrase 'A little rain never hurt anybody' was something Fenn used to write.

Sweet heavens.

Emily's pen slipped from her hand, splattering ink across the page. She pressed her palms over her mouth, shaking her head as if trying to dislodge the thought.

"No, no, no. This is absurd." She jumped up to pace the room, her skirts brushing against the furniture. "Coincidences. Pure coincidences. That's all this is."

But was it, really?

She stopped pacing, her hands clenched at her sides. Her eyes snapped back to the list.

Could it be true? Could the Duke of Wolferton really be her forest fay, Fenn?

It was inconceivable. It was entirely impossible. Fenn

had been kind, whimsical, and full of dreams. Fenn had loved her. Or so she'd believed.

But Wolferton was arrogant, cold and self-important. They couldn't be the same person.

He couldn't possibly be her childhood sweetheart, her soulmate, her first love.

Could he?

A harsh, disbelieving laugh escaped her lips.

And if he was—assuming it was true—why hadn't he said anything? Why had he remained silent, as though their shared childhood had meant nothing? Why had he begun dropping these hints—as if to tease her, as if he wanted her to remember?

Her chest tightened as if a hot, sticky weight pressed down on it. If he was Fenn, what was he playing at? Why the charade? Why not tell her the truth?

But then again, if he had approached her saying, "I'm Fenn, your childhood friend and your first love," she likely would have laughed in his face and dismissed it as a cruel jest.

Two hours of restless pacing and agonising over every detail had brought her to one conclusion: she needed proof. Hard, undeniable proof.

She would get it, no matter what it took.

Emily,

My dearest little love,

I can bear this longing no longer. There is but one course left to us: let us take our destiny into our own hands.

Meet me by the old tree at dawn tomorrow. Come with me to Gretna Green, where we may bind our hearts together forever.

I await you with loving impatience and a heart brimming with hope.

Forever yours, in heart and soul,

Fenn

Chapter Twenty-Two

PROOF.

That was, no doubt, to be found in his study, specifically his writing table. All she had to do was take a look at his handwriting.

It was easy, really.

She tiptoed along the corridor, looking left and right, and when no servant was in sight, she took a deep breath and opened the door.

His study was a library. Not quite as large as the one downstairs, but a smaller version of it, with mahogany shelves lining the walls, filled with leather-bound books. There was a desk in front of the window. It was shockingly tidy, empty of any papers, letters, notes, or anything that might give her a clue to his handwriting.

Emily wrinkled her forehead in thought as she stared at the clean, polished surface of the desk.

There was his quill and a pot of ink. She picked up the quill and let it drop.

There was nothing more on the table.

Either the Duke did not work here at all, or he was so tidy that he cleaned up after himself. Maybe it was because he didn't live here at the moment, she thought. Of course. He'd moved into his bachelor flat at the Albany for the time being, since she lived here.

Still, he'd used the study every day, locked himself in there for hours with his secretary.

Her hand went to the drawer and hesitated. A pang of conscience almost made her drop it. But then, with determination, she pushed her misgivings aside and opened the drawer.

There they were, files and folders filled with papers and documents.

Slightly nervous, she pulled out a folder and opened it. It was filled with papers in various styles of handwriting, none of which looked familiar.

A letter fell out, written in a tight, black scrawl. Emily bent to pick it up and was putting it back in the folder when the name 'Edmund White' jumped out at her. She stopped and read the letter.

Your Grace,
Following my investigation into the matter of Mr Edmund White, I respectfully submit the following findings:

1. It has been confirmed that the steward, Mr Bartholomew Jago, evicted the White family from Meadowview Cottage on December 30th, 1809 due to his inability to pay the rent. This action was carried out in accordance with directives issued by your late father, the former duke.

The tenancy was subsequently granted to Mr Hoby. The cottage has remained unoccupied since Mr Hoby's demise three years ago.

2. A review of the estate accounts reveals discrepancies: Mr Jago raised the rent for the property, yet the recorded sums do not correspond to what was deposited into the estate's coffers. One can conclude that Mr Jago must have embezzled the difference for his personal gain.

3. Regrettably, Mr Jago is no longer in the country, having departed for the New World. As such, we are unable to apprehend him or seek restitution for his misdeeds.

I remain at Your Grace's disposal should you require further inquiry into this matter.

Your obedient servant,
Peter Olney

EMILY STARED AT THE LETTER. The date on the paper, five years earlier, meant he'd known about this all along. It was an ugly reminder of the Duke and the role he'd played in her life. And that Jago had been corrupt did not surprise her in the least. He'd followed the Duke's orders, embezzled the money and disappeared.

Underneath this letter was another letter, written in the same hand, no doubt his secretary's.

Your Grace,
This is to confirm Miss Emily White's claim that her
father, Mr Edmund White, did indeed die the night after
the eviction. He was buried in the Parish Cemetery of
Hilperton.

This letter was dated only two weeks ago. A thick, hard lump formed at the back of her throat and she felt a trickle of tears run down her cheeks.

The door opened and Wolferton strode into the room, pausing when he saw Emily standing at the desk with the letter in her hands.

"Emily? What are you doing here?" His eyes fell on the letter in her hands, and he frowned. "What is the matter?"

He walked over to her and took the paper from her hand. "Ah." He scanned the letter. Then he placed it on the table. His face was unreadable.

"You really didn't know about my father," Emily said. "You sent your secretary to confirm what I said."

"Yes." He seemed to search for words. "I seem to lack the appropriate words other than that I truly am sorry, Emily. Jago was corrupt. That is what Olney, my secretary, was investigating. But none of this absolves me. Even though he acted on my father's orders, the responsibility was mine, and for what happened to you and your family, I owe you and your sister a sincere apology."

Emily blinked, momentarily unbalanced. An apology? No, she didn't want that. She wanted to unleash her fury, to rail against him, to solidify the image of him as the devil incarnate, to blame him for all the evil that had ever befallen her in her life.

His face was grave, his eyes—goodness, his eyes!—well, she almost drowned in them. A pot of molten gold. Worst of all, he looked as if he meant every word he said.

He reached out a hand and tilted her chin up, wiping away a tear with his thumb.

"I wish things could have been different. I wish I could have said and done things differently. I wish... " He searched for words. "I could have been there for you."

Why weren't you, then? The words were on her lips. The old resentment rose in her.

She pulled away. "I have so many questions. Not only about this—" she gestured at the letter "—but also about something else."

She remembered why she'd come into the study to begin with. She wanted the truth. She wanted proof.

He nodded, his face drawn. "You have but to ask."

She passed a hand over her forehead. "When I was younger, a child, really, I had a-a—"

"A?" His brow arched.

"A-a... " Why was this so difficult? She waved her hand in an aimless circle, then tapped her temple. "How do you say it?"

He looked at her, amused. "Come, come, spit it out."

She hesitated. "A relationship isn't quite the right word," she murmured. She worried at her lower lip before continuing, "To be honest, I'm not at all sure how to describe it." She stared intently at the vase on the table as if it might offer some guidance. "There was a boy," she finally said.

"So you had a lover," he stated, his expression deadpan. "It happens."

She flushed hotly. "No! That is to say—yes." She cleared her throat, avoiding his eyes. "I mean, not like you think. I did love him. I do love him. That is, of course, I thought I did. I do." Heavens, why was this so awkward? She threw up her hands and glared at him. "Oh, I don't know! I was just a child. How could I have understood love then when I hardly understand it now?" Then she winced. This certainly wasn't coming out the way she'd intended.

He folded his arms, but the amused glint in his eyes had died. "Go on. I'm all ears."

"The thing is." She stared at him, hard. "This relationship, or friendship, or letter-ship, or whatever you want to call it, it was more on paper than anything else, and I never even actually met him, which is absurd if you come to think about it, and entirely implausible, but the fact of the matter is, this thing that we had was something quite, quite out of the ordinary. Like, like—" she gestured helplessly "—God help me. Like soulmates," she finally blurted out.

"Soulmates." He blinked.

"He knew me like no one else knew me," she hurried on, "not my father, not Cissy." She stared into space. "Not even myself. It was that kind of connection, you know?"

He tilted his head, his expression half serious, half mocking. "I confess I don't quite follow. But how enviable, if such a thing does exist."

"Yes, well, it felt like fate. It was so special."

"Do go on." He sat on the desk, crossed one leg over the other with a smirk, his quizzing glass dangling from his fingers. "I find this is vastly entertaining."

Hateful man!

She skewered him with her glare.

"So," he drawled. "Your point being? What was it you wanted to ask?"

"The boy with whom I nearly eloped," she said through clenched teeth. "I wanted to ask whether you are him. I want to know whether you are Fenn."

Fenn,

I waited for you for three entire days and nights, but you did not come.

You must have changed your mind.

It is difficult, oh, so difficult, but I will try to understand.

Your heartbroken
Emily

Chapter Twenty-Three

THE QUIZZING GLASS DROPPED.

"You eloped?" He leaned forward.

"Yes." She lifted her chin. "I mean, no. I said nearly. We had plans to elope. But it never actually happened." She narrowed her eyes at the look on his face. "Why, does that surprise you?"

"No, no, not at all, not at all. Who would have thought you would ever consider eloping—but, well, I suppose that is beside the point." He waved a hand. "Back to the matter at hand. You want to know if I am your lost childhood love? Your soulmate?" His face was unreadable. "In all seriousness?"

She rubbed her damp hands down her sides. "I know it sounds completely ridiculous. What must you think of me? I take it back. Of course, you are not Fenn. How could you be?" She threw up her hands and suddenly it all came out. "You are everything I despise. You are the complete opposite of Fenn. You and I— we have nothing in common. I confess it's no secret that I hold you in profound dislike, after all you did to us. Not to mention what you stand for, your station, your very existence. I've always deplored it." She could have bitten her tongue off as soon as she'd uttered the words, but it was too late. It was as if a dam had broken and she vomited it all out, all the years and years of bitterness, all her pent-up frustrations, and once the words were out, she could not take them back.

Something flickered in his eyes. "Just to be clear. Not only do you dislike the fact that I am a duke, you dislike me as a person. Correction. You hate and despise me."

She cleared her throat and looked away. "Well. That sounds a bit harsh, put like that. But all my life you've been a symbol of everything I hated, so it's rather difficult to suddenly change one's mind... " Her voice trailed off weakly.

It was a miracle that a bolt of lightning didn't come down from the heavens to strike her dead for her blatant lies. Not a word of what she'd said was true. Quite the opposite. But she'd rather be struck by lightning and buried six feet under than admit that she'd fallen head over heels in love with him before he'd even uttered his fake proposal. Then why on earth was she uttering all this nonsense?

Emily rubbed her forehead in agitation. Wolferton, Fenn... the two names tangled in her mind until she could no longer make sense of anything.

His eyes fell on the letters on the table. "Because you find it impossible to forgive what I have done to your family." His voice was flat.

She hesitated, the silence stretching taut between

them. Fenn would never have cast her out. Fenn would have known. He would have saved them. He would have offered them another home. He would have stopped the corrupt steward from throwing them out in the first place.

It was unforgivable.

Unforgivable that he wasn't Fenn.

Because, deep down, she loved him.

Wolferton.

And he could never, ever know.

Their relationship wasn't real. It was a façade, a ruse, a make-believe—a fairytale, just like her relationship with Fenn had been.

"Yes." The single word echoed through the room.

Maybe it was the shadows flickering across the walls, but he'd never looked as diabolical as he did now. Cold, hard, cynical.

Emily shifted uncomfortably.

"Well. I suppose that was to be expected," he said in a clipped voice. "But to get back to the matter at hand. To answer your question, Lady Poppy, no, I am not your soulmate. Your—what was his name? Fenn." He sneered.

It shouldn't have surprised her in the least, but a pang of bitter disappointment churned like acid in her stomach.

"Yes, I know," she whispered.

He rose. "Well, if there isn't anything else, I will be going. Thank you for this entertaining, er, glimpse into your past life. Perhaps your childhood love still lives somewhere. Maybe you'll find him one day. Who knows? People tend to change over time and he might no longer be the same as you remember. Nor would he want to be, if he had any sense."

She tilted her head, frowning. What was that supposed to mean?

His face was a mask. "If you insist on pursuing your former love, may I remind you that you have a contract to uphold? It doesn't look good for you to be pining after someone else while you're engaged to me. I don't want to look like a cuckolded fool long before we're even married. Even if it is all hypothetical."

"Of course not," she choked out.

"Play along with my aunts, even if they lead us to the altar. I shall find a suitable way to extricate ourselves from it without anyone receiving any harm."

"Yes, but how?"

"Just trust me, Emily," he said wearily.

Then he left.

Emily sat down heavily on the chair and felt like bursting into tears.

"I will not cry," she growled, rubbing her eyes, angry at herself. No, she wasn't angry with herself. She was angry at him. Angry at him because he wasn't Fenn?

Maybe not even that was true.

Angry at life?

Angry at fate?

She heaved a heavy sigh.

She didn't understand anything anymore, and she certainly didn't understand him.

THE DUKE JOINED them for tea that afternoon.

How had a simple, routine tea become such a highly charged, utterly bewildering ordeal for Emily?

As soon as she entered the room, he beamed at her, took her hand and drew her closer, his every action that of a man deeply in love. He stayed close, touching her at every opportunity, which left her feeling thoroughly confused, because she still had the harsh words they'd exchanged earlier echoing in her ears.

Of course, that was exactly what he was supposed to do. It was all part of the plan. They were pretending to be in love; this behaviour was all a ruse.

But now Emily was faced with a new layer of confusion. Was this the Duke, playing his part to perfection in the role they had agreed upon? Or was this Fenn, hiding behind the guise of a duke, who might—just might—have genuine feelings for her? But then, he'd said he wasn't Fenn, hadn't he? And that she was contractually obliged to play the affectionate betrothed in the company of his aunts.

Maybe was it all a figment of her overactive imagination, her mind conjuring up meaning where there was none?

What an awkward situation it was!

The three aunts looked on, their faces full of approval.

"We must discuss the wedding," Araminta declared firmly. "There is no point in waiting longer. What do you say to Saturday next, Wolferton?"

"I want whatever my bride wants," was his quixotic reply.

"Poppy? What do you think?" All eyes were on Emily.

Emily barely heard the question. The Duke had leaned closer, his hand tucking a stray strand of her hair behind her ear. His fingers brushed her cheek, leaving a tingling warmth.

She swallowed hard.

"Yes," she said, the word spilling out without thought.

"Excellent," Araminta exclaimed. "We'll speed things up and have the ceremony at St George's, followed by the wedding breakfast here at Wolferton House."

Emily's heart pounded in her chest, her mind still trapped by the trail of heat his fingers had left on her skin. It took her far too long to register that her wedding had been mentioned.

She sat bolt upright. "Saturday next? What exactly do you mean by that? Do you mean this coming Saturday —three days from now—or the Saturday of the following week?" Either option was far too soon, but if they were planning the ceremony in just three days, it would be with an alarming haste that would be almost impossible to escape.

"I meant, of course, whichever Saturday comes next," Araminta clarified with a raised eyebrow. "Isn't that how we generally understand the phrase?"

Emily stared at her in horror. "But that's only a few days away!"

"Indeed." Araminta narrowed her eyes at her. "Isn't that an advantage? Is there a reason why we shouldn't speed up things, seeing as you two are so in love?"

Emily picked an invisible crumb from the tabletop.

"Oh. No, not at all." She caught Wolferton's warning look and cleared her throat. "Everything is well."

"Good." Araminta adjusted the spectacles on her nose. "For one moment, you had me worried. Wolferton has already obtained the special license, so there is no reason whatsoever to delay the wedding. It will be a small gathering, limited to the closest family and friends. Let me know if there is anyone else I should add to the guest list. So far, I have only included your sister. It would be nice to have more of your family present, though, considering you and your sister are orphans, of course... " she trailed off with an air of polite pity.

"We need to talk!" Emily hissed at Wolferton, who kept patting her hand with annoying nonchalance, apparently seeing nothing wrong with their fake engagement being tied up in a very real wedding ceremony.

Wolferton just kept beaming at her as if she were the most beautiful thing under the sun. "Yes, my dear, let us talk."

"We will leave you then. Come Jane, Mabel." Araminta nodded to her sisters, and they left the room.

Emily jumped up and paced the room, wringing her hands, while Wolferton leaned back on the sofa and watched her. "What are we to do now? How are we going to get out of this? They are quite infuriatingly bent on this wedding, almost as if they sensed that our union might not be real, and they want to ascertain that it is impossible to dissolve it, hence the haste of it all." She glared at him when he remained silent. "Have you nothing to add to this conversation?"

A finger traced the curve of his upper lip thoughtfully, and Emily stared at his hand. It was large and strong and his fingers were long and slim. She swallowed and tore her eyes away.

"Well?"

"Trust me."

"That's all? Trust you?" She trusted him about as much as a sparrow trusted a hungry cat. She narrowed her eyes at him. "Don't you think we should stop this before it becomes irreversible?"

"Yes. Of course." He pulled himself up. "But timing is everything. If the truth comes out too soon, everything will have been for nothing." He furrowed his brows. "You were protesting too much just now about them advancing the wedding. It made Aunt Araminta suspicious."

The door to the drawing room was open, and they could hear the aunts continuing the discussion of the wedding date in the corridor.

"Come here," he said.

Emily stepped up to him, tilting her head questioningly.

He cupped her face in his hands and turned her face towards him.

She could drown in his eyes. There was an unspoken question in them, something like a longing.

"What?" she whispered, lifting her own hands to cradle his face, unable to stop herself. She saw the shadows under his eyes, the hard angles and planes of his chin and cheeks, the long dark lashes, the pupils large in a sea of gold.

He bent his face and kissed her.

This kiss was oh so different! Gentle, almost shy. Like

butterfly wings brushing her lips. She rose on tiptoe, pressed closer, melting into him, wanting more. Somehow, her fingers tangled in his hair and time stood still.

After a wonderful eternity, he released her gently.

"I think we'd better stop," he said, his voice rough and unsteady.

Emily tugged at a loose strand of her hair, her thoughts racing. Of course, this didn't mean anything, she reminded herself firmly. He'd kissed her for the benefit of his aunts. Only for that.

The conversation in the corridor had fallen utterly silent. She squinted at the door. Were his aunts standing there, gawking?

A male voice sounded from outside. "I beg your pardon, my lady. Is His Grace within?"

"This is hardly a suitable moment," Araminta's voice hissed, sharp with urgency.

The Duke's secretary stepped into the room, ledger in hand. He froze, his eyes widening. "Oh. I beg your pardon, Your Grace. My lady." His cheeks turned an unmistakable shade of crimson as he bowed hastily.

Emily stepped back instinctively, widening the space between herself and the Duke. Turning to the mantelpiece, she feigned an intense study of the floral arrangement atop it, though her cheeks burned with mortification.

"Olney," the Duke said, his tone crisp. "This had better be urgent."

"It is, Your Grace," Olney replied, straightening his spectacles. "It concerns the irrigation system at Ashbourne Estate."

The Duke gave a controlled sigh and took a last look at Emily before gesturing towards the door. "Very well. I'll take care of it. Wait for me in the study, Olney." Turning to Emily, he said, a note of regret lacing his voice. "I'll see you later for supper."

Emily left the study, wobbly and breathless, surprised that she was still able to walk.

Fenn,

Have you forgotten me entirely?

Has something happened? Are you ill? Are you safe?
Please send me a sign that you are well.

I am most fearful and worried,
Emily

Chapter Twenty-Four

She ought to break it off before it was too late.

But it was already too late, another part of her brain argued. She'd come too far now and couldn't simply retreat. She had to see it through to the bitter end, come what may.

After a sleepless night of tossing and turning and evaluating her choices, Emily rose and, after a brief, horrified glance in the mirror, crawled back into bed.

Her abigail had taken one look at her face and said, "I'll bring some cucumbers for your eyes, m'lady. We can also use some powder to get rid of the dark circles."

The powder, in the end, did the trick, and with her abigail's help she looked as though she'd had at least a little sleep.

When she finally appeared in the hall, where the aunts were waiting for her, they did not seem to see anything amiss with her face. Only Mabel gave her a sharp look, but said nothing.

Their shopping trips wouldn't end. How many gowns did a woman need? According to Aunt Araminta, a grand total of thirty-six.

"Why thirty-six?" Emily asked, taken aback.

"Because that is the minimum number of dresses a duchess needs to be called presentable," Aunt Araminta explained. She was wearing a hideous bonnet that looked like a dark moss-green chimney with feathers and flowers. "It won't do for the duchess to wear the same dress twice in a month."

"It just seems so excessively excessive," Emily said lamely.

"If you don't want them, I will take them gladly," Cissy put in cheerfully. "A girl can't have too many dresses."

"I am in agreement, child. As for you, you are a different matter altogether." Emily was glad that Araminta had turned her attention to her sister. "You too must marry."

Cissy took it in stride. "Indeed. I have been told so ever since I learned to speak."

"The suitors aren't a problem, it appears," Aunt Jane put in thoughtfully. "The girl is quite adored by the men. In fact, one of them came calling only yesterday. What was his name? It was so ordinary. Mortimer or Marks or something like that."

Emily sat up straight. "Never say that Mr Matthews came to call?"

"Matthews, yes, that's his name." Jane nodded. "A diffident fellow, to be sure. He came while you were out. Left his card. Said he'd call again today. I'm surprised the butler didn't give it to you. He's probably calling now and will find you gone again."

"The butler might have told me." Cissy had two distinct red spots on her cheek. "But it slipped my mind."

"But, but—Matthews," Emily turned to her sister. "Shouldn't you at least talk to him?"

Aunt Araminta looked from one girl to the other. "Why? Was there anything special about the man? He looked quite ordinary, I must say. You also received a bouquet of flowers from a Mr Kent, Mr Allen, and a Lord Tarington, I think his name was. How extraordinarily fortunate you are to be so courted!"

Cissy averted her eyes and played with the string of her reticule. "Yes, well. It is always like that."

"What Cissy means to say is that they always come courting, but nothing ever happens beyond flowers and an occasional ride out in the park," Emily explained. "The problem, Lady Dalrymple, seems to be that while there is no shortage of suitors, none of them ever come up to scratch."

"Perhaps it is because the lady's heart is elsewhere?" Mabel's quiet voice entered the discussion, but was overruled by Jane's comment that it was neither here nor there, and that gentlemen, if interested, would have to be persuaded to come up to scratch, no matter what. Though how that was to be achieved was, of course, the question that many a matchmaking mama asked herself, too, no doubt.

"Are you well?" Emily asked Cissy that evening, after she'd slipped into her room. Cissy was sitting in an armchair with an open book in her lap, a candle beside her on the side table, staring out of the window into the darkness beyond.

"Quite," she replied cheerfully. "Why shouldn't I be? Look at this wonderful setting. This room is even more glamorous than the one at Ashbourne House. We live in Grosvenor Square, Emily. The heart of Mayfair! We are neighbours to a Russian princess on the right and a relative of the royal family on the left. How much higher can we climb in this world? You are to marry Wolferton and he worships the ground you walk on—do not interrupt, for it is the truth. I cannot for the life of me understand why you cannot see the truth that is so obvious in his eyes. I must say, I am glad that he turned out to be so amiable and that he isn't the monster we always thought he was."

Emily shook her head vehemently. "Because it's not true. It's all a lie. He is a consummate actor and you, of all people, have fallen for it."

"Tosh, Emmy." Cissy closed her book with a snap. "It's you who can't tell the difference between ruse and reality. You can be so stupidly stubborn sometimes. Don't let your prejudices fool you. He is not at all the man he would have us believe. But why that is so is for you to discover."

Emily looked at her curiously. "Have you forgotten what he's done to us?"

Cissy looked at her sister thoughtfully. "I've come to the conclusion that he might not have been at fault at all and that we were quite wrong to have come up with this plan of revenge to begin with."

Emily furrowed her brows. "How so?"

"I, too, talk to the servants, you know. I also talk to the three aunts daily. I learned that he came into his title and inheritance quite unexpectedly. I imagine he wasn't at all prepared for his role, having been estranged from his father, as they say. They barely knew each other. So when he became duke, he had to rely on his steward to keep the estate running. I don't think he knew about the eviction at all. He couldn't have known what his father's orders had been, and he had no reason to doubt the steward's loyalty or his words." Cissy's face softened. "It must have been a tremendously difficult time for him."

Emily looked at her sister, aghast. Trust Cissy to find it in her heart to not only forgive him for his actions, but to empathise with him!

"Don't tell me you actually feel sorry for him now?" Emily demanded.

Cissy thought. "Well, yes. I see now how it must have happened. I believe he wasn't to blame, Emily."

"He was the duke, and as such, he should at least have been responsible for knowing what was happening on his estates," Emily lectured.

"Yes, certainly. But back then, he was young and green and he made a mistake. I believe he would never have evicted us if it hadn't been for that evil steward."

Emily stared at her sister. "Sometimes, Cissy, I think you are too good for this world."

What was more, she might actually be right. Emily recalled a single sentence from Olney's letter in the library: *This action was carried out in accordance with directives issued by your late father, the former duke.* The words seemed to confirm Cissy's claim. The old duke must have been behind it. Perhaps Wolferton had never directly ordered their eviction.

Yet, he insisted on taking responsibility for the consequences. That was another facet of his character she found utterly baffling. Had she truly misjudged him so gravely?

Cissy appeared to be convinced that they had.

Emily shook her head with a sigh. "Let's not talk about Wolferton. Tell me how you feel. About Mr Matthews. Surely it can't leave you indifferent that he has so suddenly reappeared in your life and has even come to see you. I must say, it's very unexpected. Don't you want to hear what he has to say?"

Cissy's smile was brittle. "To what purpose? Merely to endure a litany of excuses?"

"Even if they turn out to be excuses, don't you want to hear what he might say to explain why he disappeared the way he did in Bath? Even if only to find some kind of closure?"

Cissy shook her head. "There is no point. Besides, as Aunt Araminta said so well this afternoon, I have a number of other, far more eligible suitors who are eager to court me."

Emily looked at her quietly. "As you wish." Under her breath, she muttered, "And you call me stubborn... " Then she leaned forward, a gleam in her eyes. "If it's all the same to you, then you will allow me to meddle with some matchmaking, yes?"

Cissy looked at her, amused. "Who do you have in mind?"

Emily twisted a length of ribbon around her finger

and smiled innocently. "Chippendale, of course. I confess I have a soft spot in my heart for him. I have never recovered from the fact that he is not the duke, you see."

Cissy laughed suddenly. "Chippendale! By all means. But I haven't seen him since we came to London. I wonder what the man is up to these days? Oh, Emmy," she burst out suddenly. "Why do all the men in my life have a tendency to disappear after they have made my acquaintance?"

"Indeed." Emily frowned. "There does seem to be a pattern. One wonders where the man has gone." She put her arms around her sister. "It's not you, sister heart. I know it isn't. Surely there must be a good reason for his absence." She pulled away to look into her sister's face. "You haven't fallen in love with Chippendale, have you?"

Cissy sighed. "I wish I had. He is everything that is kind and wonderful, and we are good friends, you know?" She pulled at the ribbon of her gown. "But that's all there is between us, Emmy. Just friendship. There is no romantic attachment between us whatsoever. He makes me laugh, but my heart doesn't skip a beat when he is nearby. Not like... " She did not finish the sentence, but Emily knew what she was going to say.

Not like Matthews.

"Heaven only knows what it is about that man that can affect you like that," Emily burst out. "He seems so terribly dull."

"Oh, but he isn't!" Cissy gave her a surprised look. "Chippendale is forever joking."

"I wasn't talking about Chippendale." Emily patted her shoulder.

She said good night to her sister and returned to her own room.

She was getting ready for bed when there was a sudden knock at the door and Aunt Mabel entered, looking at her shyly.

"I don't want to disturb you too much," she said in her soft voice. "I just wanted to give you the dress. I embroidered a row of rosebuds on the neckline. I think it looks nicer now." She carried a soft green dress, which they'd bought that afternoon. It was a very pretty dress, with many rows of extravagant flounces at the hem, and little rosebuds embroidered all over. Emily didn't know when she would ever have the chance to wear something so beautiful. Surely she would not be allowed to keep all these beautiful dresses when their ruse was over and she returned to her simple country life at Meadowview Cottage.

It occurred to her that she hadn't thought about the cottage for a long time. And when she did, it no longer held the warm glow of peaceful, idyllic country life. It had seemed rather cold, the chimney probably clogged and the walls damp and mouldy. Besides, when it was all over and she was back to being ordinary Miss Emily White, she found the idea of living on the Duke's land, even when he wasn't there, rather unpleasant. What would it be like if he lived at Ashbourne House nearby? She would be afraid to go for a walk for fear of running into him. Of course, he would never reside there. He'd hardly even visited before, so why would he do so now? But, how sad it would be to be living there and never seeing the Duke again... so close and forevermore out of reach. Why did this thought make her want to burst into tears?

And why on earth did her mind focus so on future events that might or might not happen? She'd got herself all upset and nostalgic for no reason at all.

There was Mabel, standing in the middle of the room, arms folded, looking at her curiously.

How long had she been standing there patiently?

"I'm sorry. I was woolgathering again," Emily stammered. "I tend to do that. It's almost an ailment."

Mabel smiled. "Don't worry. It appears you're suffering from a severe case of bridal nerves."

Emily looked at her wide-eyed. "Is that it? Bridal nerves?"

"Nothing to be overly hard on yourself about. I dare say Jasper is wearing the carpet thin by now, pacing around his bedroom. Araminta had to throw him out of the drawing room because he was insufferable in his temper." Mabel paused. "He only gets insufferable when he is nervous."

That was the most she'd ever heard Mabel say. Emily sat down on the edge of her bed, inviting Mabel to do the same. She accepted her invitation.

Mabel was a small woman with soft wisps of grey hair, a gentle smile and a narrow face. Emily realised how little she knew about her, about any of them. She wondered what her history was and if she'd ever been in love.

"Tomorrow means so much to us," Mabel said now. "You have no idea how much." She folded her hands in her lap. "Araminta is over the moon. Jane doesn't show her feelings too often, but she'll have a sleepless night too. As for me... " She gestured to herself with a small smile. "Here I am. Thank you."

"For what?"

"For making Jasper happy."

"Jasper." The name sounded strange on her lips.

"He hasn't known much happiness in his life. It was a hard one. His parents separated early, and though they never divorced, they lived in different houses. Jasper never even knew his father when he was growing up. His father, the old duke, simply wasn't interested in his own son." She sighed. "Makes you wonder why he even bothered to get married. He was one of those people who would have been better off never marrying. But Jasper's mother died young."

"So you brought him up instead, you and Araminta and Jane," Emily said quietly.

"Yes. He was a shy and sensitive boy who spent more time in the library than out in nature."

Wolferton? With a scholarly, intellectual bent? Surely not?

Mabel saw her look of disbelief. "Oh yes. He wasn't always like he is now. Look." She pulled out a locket, opened it and showed it to her.

"Oh!" escaped Emily's lips. It was a miniature of a boy with thick, curly hair and dark eyes that looked too big in a narrow face.

"He was a handsome boy, wasn't he?" Mabel asked proudly.

"How different he looks. He looks almost... "

"Sad." Mabel regarded the portrait with sorrow. "He

296

was such a lonely boy. We were relieved when he went to Eton, thinking he could make friends with other boys his own age, only to find he was badly bullied. You see, as the only son of a duke, he had only ever met two kinds of people: those who would take advantage of him through flattery and deceit, and those who would take advantage of him through bullying. This made him cautious and suspicious, and must have given him the cynical streak you see in him now. If it hadn't been for Chippendale, who befriended him, I don't know what would have become of the boy." Mabel shook her head.

"Poor boy," Emily whispered.

"It was extremely difficult for him to trust people. And even more impossible for him to love... But when he finally did, it was with an absoluteness that frightened us. We have told you about it, and I do not want to say more about it. It will not do to talk to Jasper's future bride about his past loves. You are his future and what is past is long gone."

Emily thought that was a pity, for she felt an intense streak of curiosity about his past love, followed by something more surprising: jealousy. She pushed both feelings firmly away.

But Mabel went on. "It was a shock for him when he suddenly became a duke. His father died unexpectedly. He simply dropped down dead." She shook her head, as if she still could not believe it. "The boy was barely of age. You cannot imagine the deluge of duties that fell on him from one day to the next. It is too much to ask of one man, let alone a boy like him, completely inexperienced and unworldly as he was. Everyone, I tell you, everyone took advantage of him. Including many of the servants in this very house." She shook her head. "We moved to Wolferstone Abbey, Araminta, Jane and I, to help him put the whole household in order. The problem was that there was not only the household, but all the estates and the responsibilities and duties that went with them. And he was entirely unprepared."

"So he trusted people too much," Emily said in a monotone voice. "Believing that they could be trusted to do the job as they had always done it... " And that had led to Jago driving her family away. But only now did she fully understand what it must have been like for him.

Emily looked at her with wide eyes. "He blamed himself."

Of course he did.

Of course he must have.

Mabel nodded. "He always took his responsibilities too seriously. I don't know exactly what happened, but mistakes were made and there were casualties. Five years ago, he discovered that his father's steward was corrupt and that must have rocked his world quite a bit. Yet more proof that people could not be trusted," Mabel sighed. "It led him to dismissing the entire staff at Ashbourne Estate."

Mabel had just confirmed what Cissy had suspected.

Emily sat back in her chair with a slow exhale.

Mabel took her hand in hers. "Well, you see, knowing you'll be his wife, seeing him happy at last, that means so much to us, child. You do not know how much you matter to him, to us, to all of us."

The sense of guilt that overcame her nearly took her breath away.

Emily licked her lips. "What if it's all a lie?" she whispered. "What if it isn't true? Any of it. What if—what if I am not who I say I am and I have deceived you all?"

A veil of tears blurred her vision.

"You're not deceiving anyone, child." Mabel's voice was firm and sounded eerily like Araminta's. "What nonsense you talk. Besides, we all wear masks. We all lie and deceive at some point in our lives."

Emily wiped her eyes. She would have liked to tell her the truth, that this was all a sham engagement, and that they were pretending to enter marriage just to please her, that it had all been arranged by her and Wolferton, and that after tomorrow things would be very different indeed, he would leave on his travels abroad, and she and Cissy would retire to their cold cottage...

Mabel kept patting her hands. "You are tired and weary. I won't keep you any longer. You must get some sleep. Tomorrow will be a wonderful day. You'll see!"

Emily smiled at her through her tears, not finding it in her heart to tell her the truth.

Fenn,

Forgive me for writing again when it is so clear you have forgotten me. Almost a month has passed; my previous letters must have reached you, and yet no reply.

But something terrible has happened, and I find myself with no choice but to seek your help. Our beloved Papa is gravely ill, and the new duke—heartless and cruel as he is—intends to cast us out of our home. He is wicked beyond measure, and we are utterly powerless against him.

Papa grows weaker with each passing day, and I fear he will not survive the shock of being turned out. We have nowhere to go, no means to protect ourselves. I wrote to the duke, pleading for mercy, begging for a meeting, but he ignored me entirely.

Oh, Fenn, if ever you cared for me, I beg you now—please help us. We are desperate beyond words, staring into a future on the streets with no hope in sight.

Yours in utter despair,
Emily

Chapter Twenty-Five

EMILY'S WEDDING DRESS WAS THE MOST BEAUTIFUL she'd ever worn: a white French gauze layered over satin, the hem decorated with a delicate flounce of Brussels lace, above a row of pale pink rosebuds with leaves. The same roses were woven into her hair, which for once cooperated. It was brushed up and curled beautifully over her forehead and sides of her face. The maid had to wield a sturdy papillote iron to create these curls. She was wearing fine silk stockings and slippers.

For once, Emily thought she actually looked pretty as she critically studied her reflection in the mirror. It was a shame to go through all that trouble for just a few hours. By midday at the latest, the charade would be over and she and Cissy would find themselves in the carriage home to Meadowview Cottage. Why didn't that thought fill her with the satisfaction she'd hoped for?

"You look lovely, Emmy," her sister said. "I would embrace you, but then it would ruin your outfit."

She looked lovely herself, like a ray of sunshine in yellow primrose silk.

The three aunts were waiting for her in the hall below.

Jane stepped forward and handed her a small bouquet of violets. "Here," she said gruffly. "Wolferton said they were your favourite."

Emily took the bouquet and buried her face in it. The sweet smell of the flowers brought tears to her eyes. "Thank you," she whispered.

"You'll do," Araminta proclaimed with a sniff. She was wearing a huge turban with a feather in it. "Now, let's proceed and get this thing done and over with. Afterwards, we will have all the time we need to admire each other's dresses." With those words, she ushered Emily and Cissy into the carriage that was waiting for them outside the townhouse.

St George's was rather gloomy inside, Emily thought. Perhaps it was because of the overcast, rainy weather, for there was no sunlight coming through the stained glass windows. The pews were made of heavy, dark wood and only a single chandelier was lit with candles.

Wolferton was already waiting by the altar, along with the priest and Lord Hamish.

No one else was there. She'd known it was going to be a quiet affair, but that not even Chippendale was to be there struck Emily as odd.

Somewhat unnerved, she walked down the aisle and looked questioningly at the Duke. Wasn't now the time for him to turn and make a speech, to apologise to his aunts and to call the game over?

But Wolferton returned her gaze solemnly and took her hand in his.

"Dearly beloved, we are gathered together here today in the sight of God and in the face of this congregation to join together this man and this woman in holy matrimony... "

Dear sweet heaven. The priest had actually started the ceremony. Now what? She shifted nervously and attempted to catch his eye, but Wolferton merely squeezed her hand.

Emily fidgeted, growing increasingly hot in her dress. Her fingers grew clammy and sweat pooled in her armpits. The priest talked and talked. "Do something," she mouthed voicelessly.

"Patience," he mouthed back.

Emily nearly huffed. Patience! The man was asking her to sit on tenterhooks and be patient? It was like having ants crawling all over one's body and not being allowed to brush them off.

Emily shifted again and saw that all three aunts had taken out their handkerchiefs and were dabbing at the corners of their eyes. Emily sighed. The leaden guilt weighed her down.

What they were doing simply wasn't right. To lead them on in this manner. To play this charade, only to interrupt it in the middle of the climax, to declare it a ruse and that they'd never had any real intention of getting married in the first place.

How cruel could one be?

Why had she ever agreed to this?

Emily was growing increasingly agitated. As if

sensing this, Wolferton moved closer to her, increasing the pressure of his hand as if to reassure her.

Much good that did. For now she felt his heat and his smell was in her nose, that bewitching smell of sandalwood and mint...

"If any man can show just cause why they may not lawfully be joined together, let him now speak, or else hereafter for ever hold his peace—"

"—Yes, I shall speak!" a male voice interrupted, his voice echoing in the church.

"Eh?" The priest squinted over his spectacles, evidently shocked.

Wolferton froze.

Emily gasped.

So this was what he had planned. Very clever of him.

"What is the meaning of this?" Araminta spoke up.

A gentleman emerged from behind a pillar and stepped into the aisle.

He was tall and lean and sombrely dressed, and there was something decidedly familiar about him.

"On what grounds do you have the temerity to interrupt this wedding?" Wolferton asked coldly.

Well done, Emily thought. He really was an excellent actor. The plan was splendid. A wedding interrupted by outside forces, and no one was to blame.

"On account of deception. You cannot possibly marry her. If you do, your marriage will be invalid. This woman is not who she claims to be. She is an impostor."

The word rang out loud and clear.

"What nonsense is this?" Jane cried, stepping in front of Emily as if to protect her.

The man walked down the aisle and stopped in front of her. "Allow me to introduce myself. I am Lord John Hepplewhite. This woman—" he pointed an accusing finger at Emily "—is a liar and an impostor. She has been living with my aunt for years, lying to her, deceiving her, taking advantage of her, pretending to be her niece."

A sickening feeling pooled in Emily's stomach.

Wolferton gripped her hand so tightly that he almost crushed her fingers. "Prove it." He said in a clipped voice.

"I have proof." Lord John curled his lips into a sneer. "Step forward."

Out of the shadows stepped an elderly man, leaning heavily on a stick.

Emily and Cissy gasped in unison.

"Who the devil is he?" Wolferton demanded.

"The name is Jim Campbell," the man said in a thick Scottish accent.

"Look at that woman," Lord John commanded.

The man leaned on his stick and scrunched up his eyes as he looked at her. "I am looking."

"Do you recognise her?"

"Aye. As clear as daylight, even though it's been several years." He weighed his head back and forth.

"Who is she?"

"That's Miss Eliza Starling, of course." His head bobbed up and down. "Lived with Lady MacGregor for nearly three years. And that over there is Miss Lavinia. How are you, Miss Lavinia? You're as pretty as ever."

"Jim," Emily whispered.

Lord John heard. He smiled, pleased. "You do recognise him, don't you? He was Lady MacGregor's butler."

"I don't understand," the priest interrupted. "So the bride was known by another name. What exactly are you saying?"

"I am saying that she is not Lady Poppy Featherstone, as she claims. She has many names. Eliza Starling was just one of them. I knew her as Lady Honey Hepple-white. God knows how many other names she's had." He waved a dismissive hand. "She is, as I said, an impostor."

"And?" the Duke's cool voice interrupted. "Bringing forth a man who claims to have known my bride under a different name is no proof of anything at all."

Lord John shrugged. "Then perhaps I should let her marry you. Don't you see I'm doing you a favour by preventing you from entering into an illegal union? She isn't Lady Poppy Featherstone."

They all spoke at the same time.

"Nonsense, there is nothing wrong, I tell you," Wolferton insisted.

Emily put a hand on his arm. Perhaps they should just let the charade end. She wished it hadn't been quite so dramatic. She looked around and saw only dismayed faces: Mabel looked pained, Jane shook her head and Araminta frowned. Cissy had her face buried in her hands. Was she crying?

Emily sighed. It was time to end this.

She smiled sadly at Wolferton, who continued to argue with Lord John. Then she cleared her throat. "If I could have your attention... "

But no one was listening, and everyone was talking at the same time. She looked around. There was a small handbell in the front pew, which must have been left there by mistake. She walked over to it, picked it up, and rang it. The clear, clean sound of the bell startled everyone and finally she had their attention.

"Thank you. Now. If you would allow me a word." She turned to the old man. "Jim Campbell. It is good to see you, and that you are still alive and well. He was indeed Lady MacGregor's butler. He was a good butler, and very loyal, and I believe he was as fond of us as we were of him." She stepped up to him and squeezed his gnarled hands. He looked up at her with watery eyes.

"God bless you, Miss Starling. I did. Happiest time of my life serving you and your sister and Lady MacGregor. Happiest time."

She gave him a wavering smile. "It is true that both my sister, and I lived with her as Lady MacGregor's granddaughters—under a different name."

Lord John nodded in satisfaction.

Wolferton scowled. "Now look here—"

Emily raised a hand. "Let me finish. Please." She turned back to the audience, who'd been listening intently. "It is true. We lived with Lady MacGregor under another name. It started as a simple mistake. She'd mistaken us for her granddaughters, who had died long ago. We thought it wouldn't hurt to make an old lady happy by keeping her company and pretending we were the girls she so longed for." Emily closed her eyes. "I tried to tell her the truth, but she refused to listen. She preferred the fantasy. So we lived with her. We had a home, and she had the family she so longed for." Emily's voice trembled. "We were heartbroken when she died, for we had grown to love her dearly. She died happy, thinking we were her girls."

"Aye, she did." Jim nodded. "She believed it to her dying breath. Not that it hurt anyone, I say."

"We didn't stay for the reading of the will; if she left us anything, we don't know, for we didn't take anything that wasn't ours when we met her. We never stole or took anything that wasn't given to us freely."

"That is not the point. The point is that you committed a crime by pretending to be someone you were not," Lord John argued. "According to English law, she committed fraud because her actions involved deliberate deception."

"That's debatable," intervened Wolferton. "This is more an ethical question than a legal one."

The priest shook his head. "But back to the point. If she was not Miss Eliza Starling, and if, as you claim, she is not Lady Poppy Featherstone,"—he turned to Emily— "then who are you?"

Emily opened her mouth. "I am… "

"This is all a farrago of nonsense, of course." The strong, iron voice rang through the church.

There was the sound of a stick slapping the marble, along with the rustling of silk. A lady in grey, stiffer than a pole of iron, with a nose sharper than a hawk's and eyes colder than slate, walked down the aisle with a swish, swish, swish. Next to her, holding her arm, was a smaller, lither lady who Emily recognised immediately.

"Aunt Henrietta!" she exclaimed.

The two women stopped at the front of the altar, ignoring everyone, the outbursts, the gasps, the exclamations. Both Emily and Cissy rushed forward to embrace Aunt Henrietta, who was visibly moved.

"Honey, child. Annabelle. I have missed you both. My girls."

The lady in grey standing beside her pulled out a quizzing glass and pointed it at Emily.

Ignoring everyone, the lady stepped up to Emily, took her chin in her gnarled hand, and lifted it. Her iron eyes bored into Emily's skull. She felt dizzy.

Behind her was none other than Chippendale, who, quite unlike his usual mincing self, rushed forward and wiped his brow. "I apologise. It took me a devil of a time to find her, but I finally did." He looked around. "Did I miss anything?"

"Well, thank heavens," Wolferton grumbled. "You certainly took your time to get here."

The woman in grey lifted her cane and slammed it back to the ground, making an impressive sound. Everyone stopped talking immediately.

"Lord John." Wolferton turned to the man whose eyes were popping out of his head. "Please introduce these ladies to the rest of us."

Lord John wilted visibly. "This is my Aunt, Lady Henrietta Hepplewhite." He gestured at the smaller lady. Then he made a helpless gesture toward the lady in grey. "Her Grace, the Dowager Duchess of Strathmore." He cleared his throat. "My grandmother. Why are you here, grandmamma?"

"To tell you that you are undoubtedly a fool, unworthy to bear the name of Hepplewhite." She gave him a withering look.

"But... "

"Your Grace." The priest bowed so low that his wig almost flew off. "Can you clear up this confusion?"

"There is no confusion. You are all acting like buffoons. Everything is as clear as crystal when you have eyes on your face. This—" she gestured to Emily. "Is Lady Emily Hepplewhite. She has been called Emily White all her life. Whatever other names she has adopted —Poppy, Honey, Lily, whatever other flower name—it matters not. She is of good stock, the very best. She is the daughter of an earl, my own dear son, Edmund."

"So you're saying, you're saying... " Lord John's eyes almost popped out of his face.

"I am saying, foolish boy, that this is your cousin. You share the same blood. This is your Uncle Edmund's girl." Her face softened as she turned back to Emily. "My granddaughter."

Chapter Twenty-Six

EMILY'S LEGS BUCKLED BENEATH HER. IF Wolferton hadn't reacted quickly and caught her, she would have ended up on the cold marble floor.

"Uncle Edmund's daughter?" Lord John's legs buckled as well, and he sat down on the marble steps in front of the altar.

"Lord Adam Edmund Hepplewhite, Earl of Witley. Better known as Mr Edmund White, schoolmaster of Ashbourne Village." Her voice sounded bitter. Then she saw Cissy staring at her, mouth agape. "You must be Cecilia." She walked over to Cissy and lifted her chin in the same way she had lifted Emily's. "You have your mother's beauty. I only saw her once, from a distance, and she was unaware that I was watching her."

"You really are our grandmother?" Cissy breathed.

"I am. And if I had had my way, you would have grown up at Strathmore Hall, but your father, who no doubt inherited the legendary stubbornness of the Hepplewhites, would not have it. You see, when he

313

eloped and married your mother, the daughter of a schoolmaster, so far below his station, he had a bitter quarrel with your grandfather. And with myself too, I must admit. For I was as opposed to the union as my husband. But Edmund was in love." She sighed. "And so he broke with us and all that was connected with his old life and began a new one with his Francesca. We knew of your existence, of course, but Edmund insisted on living a separate life, as if to prove that he could do it, to live from hand to mouth." She sniffed contemptuously. "As if it were possible for one to ever forget one's heritage. He died foolishly, needlessly and in poverty, believing he'd done the right thing." Her shoulders slumped. "We lost sight of you for a time. You disappeared. Turned up again under different names several years later. Disappeared again. How excessively tiresome, I must say! Then this dandy—" she nodded at Chippendale, who was tugging at his cravat "—turned up out of the blue, claiming to know the whereabouts of Edmund's children." She glared at them.

"But Grandmama—" Lord John had regained his voice. "What if they're pulling the wool over your eyes like they did with the other ladies? Old ladies are their speciality. First there was Lady MacGregor, then poor Aunt Henrietta. There are others. You are falling prey to their deception."

"Pah." The Dowager Duchess shook her head. "I told you you were a fool. The girls were homeless on the streets after that idiot of a duke accidentally evicted them." She glared at Wolferton, who flushed. "Who do you think sent Henrietta to them?"

Emily and Cissy gasped at the same time. "Are you saying it wasn't a coincidence that Aunt Henrietta approached us in Bath?"

"Of course not." She sniffed. "It took us a while to discover that you'd found refuge with Lady MacGregor." She nodded at the butler. "After she died, you travelled to Bath. This is where Henrietta finally found you. The idea was for you to stay with her, not run off again. If you hadn't chased them away—" she turned to Lord John, whose mouth had gone slack "—they would have been with me at Strathmore Hall by now instead of being involved in this fiasco here." She slammed her cane down for emphasis.

"How did Chippendale know about all this?" enquired Aunt Araminta.

Chippendale adjusted his cravat. "Wolferton sent me to Strathmore Hall with the mission to fetch Her Grace post haste."

"And how did Wolferton know that Her Grace was their grandmother?"

"I have an exceptionally talented secretary who used to work at Bow Street before I took him on," Wolferton explained. "He uncovered the true identities of Lady Emily and Lady Cecily. I sent Chippendale to fetch Her Grace, although he took his dear sweet time."

Chippendale made an apologetic face. "I'm sorry, but my carriage lost a wheel on the way and it took me longer than I expected to reach Strathmore Hall."

"I was never so relieved as when that boy contacted me. Well?" She looked at Wolferton.

"Well what, Your Grace?" Wolferton inquired.

"Are you going to marry her or not? I have come for a wedding." The Dowager Duchess rammed her cane into the ground for emphasis.

"Certainly. A wedding you shall have," Wolferton replied promptly. "If the priest agrees that all ambiguities have been cleared up, and all identities confirmed?" He raised an eyebrow at the priest, who had removed his wig to wipe his bald forehead. He put the wig back on and cleared his throat.

"As far as I am concerned, everything is clear, and there were no issues to begin with." He pulled out a piece of paper and studied it. "Since the special license was issued for the Duke of Wolferton and Lady Emily Hepplewhite from the start." He pointed at the name. "I was wondering earlier why everyone insisted on addressing the bride as Poppy Featherstone."

Emily gasped and turned to the Duke. "You already knew when you obtained the license?"

Wolferton shrugged. "I don't leave these things to chance. Besides, as already stated, I have an efficient secretary."

"If, furthermore," the priest continued, "Her Grace, the Dowager Duchess, vouches for the lady's identity, then I see no reason for any obstacle to this marriage, as her word is sufficient to resolve any doubt in the matter."

"She is my granddaughter, Lady Emily Hepplewhite, as stated on the license," the Dowager said. "Proceed without further delay."

"Excellent." Wolferton clasped Emily's hand tightly. "Shall we?"

Emily hesitated.

His eyes bored into hers. "It is your decision alone," he murmured in her ear. "Say the word and I will have you out of here." She looked at him silently, her eyes widened slightly. "But if you remain silent... " he drew in a long breath. "If you remain silent, I will take it that you consent and we will be married, you and I. For real."

Emily opened and closed her mouth like a fish, unable to speak at all.

All she knew was that there was him, there was her, and the rest of the world fell away, her heart beating wildly as she drowned in his eyes.

She must have done something. Maybe she'd nodded. Maybe she'd even said yes. She could barely remember what she had done.

All she knew was that the look of tension and strain left his eyes and he looked immeasurably relieved and he pulled her forward to the priest and then, and then... and then...

... They were married.

EVERYTHING UNFOLDED LIKE A DREAM.

The priest's voice was a distant murmur, barely audible in her ears. The clapping sounded far away, muffled and unreal, as if it belonged to someone else's celebration. She felt arms around her, hands guiding her forward, but the sensations were faint, like echoes in a mist. There was a ring on her finger now. And through it all, Wolferton never let go of her hand—not for a moment.

He led her forward to the table in the vestry, where the register awaited.

Dazed, she took the quill and signed her name.

Dazed, she passed it to Chippendale, who signed as the first witness. Then to the Dowager Duchess, who signed as the second witness.

It was only when the quill returned to its place and her eyes fell on the open register that the haze lifted. Her eyes focused on the writing under the heading 'Groom':

His Grace Jasper Fennimore George Sinclair, Duke of Wolferton.

The world tilted. Blood roared in her ears as her eyes fell to his signature below.

Wolferton.

He had signed his name in a hand she knew only too well. The W, with its three loops, was unmistakable. The same flourish she had seen at the beginning of every letter she had ever received from Fenn.

My dear Little Wren, he'd started every single one of his letters, the W decorated with the same intricate loops.

Little stars danced at the edges of her vision.

Slowly, she looked up into his questioning eyes.

"What is it?"

"I knew it." She clenched her hands into fists. "I knew it!" She turned to him with an accusing look. "I knew it all along, except I simply didn't want to believe it. I couldn't believe it."

"Believe what, my love?" His voice was strangely soft. His hand was on the small of her back, trying to guide her, but she shook it away.

Something inside Emily snapped. With the mewling

sound of an angry kitten, she threw herself at him, hammering her fists into his chest.

"You never came!" she howled. "I waited and waited and waited and you never—you neh-ever came." She kept hammering, but her blows turned into feeble flaps, and then she burst into tears.

He caught her up to him and cradled her close.

"You never came," Emily sobbed. Somehow, it was the only sentence she could get out. Somehow, it was important that he understood that.

"I know. I am sorry. I am so sorry. I am so, so sorry." He repeated it over and over, murmuring it into her hair, into her ear.

"You forgot me."

"I never did. Not for a minute. Not for a second. I swear it on my life." His embrace tightened around her. "I could never forget my little Wren."

The words brought a fresh flood of tears.

"Good heavens, what can be the matter now?" Poor Aunt Araminta cried. "I'm not sure my nerves can take much more of this."

"Not a minute married and they are already quarrelling," said Chippendale with a grin. "No, leave them alone." He held back Cissy, who'd jumped up in alarm to rescue her sister. "How about we take a turn outside? The weather is rather good. Even if it is raining. And cold. And windy." He showed his arm to Cissy, who took one last doubtful look at her sister, then decided she was well looked after and left with Chippendale.

"The knot is tied, and that is good," the Dowager Duchess said with a sniff. "It's just bridal nerves."

"We were supposed to elope." Emily's nose was pressed into his cravat and she was almost unintelligible. "We were supposed to elope to Gretna Green."

"Yes, we were, weren't we?" Wolferton replied patiently. "But life intervened. And now we are married. Finally. Ten years overdue but, by God, it's finally done. I never thought I'd see the day."

The priest cleared his throat. "If you would like us to leave to have more privacy... "

"We will leave. Emily. Let's continue this discussion at home. We have guests. Your grandmother has come all the way from Strathmore Hall. We're all hungry and upset. It's been a difficult morning. Let's go home and afterwards you can berate me and throw a vase at me for having been devious and deceitful."

"An excellent idea," said the Dowager Duchess with a sniff.

Against all odds, the wedding breakfast proved to be a lively affair.

Chippendale joked with Cissy, who giggled incessantly.

The Dowager Duchess glared at everyone, but then found a kindred spirit in Araminta when it was revealed that both ladies were passionate collectors of Meissen porcelain figurines— colourful, dainty little figurines of shepherdesses in eighteenth-century dresses with wigs. Both ladies sat apart in a corner, describing their treasures to each other in minute detail.

Lord John Hepplewhite had risen stiffly, approached Emily, bowed formally and apologised to her.

"Grandmamma was right when she said I was a prize fool," he said contritely.

Emily, tired and overwhelmed, waved him away. "For heaven's sake, John. Let's not talk about this anymore. Instead, tell me about the rest of our family. How many aunts and uncles and cousins have we got? I am looking forward to having a real family, and I confess I'm glad to have you as a cousin. I'd rather we were friends, you and I." She held out her hand, which he eagerly took.

Then he, too, loosened up a bit and told her all about their extensive family.

Even old Jim was invited to the party, although he insisted on helping the butler serve them. "Once a butler, always a butler," he announced. "I will not overstep and will celebrate with the other servants below stairs."

Emily had not had the opportunity to exchange a single word with Fenn, or Wolferton, or Jasper? She had no idea what to call him. Both of their attentions were demanded by the guests. She couldn't remember what they had said or what she had eaten. All she knew was that there was an atmosphere of general gaiety and relief, with everyone talking at once, and even the Dowager Duchess deigning to smile once or twice at a joke made by Chippendale.

Emily could hardly believe that she had a grand-mother now.

Or a cousin.

Or that Aunt Henrietta was really her aunt. "I'm so sorry for everything," Emily whispered, but Aunt Henrietta brushed it away.

"I will expect you to visit me after you return from

your wedding tour," she said, tugging at Emily's shawl and adjusting a ribbon in her hair. "I can't tell you how much I've missed you both. There is much to discuss. But we'll do that when you're settled into your married life. I look forward to your visits, and to visiting you. And to a house full of children." She nodded to Wolferton, who grinned.

Emily blushed.

Cissy took her in her arms and hugged her tightly. "I'm so glad it turned out the way it did. Isn't it a miracle? We have a family and cousins and friends to wish us well. Emily! We have a home now. I can go live with Aunt Henrietta again, for she told me she'd dearly love to have me, or with grandmamma, even though she frightens me a little, or, if you don't mind, with you... "

"And there's Meadowview Cottage," Emily chimed in.

"Which is being restored," Wolferton interjected. "It won't be ready for you to live in until it's finished."

From then on, everything happened with whirlwind speed. She changed into her travelling clothes and they set off on their wedding tour to the well wishes of family and guests. Truth be told, Emily hadn't paid too much attention to these plans, thinking they would never come to pass. All she could remember was that they were to return to Ashbourne House and from there, they would visit all the Duke's estates.

"I can't believe we're actually married," she burst out as they sat in the carriage, the doors slamming shut and the carriage moving. "I can't believe you're Fenn. I can't believe any of this. Is it a dream? No, you must have planned everything from the beginning."

He sat back and studied at her solemnly. "You look more than exhausted. Why don't you try to get some sleep, and I promise we'll discuss everything when we get to Ashbourne House."

Her hand groped for his. Emily thought it would be impossible for her to sleep, but before she knew it, her eyes closed and when she awoke, she found her head cushioned against his shoulder. She sat up, disoriented, and arranged her hair.

"We have arrived," he said as the carriage pulled into the splendid drive of Ashbourne House, where the servants were lined up at the entrance to greet them.

My Little Wren,

  My Emily,

  My Love,

Ten years have passed, and after all this time, I find myself writing to you once more.

My secretary discovered your last three letters tucked into Jago's accounting book. It seems they were intercepted by his order—on my father's command. Emily, I cannot begin to express my anguish at reading them now, so late. No wonder you believed I had forgotten you, betrayed you. No wonder you turned your heart against me.

There are no words that can undo the pain I have caused. None that can make right the wrongs of my silence or the long years of separation. I have debated endlessly whether to confront you, to tell you everything face to face, to draw you into my arms and kiss you senseless until you understand the full truth of the situation, but then you were so determined to despise me—with full reason.

How can I reveal my heart when you might hate me still? How can I convince you of my feelings when you see only the façade, not the man beneath? I have tried, so many times, to summon the courage to speak. Yesterday in the library, when I suggested we get betrothed—to me it was never a ruse—I was on the verge of confessing it all, but the weight of my mistakes—my cowardice—held me back.

So many mistakes, Emily. So much regret.

Can you ever forgive me? Truly and with all your heart and soul? I convinced myself you needed more time, yet time has only deepened the chasm between us. The longer I wait, the more tangled this web becomes.

Please, believe me when I say this: through all these long and lonely years, my heart has been yours and yours alone. I have longed for you every day. And now that I have found you, I swear I will never let you go again.

We are leaving for London tomorrow. You might not see this before we leave. But this time, Emily, I shall tell you everything in person. No more letters, no more half-truths. Only the truth, laid bare.

Yours ever lovingly,

Fenn

Jasper Fennimore Sinclair

Duke of Wolferton

Chapter Twenty-Seven

It was strange to arrive at Ashbourne House not as a guest, but as a duchess. She greeted the servants with an embarrassed smile, and Mrs Smith stepped forward and said, "On behalf of all the staff, may I congratulate you on your marriage? We could not be happier with our new duchess." There was a gleam of warmth in her eyes, and Emily knew she was speaking the truth.

Mrs Smith had prepared a warm, fire-lit suite in the smaller drawing room for their comfort.

Emily was warming her hands by the fire when the secretary entered, seeking the Duke's attention on a matter of some urgency.

"You'll have to excuse me, Emily," Wolferton said with a frown. "Just for an hour, yes? Then I am all yours. Then we will talk."

Emily waved him away. "Do what you have to do, of course, and forget about me."

She decided to go for a walk instead, for the sun had not yet set and she longed for some fresh air.

Emily's feet took her straight to her tree. Much to her surprise, she found the pile of stones stacked in front of it —and at the very top a single black stone, which had always been a sign that a message from Fenn was waiting for her.

She reached into the hole and, yes! Between her fingers was a folded piece of paper.

A letter from Fenn.

The first in ten years.

My Little Wren,
My Emily,
My Love,
Ten years have passed, and after all this time, I find myself
writing to you once more...

Emily's breath shook as she read the letter. He must have written and deposited the letter the day after he made the fake proposal in the library.

He'd never intended it to be fake.

He'd never ceased to love her.

Her mind in a whirl, she turned and ran back to the house.

They had eaten and talked politely about nothing of substance.

Their conversation was stilted, and Emily racked her brain for a way to turn it to the subject of the letters.

Her nerves were on edge and she pushed the glass of

syllabub away. It was too sweet, and her stomach clenched. "No more of this. Let us finally talk."

He nodded and rose. "Come with me."

He took her hand and led her into his study. He went to the desk and took out a mahogany box from the drawer. With his other hand, he took Emily's and pulled her towards the sofa. "Sit."

As she sat down, he opened the box and poured the contents into her lap.

Emily gasped.

Letters.

Hundreds of them.

She recognised the childish, scrawled handwriting at once.

They were letters to Fenn—written by her.

Dear Forest Fay, will you grant me one wish...

"This is the first one," she murmured, picking up the letter. "I wrote it right after Mama died. And you wrote back that you couldn't bring back the dead." She rubbed her forehead. "I must admit, I was rather disappointed. What kind of forest fay is incapable of bringing back the dead?"

He chuckled. "Your expectations of what a forest fay should be able to do were a bit too high." He picked up the letter. "Yet I knew how you felt, for my own mother had died that summer. So I knew exactly what you'd been through."

Emily pulled out the letter from the tree, which she had tucked up in her sleeve.

She met his gaze. "I want you to explain this."

"So you found it." He smiled slightly. "I wondered

how long it would take you. After we left for London, I feared you never would."

"Tell me," Emily insisted. "Tell me everything."

He stared thoughtfully into the fire. "Where shall I begin? From when we met at the inn?"

"Before that," she insisted. "I want to hear your whole story." She thought for a moment. "From the moment you were born."

He nodded. "The very beginning. Very well, then. My parents' union was arranged, like so many in our class. It was ill-fated. My father was cold and distant, and my mother was a romantic. They had nothing in common. I have no idea how they managed to create me, but well, by some miracle, here I am." He shrugged. "No wonder I had no siblings, no matter how much I wished for some. After my birth, my mother declared that her duty was done, and my parents agreed to live in separate homes. I lived with Mama at Hollyton Hall, whereas my father lived at Wolferstone Abbey.

"We will have to visit both estates later, by the way, but of all the houses, Wolferstone Abbey is the one I like the least." He pulled a face. "I grew up without ever seeing my father. I never missed him. I didn't even know what he looked like. I had my mother and my three aunts, and that was all the family I needed. After Mama died, I became restless, especially during the summer. I visited Ashbourne House. These were rare visits, however; with reduced staff. No one knew when I was there and everyone assumed the house was deserted. I preferred it that way. I preferred the quiet, simple life away from society. That was possible at

Ashbourne House, which everyone believed to be uninhabited."

Emily nodded. The secret had been well kept, for no one in the village had even suspected that the duke's son had visited over the summer.

"I was terribly lonely. I took walks in the woods, and on one of those outings I saw a little fairy flit through the forest, barefoot and with twigs and leaves in her hair. I thought I was dreaming. I followed you to that clearing where you put something in the hole in the tree. You walked away, and I was too curious not to check what you had left there." He pointed to the letter she was still holding. "And so it began. We corresponded almost every day that first summer. Then I had to return to Eton. I had to have Jack, one of the stable boys I trusted, pick up and deliver my letters."

She took a sharp breath. "So that's why it took so long to reply outside the summer months."

He nodded. "The following summer I returned, and I was able to leave the letters there myself."

"I wanted so much to meet you, but you never did."

"It was partly impossible because I was not there, you see, and partly because I preferred to keep the mystery of who I really was. If you had discovered that I was the duke's son, how would you have reacted?"

"I would have become self-conscious and awkward with false reverence."

He nodded. "That is what I thought. So I preferred to keep our friendship on paper at first. I preferred to keep my identity a secret. But Emily, my Little Wren, you have no idea how much those letters meant to me then.

How much joy they brought into the life of the lonely boy I was, especially after Mama died."

She hadn't known, of course. "And then? What happened?" she whispered.

"And then… " He took her hand, his thumb tracing gentle circles over her fingers. "You know what happened. We grew up, and this friendship on paper wasn't enough anymore. You'd stolen my heart, my mind, my soul. You were all I thought about, day and night. I started dreaming of a way we could be together."

Emily blinked, her lips parting as he continued.

"The only solution I could think of," he said quietly, "was for us to elope."

Emily tilted her head. "You knew I was a schoolmaster's daughter—far beneath you socially—yet you wanted to marry me?"

"I didn't care about duty or expectations. I had it all planned. We'd get married in Scotland and live at Ashbourne House. My father wouldn't even notice. By the time he realised what had happened, we'd be long married. That was my plan."

Emily's voice trailed off, her words flat. "Except… that day, you never came." She'd waited by the tree all day, well into the night. She'd returned the next day, and the next… In vain.

He exhaled heavily, his eyes dropping. "No. I didn't come. My father intervened, of course. The steward, Jago again, had got wind of our correspondence, and he'd forced Jack, who delivered the letters, to give them to him first. When he read of our plans to elope, Jago acted in my father's name. The night before we were to meet, he had three footmen grab me and bundle me into a carriage without explanation. They took me to Wolferstone Abbey. Finally, after all these years, I met my father, and it wasn't pleasant. My father had an explosion of fury that was unprecedented, as the servants later told me. He forbade me to see you again. He could not and would not allow his only son, his heir, to make a misalliance and marry someone he considered socially inferior. I refused and marched out of the house, intending to catch the next mail coach back to Ashbourne House. If the worst came to the worst, I'd walk back. I hadn't even reached the gates of the estate when a footman caught up with me and told me that my father had had an apoplexy. He'd fallen over—and died. Just like that." He pulled his lips into a sneer. "So you see, I not only killed your father, but mine, too."

She shook her head. "Nonsense." Grasping his arm, she gave it a firm shake. "I'm sorry I ever said that. It was a cruel thing to say. Don't ever say it again. But your father... " Her shoulders sagged. "Trust him to die, just to spite you, at that very moment. I don't know why it never occurred to me that, of course, something serious must have happened to keep you from coming. I was too engrossed in my own worries. I was ready to believe the worst, that you'd trifled with me or changed your mind." Her voice broke as she looked at him. "Fenn, I waited by the tree for hours. But you know what? I wasn't planning to elope with you. I was waiting to tell you that as much as I loved you, I couldn't leave. I couldn't leave Cissy and Papa. I just couldn't."

His eyes softened. "Of course you couldn't. You'd

never leave those you love. I'd come up with an alternative plan, one where we'd take them with us. All the
plans I'd made... " He shook his head.

Emily smiled through her tears as her heart twisted
with a bittersweet pain.

"Not that it matters." He brushed it off with a bitter
laugh. "Because even as a duke, I had as much power as
an earthworm. In the days that followed, I couldn't even
get a message to you. It wasn't until much later that I
discovered the truth."

Her brow furrowed. "The truth?"

"My father had intervened again while I was at
Wolferstone Abbey."

Her head snapped up. "Your father? But he was
dead!"

He nodded gravely. "Yes. Not only did he intercept
our letters, piece together our plans, but he also ordered
Jago to have your family evicted. It was his last act."

Emily let out a shaky breath.

Jasper stood and took another bag and placed it in her
lap.

There were dozens of letters.

Emily looked at him with wide eyes.

"These letters are the ones I sent, but you never
received. They were never delivered because, of course,
you were long gone and I did not know." He ran a hand
through his hair. "I couldn't get away from the deluge of
duties and obligations. I was imprisoned here by lawyers,
secretaries, and piles and piles of work. I kept writing
letters, not knowing that they never arrived. When I
returned to the Ashbourne Estate several weeks later,

your cottage was deserted. I did not suspect the steward then. I thought he was loyal to me. He said you'd left, that your father wanted to return to his family in the north. No one in the village dared tell me the truth because the steward had threatened them all with eviction if they did. I searched for you, but couldn't find a trace. You'd just disappeared, from one day to the next.

"It was the darkest time of my life. I didn't know who to trust. Everyone seemed to be taking advantage of me. I wasn't prepared for the responsibilities that were thrust upon me, and I had no idea what I was doing. I lived in constant fear of making a mistake." He paused, his voice tightening. "And I grieved for you. I couldn't understand why you'd left without a word, without even saying goodbye."

A cold, haunted look crossed his face.

Emily raised her hand to his cheek, and he kissed her palm.

"In my darkest moments," he continued, "I even wondered if it had all been one-sided. Maybe you'd never really loved me. Or if you did, maybe it wasn't as much as I loved you. I told myself it was for the best that it had ended this way. Because what was it, really? A strange friendship based on letters? I told myself I was a fool for seeing more in it than there was."

Emily's heart tightened. She shook her head, her voice thick with emotion. "Never," she whispered. "Never."

He rubbed his forehead with one hand, as if the memory itself pained him. "I had to bury all those feelings. I was overwhelmed with work, and the endless duties and social obligations left me no time to breathe. I was surrounded by people I thought I could trust, but they turned out to be toad-eaters. Friends turned out to be false, and servants I thought loyal turned out to be corrupt. I forced myself to forget you, and for a time I was even proud that I had succeeded."

He exhaled heavily, the weight of the past pressing down on him. "Then my secretary discovered irregularities in the accounts and revealed that Jago was behind it all. By the time we put it all together, he was long gone —sailing for the New World with the wealth he'd stolen. It was around that time that I learned of the eviction."

His hand found hers, his grip firm yet pleading. "Emily, I was horrified. Desperate. I sent runners to look for you. But it was as if the earth had swallowed you whole. There was no trace of you or your family.

"You couldn't have known that we'd changed our names and been taken in by Lady MacGregor in Scotland," Emily said quietly.

"No," he murmured. "But thank heavens you were looked after, even though... " His voice broke slightly. "Even though your father did not survive that night. I will never forgive myself for that."

Emily squeezed his hand. "But I did, Fenn," she said, her voice steady though her eyes glistened. "I survived. So did Cissy. I have forgiven you. So has Cissy. You must forgive yourself, too."

He bent his head and Emily put a hand on his thick hair, and he reached out and pulled her to him until she was sitting on his lap.

"Tell me what happened next," Emily said after a while, burying her face in his neckcloth.

He looked up, a faint, tired smile on his face. "My aunts decided they'd had enough of watching me run myself into the ground and insisted on marrying me off. I decided to humour them, go to Ashbourne House, meet the ladies they'd invited, dance with one or two and then discreetly remove myself. When we stopped at the inn to change horses, an impertinent maid mistook me for the coachman and scolded me for deliberately driving my horses through the puddle to splash her. She was covered in mud, her hair blowing in the wind, and she was the most beautiful sight I'd seen in a long, long time. When she started to sing a song I thought I'd forgotten, I couldn't believe my ears. I thought it must be a coincidence. Surely the song was well known in the area. But I knew that voice. The longer I talked to you, and the more I looked at you, the more convinced I became that you were my Little Wren. But I had to be sure."

"So you arranged for us to be invited to Ashbourne House," Emily said. "And here I thought I had orchestrated it so cleverly that we were invited to the house party."

He chuckled. "You had mistaken Chippendale for the duke and me for the coachman, which I found amusing, and so I decided to use the mix-up to see if I could get more information out of you, more proof of who you really were, if you were really my Wren. But I was already certain of your identity after our first meeting."

Emily smiled as she remembered that meeting. "I was so angry with you. I thought you were a cheeky coachman trying to take advantage of me and then black-mail me by threatening to expose me."

"That never occurred to me, but after you mentioned it, I thought maybe it wasn't such a bad idea if it meant I could see more of you."

He pressed his lips into her hair for a quick kiss. "I wanted to tell you who I was. But then you told me about your father, and it became clear that you hated me to the core. I did not know what to do. I was entirely confused. It was torture to have you so close yet be unable to tell you who I really was. I confess, at first I was simply too cowardly to do so."

"Yet, later, you denied it. When I asked you directly. When I asked you if you were Fenn, you said you were not. Why?"

He rubbed his brow wearily. "That was because I suspected you'd idealised Fenn in the same way you'd demonised the duke. I was afraid you'd be disappointed when you realised who I really was, that I was nothing like you'd imagined. You'd created an image of Fenn in your mind that never existed. Fenn seemed to be all that was good, pure, wonderful in your life. And Wolferton, the duke, was demonic and evil. Don't you see? I'm neither."

Emily worried at her lower lip. He might have a point.

"I lied because I was afraid. Afraid that if you knew the truth—that I was Fenn, that I'm the duke who wronged you—you'd hate me even more. I couldn't bear that." His eyes were troubled. "I didn't tell you because I needed to know if you could care for me, the man standing before you now, not the memory of a boy who existed in your letters. I feared I could never measure up to the Fenn I'd created on paper." He pulled a frustrated hand through his hair. "Dash it all. I'm not good at this. I'm not good at talking about my feelings. I just wanted to know whether you could learn to care about me as I am right now. Right here. I'm just a flawed man who loves you. That is partly why I preferred to keep our relationship on paper, and why I have kept up the pretense as long as I have. I'm an intolerable coward. It just seemed safer that way."

"Fenn," Emily whispered, tears entering her eyes.

He shook his head. "Fenn is what my mother called me. Everyone else called me Jasper, or just Wolferton. I'm not a good man. I have learned to be ruthless to get what I want. I wanted you, so I did it. I'm well aware that I tricked you into this marriage. I won't apologise for that. It was all planned. If you find that you cannot bear this union, then I will not force you to live with me."

"Fenn," Emily said sharply. "You're such a fool."

The ghost of a smile crossed his face. "That too."

"You're talking nonsense. First of all, you did not trick me into this marriage. If I hadn't wanted to marry you, I wouldn't have done it. In the end, it was my choice to go ahead with it. I could have just taken Cissy by the hand and walked out, and by now we'd be living under a different name with someone else. Give me some agency. Secondly, although you'd denied it so vehemently that afternoon, I only believed it for a moment. I knew you were Fenn, deep down, even though I didn't see the proof until I finally saw your signature on the marriage register." She made a loop with one hand. "The W gave it away. If you hadn't dragged me to the altar, I would have dragged you there. Duke or not, you've owed me a marriage since I was seventeen, and I would have hounded you and held you to that promise." She thought for a moment, her lips quirking upwards. "Although I must add that it's a nice touch that you turned out to be a wealthy duke and not a poor blacksmith. Though Meadowview Cottage is lovely and will always be the home of my childhood, I find it infinitely preferable to live here. It's a bit bigger and more comfortable, you see."

His fingers tightened around her waist.

"As for me idealising Fenn," Emily continued, "I suppose you're right. I suppose you really aren't the wonderful, delightful boy I imagined you to be. Kind and generous to a fault. Sweet and kind and sensitive." She shook her head sadly. "How cruelly you've deceived me."

He shifted uncomfortably.

She placed one hand on his cheek. "The Duke of Wolferton is hard, cynical, ruthless, and infuriating. He is most off-putting." Then she placed her other hand on his opposite cheek, framing his face, and stared at him intently. "Until one realises it's the outer shell. The sad truth, I'm afraid, is that you're an onion."

He blinked. "An onion? You mean I make you cry?"

"That too. I mean the layers. You've obviously never peeled an onion in your life, have you, Your Grace? It has layers and layers, one on top of the other. Until you get to the core." She smiled. "And the core is sweet. Shocking, isn't it? Wolferton and sweet. It seems such a paradox. But there it is."

"Are you saying you don't mind being married to me? That you love me back, just a little? You never answered my letter." There was a catch in his voice.

"What a fool you are, Fenn. You have confused me so. First, I loved Fenn, a sad, innocent, hopeless kind of love. Then I fell head over heels in love with that scallywag George. How could it be that all you had to do was drench me in mud and I would fall in love? And then the scowling Wolferton began to make all these demands on my heart. He made me want to kiss off that frown between his eyebrows, like this,"—she pressed her lips to his frown—"ever since he first entered the drawing-room. Oh, to confuse me so! I haven't stopped loving you in all these incarnations." She planted a second kiss on the tip of his nose. "Not for a minute."

She drew his face down further and finally, finally, kissed him fully on the lips.

Epilogue

IT WAS SUMMER AT ASHBOURNE HOUSE, AND THE Duke and his family were having tea on the veranda. Baby Edmund, named after Emily's father, was cranky and weepy and would not go to sleep.

"What's the matter, little prince?" Emily took him from the nurse's arms and rocked him gently, but not even her singing of his favourite lullaby would do the trick.

"Maybe he's teething," Aunt Mabel suggested.

"Maybe we need to change his napkins," Araminta diagnosed.

"I just changed him," Jane protested. "It's not that. Maybe he has gas. Maybe he needs to be burped more."

"He just burped," Emily said. "Didn't you hear? It was louder than an old drunkard's." Emily shook her head over the noises her little son was capable of producing. "Here, Mabel, you take him. You usually have a calming effect on him." She placed him in Mabel's arms.

And, lo-and-behold, the baby calmed down immediately and smiled into his great-aunt's face. She rocked him gently in her arms. "Leave him with me, Emily, and you enjoy your tea."

As soon as Emily raised her cup, the butler appeared, holding a silver salver. "The mail, Your Grace."

Emily picked up a letter. "It's from Cissy." She turned it over in her hands, frowning. "Why isn't she here yet? Why is she sending letters instead?"

She opened it and read it, inhaling sharply.

"What is it, Emily?" Araminta inquired.

Emily started to laugh. She laughed so hard that tears streamed down her face. She wiped them away with a handkerchief.

"I'm glad you're enjoying yourself, but it would be nice to share the joke," Araminta said.

"It's just that Cissy wrote—she's in Scotland." Emily laughed again.

"I don't understand. Scotland? What is she doing there? Shouldn't she be here now for tea?" Araminta inquired.

"It appears she has eloped."

There was a puzzled silence. Then, "She has eloped?" the three aunts said in unison.

"But, my dear. With whom?" exclaimed Aunt Jane.

"That is the point. After all my efforts to set her up with Chippendale—what better, more eligible man could there be for Cissy? She decided to elope with Mr Matthews."

"Matthews. Matthews." Araminta tasted the name on her lips. "The name doesn't ring a bell."

"Oh. I know who he is," Mabel interjected. "Is he the

sad-looking man who waited for hours on end at the door of our London townhouse last season?"

"No. Was he?" Emily's eyes widened. "I did not know! I thought he called once, but that was it."

"No, no. I saw him waiting several times. The butler kept insisting that Lady Lydia—that's what she called herself then, if you remember—so he kept saying that Lady Lydia wasn't available. And this man, this Matthews, kept insisting that he be allowed to see her. But she turned him away every time. I felt quite sorry for the man."

"How intriguing! And now they have eloped? But how?" Jane asked. "I thought she didn't like the man."

"It's true," Emily said. "Matthews had courted her in Bath and she'd been very much in love with him. Then he left suddenly. The excuse he gave, Cissy told me later, was that he'd had a family emergency and had to leave abruptly, though why he couldn't have told her that or written to her, neither she nor I understood. It broke her heart. So when he turned up unexpectedly last winter, she was quite angry with him and found it hard to forgive him. I thought that was the end of it and kept pushing Chippendale towards her. But she must have forgiven Matthews in the end. She wrote in her letter that they began to correspond in secret—how shockingly improper! —and one thing led to another and... " Emily waved her hand.

"But why did they have to elope? It wasn't as if anyone would have objected to the union," Mabel said.

"Wolferton might have. I remember he wasn't too fond of the man when they met at the Royal Menagerie,"

Emily guessed. "Where is he, anyway? The tea is getting cold."

"I haven't seen him this entire afternoon. I think he's locked himself in with his secretary again. The man works far too much." Araminta sniffed.

Baby Edmund had fallen asleep on his aunt's arm. "Leave him with me," Mabel told Emily as she went to relieve her of him. "He'll wake up when we move him. Why don't you rest, Emily? You look pale and tired, and I'll watch him until he wakes up."

Emily decided to take a short walk through the park instead. She wandered through the trees, enjoying the autumn foliage and marvelling at how beautiful the forest was.

She walked to a clearing where her oak tree stood, and, after a moment's hesitation, she reached inside and pulled out a letter.

My dearest Wren,

Do you know that you are and always will be, the love of my life? You and little Edmund have filled my world with a joy so profound, it scarcely seems real. When you smile that sweet smile of yours, like you did this morning, in that moment, my world becomes brighter, fuller, and wholly yours.

I spent far too long over these lines, grinning to myself like a fool, so that my secretary, quite perplexed, inquired what on earth I found so amusing about the irrigation problem we're so desperately trying to solve. Little does he know that every thought, every breath I breathe, belongs to you.

I love you deeply and unreservedly. That is all I wished to tell you today.

Yours eternally,
Your devoted servant,
Your ever loving,
Fenn

P.S. My apologies—I shall be late for tea.

Also by Sofi Laporte

Merry Spinsters, Charming Rogues Series

Escape into the world of Sofi Laporte's cheeky Regency romcoms, where spinsters are merry, rakes are charming, and no one is who they seem:

Lady Emily's Matchmaking Mishap

A scheming spinster's matchmaking plans for her sister take an unexpected twist when she finds herself entangled in a charade of love.

Miss Louisa's Final Waltz

When a proud beauty weds a humble costermonger, their worlds collide with challenges and secrets that only love can conquer.

Lady Ludmilla's Accidental Letter

A resolute spinster. An irresistible rake. One accidental letter... Can love triumph over this hopeless muddle in the middle of the London Season?

Miss Ava's Scandalous Secret

She is a shy spinster by day and a celebrated opera singer by night. He is an earl in dire need of a wife - and desperately in love with this Season's opera star.

Lady Avery and the False Butler

When a hopeless spinster enlists her butler's help to turn her life around, it leads to great trouble and a chance at love in this rollicking Regency romance.

(*more to come*)

The Viennese Waltz Series

Set against the backdrop of Vienna's 1814 elegance, diplomacy, and intrigue, this series twirls through the entwined destinies of friends, enemies, and lost lovers in charming tales of love, desire and courtship.

My Lady, Will You Dance? (Prequel)

A Lost Love. A Cold Marquess. A Fateful Christmas Country House Party...

The Forgotten Duke

When a penniless Viennese musician is told she may be an English duke's wife, a quest for lost love begins.

The Wishing Well Series

If you enjoy sweet Regency novels with witty banter and a sprinkle of mischief wrapped up in a heart-tugging happily ever after, this series is for you!

Lucy and the Duke of Secrets

A spirited young lady with a dream. A duke in disguise. A compromising situation.

Arabella and the Reluctant Duke

A runaway Duke's daughter. A dashingly handsome blacksmith. A festering secret.

Birdie and the Beastly Duke

A battle-scarred duke. A substitute bride. A dangerous secret that brings them together.

Penelope and the Wicked Duke

A princess in disguise. A charming lord. A quest for true love.

A Mistletoe Promise

When an errant earl and a feisty schoolteacher are snowed in together over Christmas, mistletoe promises happen.

Wishing Well Seminary Series

Discover a world of charm and wit in the Wishing Well Seminary Series, as the schoolmistresses of Bath's most exclusive school navigate the complexities of Regency-era romance:

Miss Hilversham and the Pesky Duke

Will our cool, collected Headmistress find love with a most vexatious duke?

Miss Robinson and the Unsuitable Baron

When Miss Ellen Robinson seeks out Baron Edmund Tewkbury in London to deliver his ward, he wheedles her into staying—as his wife.

About the Author

Sofi writes sweet, mischievous Regency romances filled with witty banter and heart-tugging happily-ever-afters. A globetrotter at heart, she was born in Vienna, grew up in Seoul, studied Comparative Literature in Maryland, and lived in Quito before settling in Europe.

When not crafting stories, Sofi enjoys exploring medieval castle ruins, taking leisurely walks with her dog, and embracing the rewarding challenge of raising three multilingual children.

Get in touch and visit Sofi at her Website, on Facebook or Instagram!

- amazon.com/Sofi-Laporte/e/B07N1K8H6C
- facebook.com/sofilaporteauthor
- instagram.com/sofilaporteauthor
- bookbub.com/profile/sofi-laporte